Wish Trilogy | Book One

WISH I WAS HERE

Ilsa Rey

Black Rose Writing | Texas

ISBN: 978-1-68513-690-1
LIBRARY OF CONGRESS CONTROL NUMBER: 2025941488
PUBLISHED BY BLACK ROSE WRITING
www.blackrosewriting.com

Printed in the United States of America
Suggested Retail Price (SRP) $20.95

Wish I Was Here is printed in Chaparral Pro

*As a planet-friendly publisher, Black Rose Writing does its best to eliminate unnecessary waste to reduce paper usage and energy costs, while never compromising the reading experience. As a result, the final word count vs. page count may not meet common expectations.

For my family.

WISH I
WAS HERE

CHAPTER 1

I sometimes wished I was invisible, just to make life easier. That was the ironic part.

Four down three to go, I thought when the bell announced the end of fourth period. That and, *Shoot. There goes my stuff.* The shrill ring jolted me back to the present, scattering my thoughts along with the notebook and pen on my desk. Someone behind me snickered, but I was used to that.

It's almost over, I reminded myself, running through my home-stretch mantra. *Only two months to go.*

So much for Mom's prediction that high school would be the best time of my life with friends, plural. I had precisely one friend, Isaac, which was fine with me. He was all I needed. But what would our friendship look like once high school was over?

One thing at a time. Just graduate. Worry about college without Isaac later.

It was hard to imagine life without my sidekick. Okay, fine, I was his. Still, we'd been basically inseparable for the past four years. But Isaac didn't belong at University of Michigan any more than I belonged wherever he was going, probably MIT. I tried asking, but whenever I brought up the college subject, he quickly changed it. Apparently, he wasn't keen to discuss our imminent separation any more than I was.

I sighed, collected my stuff into my bag, and filed out of the classroom.

"Hey, Ana," someone said. "Where were you last period? The moon, or had your mind gone to Uranus?"

"I heard that one in eighth grade," I called over my shoulder as I walked away.

The bullying toward Isaac and me was comically lame at this point, like they did it more out of habit than actual desire. They'd all but given up after the Great Social Media Blitz of Junior Year had failed to rattle us. Someone's deepfake AI-generated image of Isaac and me together in a less than flattering pose had gone viral around the school. It caused us the briefest of awkward moments consisting of, "Did you see it?"

"Yeah."

"You?"

"Yep."

Then we shrugged it off. At least we had each other to help endure this annoyance.

As if on cue, Isaac fell into step beside me, his sandy blond hair flopping over his green eyes. He pushed it aside, only to have it fall back again, as always, which made me smile. I loved the predictability of him.

"Any good ones today?" he asked.

"Nope. Just a throwback to the old space cadet stuff. You?"

"Jim called me Beaker Brain."

"I've always liked that one. The alliteration alone."

"Then Brad shoved me after third period."

My forehead scrunched. "You all right?"

"Yeah. He'll have to try harder to make me fall."

"Nice." I held up a hand. He slapped me a half-hearted five.

"Aaaaannnddd, looks like he's about to try harder." Isaac nodded ahead.

Sure enough, Brad threaded the crowd toward us, a look of determination on his face, but it was directed at me this time.

"Hey, Ana," he called with a sick grin.

Isaac pulled what looked like wax paper from his pocket and, with a quick flick of his wrist, tossed something clear and gelatinous on the floor. Brad slipped and fell. Hard. Everyone laughed until he glared them down.

We casually stepped around him.

"Thanks," I said.

"I got you." He nudged my arm with his elbow and smiled, but it didn't reach his eyes. When the laughter reignited, we turned to see Brad trying to get up. He slipped again, the goo having stuck to his shoe.

"What's your hurry, Brad?" Isaac asked him. "Why not stick around?"

Brad scowled.

I gripped Isaac's arm as we walked away. "Oh my gosh. That was amazing."

He grinned for a millisecond.

"What was that stuff anyway?" I asked.

"Just a little slime of my own creation," he said, crumpling the wax paper and returning it to his pocket.

"Well done."

He shrugged, not with his usual modest grin, but in an "eh, whatever" sort of way.

What's up with him? He should have enjoyed that more.

"You know what's wrong with our classmates?" he said.

"Where to begin."

"They lack brains and imagination."

I smiled. "Fortunately, we have plenty of both."

I waited for a quippy line about his over-sized brain and my over-active imagination, but it didn't come.

"Are you okay, Isaac?"

Without looking at me, he raised a hand in farewell as he headed off to his next class. "See you in chem."

I slowed to a stop and watched him go, my forehead creasing.

Something was off with him.

Muffled laughter followed me down the hallway. Brad was walking off balance, a shoe in one hand, or rather, hanging from his hand. Apparently, he had tried to take the slime off, only to have it adhere to his skin.

I might've felt bad for him if a little retaliation weren't sorely overdue. He was the worst of them all.

Smirking, I stepped into my economics classroom, taking my usual seat in the back corner by the window. Paying attention here would be hard enough without Isaac's strange mood on my mind. Did he somehow know I was keeping the news of my U of M acceptance from him? I groaned. It was stupid of me to believe I could hide anything from him. I just wasn't ready to have that conversation. Is that what was bothering him? Knowing we still had to talk about it but not wanting to bring it up?

Once economics passed in a haze of supply and benefits, costs and demands, I eagerly entered the chemistry lab. Over the low buzz of the malfunctioning fluorescent lights, feet shuffled and chairs scraped across the tile floor. I slipped into my seat next to Isaac and tried to act natural. "So, how's it lookin' today?"

He nodded toward the front of the room with little enthusiasm despite this being his favorite subject. "I'm thinking sludge lab."

I bobbed my head as though I knew what that meant.

Large, multi-colored jars of unknown concoctions sat on Miss Mendle's desk. Some held swirling particles. Others had unsavory-looking chunks at the bottom.

Weird brew of stuff—sludge. Got it.

On a normal day, I would've come up with a story behind at least half those jars, but now I was certain today was not a normal day. The off-ness I had sensed in Isaac before had become more pronounced.

He tapped his worn-out sneakers against the floor, his legs bouncing so much even the ancient Soundgarden T-shirt he wore wiggled over his narrow frame. This had to be more than just the college issue. I furrowed my brow at the uncomfortable feeling of not knowing what was up with him. Normally, we could read each other's thoughts.

Instead of scribbling secret formulas in his own brand of hieroglyphics/cuneiform/Chinese calligraphy, oblivious to the rest of us, he focused on Miss Mendle as she placed one mystery jar on each double desk. The pretty blonde girls got an attractive blue jar. Isaac's and mine looked like it contained a pureed baby rhinoceros.

"The goal for this week is to use all the methods you've learned to identify the chemical content of every substance dissolved or mixed inside your jar. I want it down to the element." Miss Mendle pressed her fingers together under her chin and smiled. "Now get to it."

I had to hand it to her. This close to the end of the school year, most teachers had started counting down to summer vacation with more eagerness than the students. Even in April, Miss Mendle still had that new car smell.

I looked at our jar and sighed. At this point, Isaac would normally leave me to fumble with the graduated cylinders and test tubes. He'd be knee deep in his notebook but would still gesture with his pen and half a glance, saying, "You should pour that one into this one first." I'd try my best, but down to the last twenty minutes, he'd take over. It was nice of him to give me a crack at it first.

Today, however, I sat back, startled, as Isaac pushed me aside with a sweep of his arm. Lighting the Bunsen burner in seconds, he began distilling some component out of our jar. A rubber cork, glass straw, and test tube were soon in place. While that percolated, he spoke in a near whisper.

"I screwed up, Ana." He rubbed his hands across his jeans.

"How? You just started. Besides, wouldn't that be like Michelangelo screwing up painting a fence?"

"Not the lab," he hissed. "My experiments. At home. I really messed up, and now I'm in trouble."

"What are you talking about?"

Miss Mendle, doing the rounds, approached our table. "Looking good, you two." Since our labs were always perfect, she paid little attention to us. The labs of those close enough to watch Isaac were often near perfect, if they could keep up with him. He always ignored their whispered pleas to slow down.

A yell and the sound of breaking glass from the other side of the room sent Miss Mendle scurrying.

"I told you to use the crucible tongs, Sean," Tommy said.

Amateurs.

I turned my attention back to Isaac, who was dropping a completed test tube into a wooden holder with one hand while inserting a glass straw into a new tube with the other. He cranked up the flame on the burner, ready to evaporate out the next substance.

"What do you mean you're in—"

"Not now. Can you come over after school?"

Since when did he need to ask? But I nodded and watched in silence as he continued the experiment. I struggled to keep up as he dictated observations and conclusions for our lab sheet. When he finished, I carried our equipment to the sinks, watching him over my shoulder as I scrubbed out a tube with a skinny wire brush. His feet had gone back to tapping. He stared at the clock and ran his fingers through his hair, making it stand up.

When I rejoined him, he seemed tense, like a jack waiting to spring from its box.

"I'm going home now. I probably shouldn't have come at all." He slung his backpack over his shoulder. "I may be underestimating him," he added so quietly I'm not sure he meant for me to hear.

"Underestimating who?" And because I couldn't help pointing out how weird it was, I added, "You're actually skipping last period?" I almost felt his forehead.

His eyes were intense when he looked at me. "I need to get ready. Just come over as soon as you can, okay?"

"Get ready?"

But the bell rang, and he was out the door before I could even pick up my bag.

Isaac's street was a cloud-covered ghost town when I pulled up after school. I used the spare key he'd given me sophomore year to let myself in and locked the door behind me. All the lamps on the main floor were off, giving the orange light echoing up from the basement an ominous glow.

I headed downstairs. "Hey, Isaac. Are you going to tell me what's go..." I stopped, my feet glued to the step. A suitcase stood next to the fire extinguisher at the bottom of the stairs, a piece of T-shirt poking out between the case's zippered teeth.

"You going somewhere?" *Without me?* "Spring break is next week. Couldn't your parents have waited a couple more days?"

"My parents aren't going," he said as I reached the bottom step. Another suitcase, this one filled with worn spiral notebooks, lay open on a wooden table in the middle of the room. Isaac's tools, gadgets, gears, and metal parts from clocks, maybe, or engines, or who knows what, were shoved off to the side instead of taking their usual place at center stage.

"I guess traveling on your own is technically legal now and all." I waited for him to say something. Instead, he collected more notebooks from around the room—stacked on top of books and between his homemade robots that could scratch his back, open and hand him pop cans, or pick things up off the floor. One of them could probably defuse bombs if Isaac wanted it to. He grabbed a notebook from the top of Einstein's empty cage. Though the rabbit's musty odor lingered, he must've set his pet free.

Fear shot through me at what that implied.

"How long are you going to be gone?" I said in a quiet voice. When he didn't answer, I said, louder, "Isaac. What's going on?"

He pushed his hair away from his eyes to look at me. "I'll make this quick. I don't know how much time I have." His movements were jerky, agitated as he piled more notebooks into the suitcase.

My heart started pounding.

"Last night in the chat room, I sort of got into an argument with Apple Pi."

I nodded. He'd mentioned the cutesy username a few times. I imagined Apple Pi as a middle-aged balding man with a beer gut. To me, these Basement Builders, as I called them, were just a bunch of guys trying to one-up each other.

"I have a strict policy of not revealing anything of importance online," Isaac continued, "but he pushed me too far. He was bragging about some stupid hovercraft he built, as if that weren't an elementary project." Isaac spat the words. "Then he accused *me* of not being a scientist of any real value." He paused, exhaling through his nose. "I got mad. He got the better of me, and I..." He looked at me and drew in a breath. "I showed him Einstein."

When he didn't continue, I said, "So?"

Isaac dumped some rabbit food on the table. He set the empty cage near it and opened the door. I looked at the table and back at him.

A sound like bits of gravel scraping against each other reached my ears. I squinted, listening hard. It was more like crunching. Chewing. My gaze darted back to the table. I blinked.

The food was disappearing.

I clamped a hand over my mouth to silence a scream.

"I opened a video feed and showed Apple Pi this last night," Isaac said in a defeated tone.

At least I think that's what he said. The blood pulsating in my ears distracted me from hearing straight. And apparently seeing straight.

"What's happening to the food, Isaac?" I whispered.

He grabbed my wrist. "Feel." He held my hand, palm down, above the table. At first there was nothing and then, a slight tickling as though from fur. He lowered my hand, and I felt the movement of the rabbit, the soft fur slipping in and out between my trembling fingers as its muscles bunched and relaxed.

I snatched my hand away and stepped back, shaking my head. "I don't believe it. How'd you do this?"

"I've been experimenting with cells, messing around with different hormones, blood samples."

I grimaced.

He held up a hand. "Just listen."

I nodded more times than I intended to.

"The first step was Einstein's blood, transmutating his neuropeptides and neurotransmitters. Then I injected some oxytocin, manipulated the RNA, added cuttlefish DNA for its adaptive camouflage properties..."

My forehead screwed up. "What?"

"Basically, I found a way to create a sort of shield around Einstein's cells." He mimed forming a ball, as though that helped. "It's like a transparent glass wall. He's still there, but you can see right through him."

Fumbling for a chair, I sat, gasping for breath as though the air had been sucked from my lungs.

I glanced back to where Einstein was eating. My chair toppled when I jerked upright.

Part of the table had vanished.

I pressed a hand to my throbbing chest as the table reappeared.

"Einstein must have drooled," Isaac said so casually it was annoying. "Even his saliva can make things disappear." He walked around the table, gesturing with his hands as he spoke. "The invisibility atoms move at elevated speeds, bouncing into molecules of other objects, causing a chemical chain reaction of invisibility. But, as you can see, once his saliva dried, the table became visible again."

"Well, of course." Sarcasm became my coping mechanism.

Isaac righted the chair, and I sat down just in time for him to say, "Now theoretically for humans—"

There went the chair again. "Pardon? Did you say *humans*?"

He nodded, this time stepping over the chair on his circuit around the table. "Because of our sweaty, oily skin being in direct contact with our clothes, they'd turn invisible with us."

"How nice." Again with the sarcasm because this couldn't actually be real. Yet he kept going.

"Even the edge of your sleeve, being part of a piece touching your skin, would be affected, as would anything you touched."

Am I supposed to be taking notes?

"Einstein doesn't have that effect because he's not an oily animal."

"Yay for him. But, uh, is it... permanent?"

"He's been like this for two days."

"Two days? And I'm only hearing about it now?" I wanted to knock over another chair.

He grabbed Einstein's food dish and sprinkled it with several drops of clear liquid from a vial. "He'll go back to normal so long as he eats this soon. The antidote only works if taken within one week of turning invisible." He put the dish in the cage. "Otherwise, he'll be this way forever. That could mean insanity or death, so I hope this stuff doesn't taste too bad."

He turned to his suitcase and started counting the notebooks inside as though he hadn't just said something completely bonkers that would make members of PETA faint.

"You mean he might die? Your beloved rabbit?" I grabbed my head with both hands. "But wait. One shock at a time. How could you not tell me about all this?" There was no hiding the hurt in my voice.

"I'm telling you now," he said simply. "Oh, and one more thing. Any rabbit that's related to him can still see him. It has to do with shared genetics."

My fingernails dug into my scalp. What was he *talking* about? And could this *get* any weirder?

"After so many years, so many failed attempts, explosions, dozens of potentially toxic ingredients in a hundred different molecular combinations, and in the end, it all seemed so simple."

"If you say so. Wait, toxic? Explosions?" I shook my head to clear it and let my arms fall. "I can't believe you've been working on this for years and I never knew. I thought we shared everything."

He looked up and sighed. "I didn't want you to get involved."

I met his gaze. "When it comes to you, I am involved."

He held my look for a moment then went back to his blasted notebooks. "It's important that no one else finds out about this," he said.

My brain kept flip-flopping between irritation and disbelief. It was disbelief's turn. My eyes, unfocused, darted around the room but saw nothing.

"Listen to me, Ana. No one can know. Do you understand?"

My eyelids slid shut as I hugged my arms to myself.

"Ana." His tone was sharp. "Do you understand?"

I rapid-fire blinked, trying to focus on his face. "Yes, yes, I understand."

"You're the only person I trust with this. Promise me you'll keep it secret. Under no circumstances should you tell anyone." His voice matched the intensity in his eyes.

I stared back at him.

"Ana," he yelled.

I jumped. "Right. Tell no one. Got it."

"Good."

I closed my eyes again, wishing this was just one of my characteristic daydreams. When I opened them, Isaac was on his knees, reaching to the back of a large double-door metal cabinet. He yanked on a steel box, stuck to the underside of the bottom shelf, until it slid free in his hand. A thick magnet lined the top of the padlocked box. He unlocked it with a key from around his neck. Inside was a black velvet ring box. He stood as he opened it to reveal a single capsule. It looked like an ordinary, oblong pill, speckled with various shades of gray, dull yellow, and larger red spots.

"All you'd have to do is swallow it," he said, his voice low and serious. "You'd be invisible in a matter of seconds." He handed me the ring box.

I looked from the box in my shaky hand back to him. *Is he asking me to use it? Does he want me to be his human guinea pig?*

Is he nuts?

"You should go. Quickly." He broke his gaze and turned back to the suitcase, clasping it shut. "Take that with you, and keep it safe, please. For me."

"Where are you going?" My voice cracked.

"I have to—"

The front door crashed open.

Isaac spun and grabbed my arms. "I'm sorry. I'm so sorry. I didn't want this to happen to you."

The fear in his eyes made my heart crash against my ribs. "What's going on?"

"Remember this one thing—you hold the key, okay? Remember that."

"Hold the key to what?"

Three burly men, wearing gloves and black ski masks, burst into the basement.

"Which kid?" one of them asked.

"The boy," said another in a gruff voice.

The first man lunged and grabbed Isaac.

I cried out and reached for him, but my feet refused to move.

The man spun Isaac like he was a stuffed toy and pinned his arms behind his back. Isaac, dwarfed by the larger man, squirmed and kicked, causing his cell phone to fall from his back pocket. His captor stomped on the phone and grinned at Isaac's useless attempts to break free.

"Don't worry, kid. Our orders are to deliver you unharmed. Just relax, and this will be a lot easier."

"Deliver me where?"

"You'll know when we get there."

The man yanked his arms back tighter. Isaac winced.

"Get the girl too," the second man said. "Sounds like she's got something we need."

"Leave her alone. She has nothing to do with this," Isaac said.

"But what about that key?"

"Nooo..." Isaac's cry was strangled out of him as the man holding him squeezed.

The third man advanced on me. Wide-eyed, I backed away until I bumped into the far wall. He was a few steps away. I glanced at Isaac. He nodded. I looked at the box in my hand and realized what I had to do.

Oh, crap.

The man reached for me. I thrust the pill in my mouth and swallowed.

A tingling sensation filled my center then exploded like a lightning bolt through every inch of my body. The electrified feeling lingered for a millisecond at the tips of my fingers and toes then disappeared in a cold flash.

I twisted away as the man's hand grasped where my arm had just been. He paused, blinked. I dropped silently to the floor just before he swept his hand back and forth through the empty air above me.

"Holy—" He spun toward the others. "Did you see that?"

"Find her," the man at the stairs said with grim calmness.

Wasting no time, I ducked around the man in front of me and hid under the table. I peered up at Isaac whose eyes were locked straight ahead. My would-be kidnapper stalked around the room with his arms out.

My breathing was so labored I feared it would give me away. I took a few seconds to calm myself, but my mind was screaming.

Then my flight instinct kicked in. All I wanted was to get out of there. But what about Isaac? I searched the room and spotted the fire extinguisher near the leader's feet.

Fight it is.

I'd have to be quick. From what Isaac said, only the part I was touching would turn invisible. I crept from under the table, sucked in a lung-full of air, and grabbed the top of the canister.

The leader reacted at once. He swiped his arms at me, but I dodged them and bashed him in the stomach. He doubled over with a groan.

The other man came for me. I swung the extinguisher against his knees. As he fell, he whipped an arm toward me. I kicked it away and turned on the big man holding Isaac. I heaved the canister with all my strength against the back of the man's legs. He stumbled, his grip slackened, and Isaac fell onto his hands and knees. He tried to crawl away, but the man grabbed his ankle, tugging hard. "Get back here." He yanked Isaac up by the armpits and put him in a stranglehold.

The leader, back on his feet, rushed at me. I smacked him in the knees with the extinguisher then dropped it on his head, knocking him flat. The second man took another swipe at me. I lunged under his arm and made it to the bottom step.

This was my chance to make a break for it. A quick glance at Isaac and... for a second, I thought he looked right at me.

"Run," he yelled. "Go!"

I'm sorry, Isaac.

I bolted upstairs and out the open front door, breathing hard, more from fear than exertion. A shaft of sunlight broke through the clouds, blinding me. I ran headlong into a van parked in the driveway, knocking me to the ground.

Footsteps pounded.

They were coming.

Panic seized me. I cringed, wrapping my arms around my legs and curling into a ball.

Two of the men burst outside and stopped a foot away from me.

I held my breath.

"Forget it," one said. "We'll never catch her now."

"The boss won't be happy. Sounds like the girl has something we need."

"What do you suggest we do?"

"Get it from her later."

The other man nodded. "Come on. Let's get the boy." They headed inside.

My breath came out in a whoosh. Get the key I supposedly had from me later? Good luck with that. The only key I had from Isaac was to his house, and obviously these guys made do without it.

I stood to give the van a quick once over. Brown Chevy. No license plates.

Convenient.

I dashed to my car and shut the door behind me. My hands shook so badly, it took several tries to get the key in the ignition, but I didn't turn it yet. Gripping the wheel, my hands looked so normal. I snapped them back.

Did I just make the car disappear? Having everything still visible to me made it tricky to know what disappeared and what didn't. That my clothes turned invisible was obvious, or I would've been caught easily. The fire extinguisher canister stayed visible, but the pieces I was holding on top must've disappeared. Right? Isaac said something about... Dang it. I couldn't remember what all he'd said. I pressed the heel of my hands against my temples.

This is all so confusing.

I took a deep breath and regrouped.

It should just be the steering wheel that vanished. Still, I didn't want to take any chances. I flicked open the glove box, relieved to find my winter gloves there. I slipped them on and caught a glimpse of myself in the rearview mirror. If I was invisible to everyone else...

I grabbed my yellow raincoat from the back seat, pulled up the hood, making sure my hair covered my ears, and folded back the sleeves over my shirt to be sure they wouldn't touch my skin.

Movement caught my eye. One of the kidnappers had stepped out the front door and was scanning the area. I slumped low in my seat. The street was empty, so he beckoned his team out. They carried Isaac, now gagged, and threw him into their van. As soon as they turned left at the corner, I started my car.

How far back should I stay? Three car lengths? Five hundred feet? I had no clue, but I left as much distance as I could without losing them.

After a few turns, they got on the highway. Rush hour had started. It was easier to remain unseen, but I worried about keeping up. Despite the larger vehicle, the van's driver was skilled at weaving his way through traffic. He sped into the left lane. With a death grip on the wheel, I made my way over, four cars behind.

The van slowed, keeping pace with the pokey pick-up truck next to it. The cars behind them formed tighter ranks, boxing me in.

With no warning, the van gunned forward and cut over two lanes. It squealed down the nearest off ramp.

"Dang it," I shouted as I zoomed past the exit.

I banged on the steering wheel, gritted my teeth, and forced my way to the right, cutting off one car and slamming the brakes to avoid hitting another. With the angry blast of horns behind me, I took the next exit and doubled back, scanning the area.

I spotted the van. It was—back on the highway. I screamed as it drove past me while I idled at a red light.

My heart sank. I dropped my forehead onto the wheel.

A honk from the car behind me alerted me to the light change.

I rolled back onto the highway, heading south toward home.

And away from Isaac.

CHAPTER 2

I shut the car off in my driveway and sat for a moment, still in disbelief over what had just happened. Yet, my brain kept replaying the events of the last hour like a movie marathon with only one darn film. Again, I flinched at the memory of Isaac's frightened face as he yelled for me to run. What made it so heart-wrenching was he was scared not for himself but for me, the one not being held captive.

The one who abandoned him.

Did he know I tried at least? Were the men in the van talking about me following them? Did Isaac hear and take comfort in that? I could only hope. But how to find him?

Isaac insisted I tell no one, but that was before he was kidnapped. Had the rules changed? I wanted to call the cops, but they might want to bring me in for questioning. That would blow Isaac's secret for sure. And even if I told them about the van, I didn't know where it was headed, besides north. Other than that and "brown Chevy," I had nothing.

I gnawed on a thumbnail. When the Masons realized Isaac was missing, they'd call the cops, and I wouldn't have broken my promise. Surely, the police could find him without my help.

Then there was me being invisible forever unless I got an antidote from Isaac within a week. Permanent invisibility could mean "insanity or death," Isaac had said.

Insanity or death.

What the heck had he given me? And why on earth had I taken it?

I rested my face in my hands but, after a moment, pulled my head up with resolve.

Seven days. Isaac was sure to be rescued by then. No problem.

That's what I'd keep telling myself anyway.

And finally, the matter of his kidnappers saying they'd be coming for me and this mysterious key. They seemed confident, too, but since they didn't know who I was, they wouldn't be able to find me.

Would they?

Isaac said I "hold" the key, not that I have a key. Was it some goofy "the key to everything is inside of you" sort of thing? But that didn't seem like Isaac's style.

My fingers trembled as I pulled the car keys from the ignition and stared at the garage door, practicing breathing slowly the way a normal person does. I shook off the raincoat and set it on the passenger seat.

I was now in stealth mode.

A car drove by. I waited until it went around a corner and was about to open the door when I remembered old Mrs. Granville across the street, potentially doing her usual neighborhood spying. The velvety red drapes were closed, no bony fingers parting them, no beady little eyes peering out.

I left the car and hurried inside.

"Welcome home, Anastasia," Mom called from the kitchen as soon as I closed the front door.

I froze. Would she be able to see me? Isaac said Einstein's relatives, for whatever science-y reason, would be able to see him.

"Ana?" she called again. "Is that you?"

I hesitated, cringing. "Yes, Mom."

Her high heels clicked down the hallway. Her floral dress swayed around her.

I held my breath.

"Want to join me? I'm marinating chicken breasts," she said, looking right at me.

I exhaled, though with a twinge of disappointment.

Now what? Just act like everything's normal? How, when everything was most definitely *not* normal. Still, what choice did I have?

Not knowing what else I could do, I trudged after her to the ever-spotless kitchen. Mom had it remodeled to look like something out of a magazine with its spacious design, modern appliances, gleaming granite countertops, and custom cabinetry.

"Notice anything different about me?" she asked.

Something was different about *her*?

"Umm, new nail polish color?" I didn't even check her nails.

"No. Well, yes, but no. Guess again."

I squinted and tried to focus. "You got a haircut." My words fell flat, but she didn't notice.

"Yes, I got bangs. What do you think?" She turned her head from side to side, her sculpted chin-length auburn hair flouncing back and forth.

"It's nice, Mom." I did my best impression of enthusiasm.

"The stylist said it makes me look ten years younger."

I'll bet he did.

I disagreed, but the lack of a single gray hair helped her cause. She didn't need to dye it; her hair just knew better than to turn gray. It wouldn't dare.

"Why are you wearing gloves, honey? It's not cold outside."

"Oh. Right." I pulled them off, placed my hand flat on the counter, and watched her for a reaction. There was none.

Interesting.

"I guess I just got chilly," I said.

"Take a sweater with you next time."

I nodded my response.

"How was your day? You look a little haggard." She kept her eyes on me, waiting for an answer.

What could I tell her?

"Umm, do I? It was an... odd day."

Normal, remember? Act like everything is normal.

This was going to be a lot of work. I slumped onto a barstool, slid my arm across the counter, and laid my head against it, feeling the beginnings of a headache.

"Do you want to tell me about it?"

I was surprised she wasn't admonishing me to sit up straight. She'd named me Anastasia after the legendary Russian princess and had been trying, and failing, to make me more princess-like ever since. I struggled to form a response.

Loud knocking on the front door sent me bolt upright. The sudden movement made my head throb. I winced and pressed my fingertips to my temples.

"I wonder who that is." Mom hastily washed her hands and dried them on her apron as she headed to the door. When she opened it, she said, "Oh," in a confused tone. "Hello, officer."

Officer? My stomach tightened as I slid off the barstool.

"Are you Mrs. Roberts?" a male voice said.

My eyes widened. *Don't I know that voice?*

"Yes."

"And is that your Volvo?"

I definitely know that voice. What is he *doing here?*

"Yes, it's the one my daughter uses for school. Why?"

"Was she driving it recently?"

"She just got home a few minutes ago. What's this all about?"

"Well, Mrs. Roberts, the station received several complaints of that car in town, apparently driverless."

What? But the raincoat. I was so careful.

I felt the top of my head. It was hot. Of course. I was sweating during that intense drive. The sweat from my head must've gotten to the hood. What a fool I was. I pressed my hand against my throbbing chest.

Mom snorted. "You're joking, right?"

"I'm afraid not, ma'am."

"There must be some mistake. That's impossible."

"Whatever the case, I'd like to speak with your daughter."

"Oo-kay. Let me get her for you."

What do I do? He can't see me. I tried to flatten my messy hair.

"Ana," Mom called, her voice nearer.

But he literally *can't see me.* I bolted up the back staircase just before Mom reached the kitchen.

"Ana?"

Creeping along the upstairs hallway, I tried to slow my breathing. I was about to press my sweaty palms against the wall behind me but stopped myself. It wouldn't help matters if I made part of the house disappear.

I poked my head around the corner to the foyer below and saw him. Despite all, my heart did a back flip. It was my first Ben Cody sighting in months. *The* Ben Cody—my ultimate fantasy since freshman year. I was so sad that he was a senior and I only got one year in school with him. Normally guys that good looking were jerks, but he was polite and kind to everyone, even the social outcasts like me. Not that I ever had the nerve to talk to him. And now he was a full-fledged cop, having finished college in three years and graduating from the Academy in record time. Why did *he* have to be the one to come here?

Mom's heels clicked back along the hardwood floor. "Ana?" she called up the front stairs.

I stepped farther into the shadows. Would she come looking for me?

"I'm sorry. I don't know where she went," Mom said.

I closed my eyes and exhaled.

"That's fine, Mrs. Roberts." Then he raised his voice, as though knowing I was within hearing range. "Please let your daughter know that driving hunched down in her seat so other drivers can't see her is not only dangerous to herself but poses a serious distraction and therefore a danger to fellow travelers as well."

"Yes, officer, I'm very sorry. This isn't like her at all. I'll pass along your message. It won't happen again."

I could practically hear her nod and shake her head with every other sentence.

"Okay, ma'am. I trust you're right. Thank you. Have a good evening."

"You, too."

At the last second, I tried to steal another glimpse of him, but the door shut before I could.

Silence followed. Mom leaned her back against the door, her cheeks red. She spotted me and tramped upstairs.

"What on earth were you thinking?" She flailed her hands. "That was so embarrassing. To have a police officer come to my house and complain about my daughter driving recklessly. You could have caused an accident. Did Isaac put you up to this? Was it supposed to be some practical joke? A dare, maybe?"

"No, Mom, I, umm... was just feeling really tired is all. I didn't realize people couldn't see me when I was slumped down like that." I wasn't prone to lying to her, but I didn't know what else I could say.

"Well now you know. Next time use your head, Ana." She smoothed imaginary wrinkles out of her dress. "I hope the ladies don't hear about this," she muttered as she stormed away.

When she passed out of view, I stared, unfocused, at an empty wall. Then I stumbled to my room and collapsed onto the bed, feeling a cushion of air flow from my leaf-patterned comforter.

Now what was I supposed to do? To everyone except my mom, I was invisible. Going to school tomorrow was out. Raising my hand in class would be pointless, not that I was likely to anyway. And a book opening to page 230 by itself? That would raise a lot of questions.

My head pounded as I stared at the pale-yellow glow-in-the-dark star stickers on the ceiling. They formed the constellations of the summer sky— a gift from Isaac.

And where was Isaac now? A cold abandoned warehouse? I shuddered and tucked my limbs in close, suddenly as chilly as I worried he might be.

His captors would no doubt be forcing him to recreate his invisibility pill. Would they sell it to the highest evil bidder like drug cartels? Warlords? North Korea? Was the U.S. friends with Russia, or not? And if they could mass produce invisibility, then what? Disappearing armies doing who knows what damage? Terrorist cells wreaking who knows what havoc? I shut my eyes to the horror of the thought.

Not willing to let my brain entertain those possibilities any longer, I rolled onto my side and forced my train of thought to jump tracks.

Ben was here. In my house.

Was it only this morning I was daydreaming about him? It felt like forever ago. Desperate for a distraction, I let my mind drift back to the memory: in the kitchen with Mom for breakfast, having one of our typical "discussions."

"I'm graduating in less than two months, Mom. Nobody cares about my social standing at school."

"But wouldn't you like to go out with a bang?" she said with a big, fake encouraging smile.

I made myself busy with eating. It was like she'd never met me. Just because *she* was prom queen... If she had hopes of me continuing that legacy, she should've let them die long ago. Like the first day of freshman year.

"I guess there's still hope for you in college," she conceded, mostly to herself, then added, "Have you checked to see if some better schools allow applications this late in the year?"

"University of Michigan will be fine," I said in a tone I always hoped in vain would end the conversation there.

"Yes, but," her head cocked to the side and her forehead creased, signaling she was about to launch into her standard attack on my college choice: I could get into a better school. Yaddity yah. My grades are terrific, even if I don't have a lot of variety in my extra-curriculars. Blah blah blah. Poetry Club and the school paper were about it. Forgive me for not being into sports.

I was sure U of M was a good school. It had to be. It's where Ben went. That they carried my intended major, creative writing, was merely an added bonus.

Since I'd already resigned myself to not being able to follow Isaac wherever he was going, I figured I might as well follow in Ben's footsteps instead. It would at last be one thing we had in common, something we could talk about, if I ever worked up the courage to speak to him.

I shut my eyes and pictured him and his slightly curly chocolate brown hair. A happy murmur escaped my lips. I hoped Mom wouldn't notice.

She did.

"Ana, are you daydreaming again?" She snapped her fingers, forcing me to open my eyes. The image of Ben disappeared in a puff of smoke.

I sighed. "Yes, Mom, I'm listening."

Barely. I wonder what Ben looks like in uniform.

My eyelids drooped.

"Ana." This time she smacked her hand on the countertop. My eyes popped open. "Where do you go, girl?"

Like I'd tell her.

"Sorry, Mom. You were saying?" I looked at her pointedly, forehead tilted down, eyes narrowed and focused.

"I was saying..."

Lost her again. Though I kept my full-of-attention pose, I was playing photoshop in my mind. I pictured Ben in swim trunks. Then I moved an image of the Hinckley, Ohio, police duds over top.

Hat? No hat. Baton?

My lip curled in a mischievous grin. Around the edge of the image, Mom's face appeared, frowning.

Uh-oh.

"What's that goofy smile for? You weren't paying any attention to me, were you?"

"No, no, I got it. Dress better, wear more make-up, try not to daydream when people are talking to me."

She shook her head, hands on hips.

"Make friends?" These were the likely choices—what she harped on me for the most. Well, that and never having a boyfriend. Isaac, my only friend, who happened to be a boy, didn't count, apparently. You'd think she'd be glad I was staying out of trouble, not getting pregnant and all that. Judging by the belly bumps on so many of the girls waddling the halls of my school, I figured she'd be pleased I wasn't "normal."

But I still hadn't hit the nail on the head, judging by the way she shook hers. She said nothing as I dropped my white plate, covered with scrambled egg scraps and ketchup blobs, into—

The phone rang, jerking me back to now. I blinked to remind myself where I was. Mom answered after the second ring. She used her usual cheery phone voice, only this time it sounded forced.

"Oh, hello, Helen."

I swung my legs over the side of the bed and sat up.

"No, he isn't here… I don't know. Let me get her."

I was already on the move when Mom called my name. I scurried down the back stairs to the kitchen and took the land line from her outstretched hand.

"Hi, Mrs. Mason," I said, trying my best to keep my voice even.

"Hello, Ana. Have you seen Isaac?" she asked.

"No, not since school." I turned away from Mom and grimaced. I hated lying to Isaac's mom.

"You sometimes come to our house after school, don't you?"

"Yes, but not today."

"I see. Well, did he tell you anything about where he was going?"

"No." My voice quivered.

Keep it together.

"He's not getting a head start on Operation Descartes, is he?"

I laughed awkwardly. "Not that I know of," I said in as ordinary a tone as I could muster. Operation Descartes was the plan where the four of us— Isaac, me, and his parents—would fly away should Isaac need to drop everything and run. It started when Isaac landed on a government watch list, or several, when he launched his far-too-successful-for-a-fourteen-year-old rocket that brought the authorities to his house. They let him go, but they would be keeping an eye on him, they said.

The plan was named after René Descartes, who came up with the coordinate grid system after observing a fly on his ceiling. Isaac was a big fan of the mathematician. I appreciated the pun in "flying" away. Operation Descartes was in place before the Masons moved here. Now that I was eighteen, I was invited to join them, if I chose to, and if it should come to that. But since Isaac was also eighteen, we didn't need his parents, whether his mom realized that or not.

"Okay, well, if you hear from him, you'll let me know?"

"Yes, of course."

"Thank you."

"Bye." I hung up the phone and stared at the floor. Should I have told her the truth, even though Isaac insisted I tell no one? If he hadn't shared his discovery with them, did I have a right to? They were *his* parents.

The sharp clang of Mom putting a pot on the stove startled me. "Everything okay at the Mason household?" All traces of her former irritation appeared to be gone.

"Yeah. She was just trying to find Isaac. Maybe he's... at the library."

"It's understandable that Helen would want to keep tabs on him. I'd be protective, too, after what happened to his parents."

I nodded. Isaac's parents had died in a car crash when Isaac was in eighth grade. Then his science teacher and his biology professor wife adopted him.

"Before I forget, your father called. His return trip has been delayed."

I pursed my lips. Dad was a good buffer between Mom and me. I'd roll my eyes at him across the table, and he'd respond with a sympathetic smile. He didn't stand up for me, but I didn't mind. He's the one who had to share a bedroom with the woman. I couldn't begrudge him wanting to stay out of the line of fire.

"Apparently the head of the accounting firm was so impressed with your father, he asked him to stay an extra day to play golf. Isn't that great?"

"Yep."

"Ana, this is a wonderful opportunity for him to move up in the company." She grinned. "Then maybe we can hire a chef."

"I thought you loved cooking." That's what she told her friends anyway, an excuse for not having a cook like many of them did.

"Of course, I do, honey, but sometimes it's fun having someone else do it for me."

Nice recovery. If she wanted more money, she could always get a job, but it seemed shopping and gossiping with her friends *was* her job. She did it full-time.

Unfortunately, I didn't have the energy to climb back upstairs. That left me to sink again onto a barstool and watch Mom work on "her masterpiece"—what she called every meal she made. Though my eyes were on her, all I could see were flashes of Isaac being beaten, thrown against a wall, knocked down, kicked in the stomach. Closing my eyes only made the pictures more vivid and horrifying. Could this truly be what was happening to him? While I did nothing but sit in my comfortable home?

I wanted to pound my fists on the counter.

One of the kidnappers said something about delivering Isaac unharmed. But could I believe that? Criminals weren't universally known to be a trustworthy bunch, so how could I be sure? Then again, what more could I do beyond hoping it was true and that the police would do their job? And quickly.

The helplessness made my organs feel like they were collapsing in on themselves. With effort, I forced myself to pay attention to Mom, hoping the distraction would soothe my aching head and send the disturbing thoughts away.

"Can you believe she's leaving him?"

"Mmm," I murmured, widening my eyes in mock disbelief. I didn't know who she was talking about, but it didn't matter. Mom was like the girls at school, only older and with more adult news to share. How we could be related was a mystery to me. Aside from an obvious resemblance of green eyes and reddish-brown hair, complete with a slightly freckled nose, the similarities stopped there.

I couldn't see myself in Mom's world, and she refused to see me in mine. It wasn't much better with my dad. Since I didn't share his obsession with numbers, we had little in common. If anything, he was more interested in what Isaac was up to than what I was doing, often asking what Isaac's latest creation was. Still, I wished Dad was there. He had a knack for toning down Mom's crazy.

"You know, Ana," she said a minute later, "you and Isaac should go on an adventure sometime. You never *do* anything."

"I got the cops sent here. Does that count?"

She made a face. "That's not quite what I meant. Why don't you two at least go to a baseball game?"

"Isaac? At a professional sporting event? Are you joking?"

She lifted her arms in the air. "This is why you need more friends."

"I don't want more friends, Mom. I'm fine."

"I'm just saying it would be nice if you had a friend other than the boy who tinkers with scrap metal."

That's when I stopped listening. It required too much effort, and I'd been taxed enough already. I once complained to Isaac about Mom, but his face went stark and cold as though a heavy metal security door had slammed shut in front of it. I should've known better. He loved his mom, and his dad. He talked about them often, and I'd feel his joy as he relayed childhood memories. But sometimes he'd cut off midsentence, seeming to remember that he wouldn't be making memories with them again.

Though, overall, he was pleased with how things turned out with his adoptive parents. They doted on him at first. Isaac figured he was a replacement for their own son who'd died of leukemia at age ten. He enjoyed talking all-things-science with them, but eventually felt he'd become more colleague than child, a fellow walking lab coat.

Mom droned on through dinner. If I noticed a pause and sensed a response was needed, I nodded and said, "Yes," or "No kidding," or "Really?" while I nibbled the food on my plate. Her meals were always delicious, but today everything tasted the same—like nothing at all.

Meanwhile, what was Isaac eating? Was he eating?

Back in my room that night, I sat on the bed, then at my desk, then back on my bed, until I found myself motionless, staring into my closet. Thoughts bombarded me like the weak kid getting pummeled in dodge ball. I knew Isaac was a genius, but how had he learned to do something like this? What other secrets was he keeping from me? And how were his parents coping? Did they call the cops yet? Would the police be concerned with a teenager who hadn't come home for supper? What was the rule for missing persons? Did they have to be gone for twenty-four hours before the police investigated?

I couldn't wait that long. Since I'd already ruled out going to school tomorrow, my day was wide open. In shows, the detective always started at the scene of the crime. I'd go back to Isaac's house in the morning and search for clues. It wasn't much, but now that I had a plan of action, I didn't feel so helpless.

At last, I was able to settle under my blankets, but a new set of questions sprang to mind. Where was Isaac sleeping, if they were letting him sleep at all? A drafty room with a stained mattress on the floor and rats for companions? Were the kidnappers being true to their word of not hurting him, or were they beating him, like I feared? I shivered and pulled the covers tight around me to force away that thought, replacing it with:

Would he be rescued, and when? Would I be invisible forever? Could I really *die* from this?

Too worn out to think any more, I eventually drifted off. My dreams were laced with police cars chasing me, Mom floating by stirring a pot and laughing, an invisible rabbit except for its blood-dripping fangs, and Isaac, alone and cold, huddled in a dark corner.

6 Days

When I woke up the next morning, it took me a second to understand the gnawing pit in my stomach. Then the events of the previous day came crashing back onto me, and the pit grew into a chasm. Though the gravity of that black hole tried to suck me into myself, I needed to get moving. I had six days to find and rescue Isaac before who knows what happened to him and before I was sent to crazy town.

I threw on my nearest jeans and T-shirt and headed to the kitchen, where I found Mom making Belgian waffles.

"I'm practicing for the ladies' brunch I'm hosting next week," she said. "What do you think is more chic, raspberries or blackberries?"

"I don't know. How about boysenberries?"

"Oooh, good thinking. But are they in season?"

"I have no idea." I grabbed a plain bagel and poured coffee into a travel mug.

"Don't you want to try my waffles?"

"Sorry, Mom. Can't be late for school." I swiped my gloves from the counter and headed to the door. She began to protest, but I shut the door behind me. It was rude, but I was afraid she'd ask me to help her pick a napkin pattern. I had more important things on my mind than the comparative virtues of floral versus vine.

Before getting in the car, I scanned the street, including Mrs. Granville's house. The coast was clear. Riffling under the passenger seat, I found my winter hat and put it on under the raincoat as a precaution. I only had a short distance to drive, but I didn't want to risk another police visit, even one from Ben Cody.

Three blocks later, I parked in a little-traveled side street where Mom had no reason to go. To play it safe, I'd have to make the four-mile trek on foot. The gloves stayed, but I ditched the hat and coat. I fueled myself on several large bites of bagel chased with a gulp of hot coffee. My tongue screamed not just from the burn. The coffee was gross, though it meant well.

As I trundled along, still trying to wrap my head around what had happened yesterday, I nearly ran into a jogger. Later, a confused woman tugged on her golden retriever's leash when it paused to sniff at seemingly empty air.

Then a horrifying thought struck me, rooting me to the spot. What if Isaac had been taken far away? Overseas even? I eased myself onto someone's lawn.

What if Isaac had been shoved into a crate and loaded onto a ship? I curled my knees to my chest and felt claustrophobic just thinking about it. Or maybe he was in one of those big metal shipping containers, boxed in by a hundred others on a giant barge? His yells and pounding on the door drowned out by crashing ocean waves?

If he was taken out of the country to some secret lab in the middle of Siberia, how would he be found? Would that become his life? I looked down at myself. Would *this* become my life?

A death sentence without the antidote didn't seem so bad if the alternative was a life without Isaac.

I put my head between my knees and breathed deeply. Part of me wanted to start screaming and tearing up grass. At that moment, I had no interest in being brave. I couldn't kid myself that it had all been a dream or my imagination. This was real, and I didn't know if I could take it.

My eyes stung. But I refused to give in, to give up hope. I hauled myself up. Isaac needed me. I had to keep going.

An hour later, I reached Isaac's one-story beige house and examined the front door lock. It wasn't even scratched. How had the kidnappers jimmied it so well?

Across the street, a man was getting into his car. Not wanting to take any chances at the front, I went around back, removed the key from my gloved hand, and let myself in, surprised but grateful the Masons had gone to work.

I expected the basement to be a mess, but if anything, it was tidier than usual. Instead of finding the fire extinguisher under the table where it had rolled yesterday, it was back by the door. Isaac's suitcases had been shoved into the metal cabinet next to the bookshelf with Einstein's open cage. Where was the rabbit now?

"Einstein," I called, then shook my head. He wasn't a dog. I moved his cage to the floor so he could get his food. A shudder ran through me at the memory of the green/gray pellets eerily disappearing before my eyes yesterday.

On the table, Isaac's tools and machine parts were spread out neatly. I could understand the kidnappers wanting to cover their tracks, but this seemed a bit much.

I got down on my hands and knees, and though I felt silly, began searching for clues: A stray hair? A muddy boot print? A torn piece of fabric? Heck, a dry-cleaning receipt? Like these guys were the type to pick up dry cleaning. Taking someone to the cleaners was probably more their style.

I knelt with my hands on my hips. It was as though the floor had just been mopped.

Being without further ideas, or a more sophisticated forensics kit, I looked at Isaac's creations. When had he made those robots? It seemed like ages ago. Wasn't there anything new?

Wait a minute. If Isaac was mixing chemicals, hormones, and neuro-whatevers, where was his equipment? Where were the test tubes, beakers, and Bunsen burners like in the lab at school? They had to be around here somewhere. I opened every drawer and checked every shelf. No chemicals.

Not so much as a junior chemistry set. I paced the room, pushing against the tiled floor, checking for loose ones I could pry up with my fingers to reveal a hidden tunnel below. If there was one, I couldn't find it.

Next, I searched for scratches, as though one of the heavy cabinets had been scraped across the floor. Again, nothing. Finally, I resorted to pulling back on substantial looking books, hoping a secret passageway would open. Not surprisingly, none did.

I thought I was getting somewhere when I examined Isaac's record collection, something belonging to his parents, which he'd insisted on keeping after they'd died. They had been avid vinyl music collectors and had met at a place called Easy Street Records in Seattle. Along the bookshelf stuffed with tall narrow albums, a line of dust was missing in front of one particular album. I gingerly edged this one out from between its neighbors. The cover read *Smashing Pumpkins: Mellon Collie and the Infinite Sadness* and featured a woman emerging from a star.

When I pulled the album open, a photograph fell to the floor. A smile crossed my lips as I retrieved it. There was young Isaac, maybe six years old, wearing a little suit and holding an Easter basket filled with colorful plastic eggs. On one side stood his mom in a yellow, flowery dress; on the other, his dad in a gray suit and thin black rimmed glasses. I could see them both in their son's features.

After a moment, I placed the photo back in the album and carefully returned it to its proper home on the shelf.

With a sigh, I collapsed against the wall and slid to the floor. I stared under the table in front of me and cocked my head to the side. That was a spot of floor I hadn't checked. Something was strange about it. At the intersection of four tiles, a darker shade of grout stretched about an inch in each direction. I scrambled over and scratched at the grout with my fingernails, but it was just as sturdy as all the rest of the flooring in the room.

Isaac must've spilled something here, that's all.

When I tried to stand, I smacked my head against the table. "Ow," I yelped and fell back onto my elbow.

That's when I noticed the masking tape X across the underside of the table. And where the lines intersected, I could just make out the numbers "-3, 11" in Isaac's writing.

"What is that supposed to mean?" I said aloud as though Isaac was standing there. When I remembered that of course he wasn't, my heart sank a little lower in my chest.

I stood, rubbing my head, and faced a poster half-hidden by a bookshelf. I'd seen it a thousand times but had stopped looking at it. Now I traced my finger over the spacecraft I knew well thanks to my dad's extensive Star Wars LEGO collection—a collection Isaac knew about, which means he knew I'd be able to identify this ship, due to my dad's careful and exhaustive tutelage. This was a Y-wing, or, in Isaac-speak, a Y-axis.

Could Isaac have turned the basement into a giant coordinate grid?

I crawled under the table again and examined the suspicious grout. If I was right, this would be my starting point, the origin, (0,0). Assuming I was to face this grid from the doorway, I counted three tiles to the left, -3. Keeping my feet along that line, I stepped forward until I ran into the metal cabinet. From there to the brick wall behind it was only five tiles. I glanced at the Y-wing—potentially my clue that I needed to go vertical now. Three stacked bricks were about the length of one floor tile, so calculating the rest of the distance brought me to the top of the cabinet.

Grabbing a chair, I eagerly climbed up to examine the cabinet's top. But there was no pouch of diamonds or rubies, no imperial jade seal of China, no lost Van Gogh painting, just a massive amount of dust, and a hook forced into the wall with a metal ring attaching it to the cabinet. The ring and hook were the sort of thing you'd see on bookshelves in earthquake territory like California, to keep the bookcase from falling on someone during a heavy shake, but here in Ohio...

I forced the ring off the hook and waited. Expecting something Indiana Jonesy to happen, I braced myself for the giant boulder to appear and smash me, but nothing. What a letdown. Did I calculate wrong? No, even my lowly brain was able to do that math correctly. I must've been wrong about the whole thing.

I hopped down, kicked the chair away, and puffed air out of my cheeks as I leaned heavily against the cabinet. I had to catch my footing as it rolled several inches away from me, riding along hidden wheels. I shoved the cabinet again, moving it another foot.

Is that the edge of a...

I pushed with all my strength until a narrow wooden door was indeed visible.

My arms, raised in triumph, fell to my sides. In place of a doorknob was an electronic keypad.

CHAPTER 3

Not surprisingly, the keypad was homemade. It had a narrow rectangular screen with a blinking cursor. The buttons were from a telephone, with both numbers and letters.

Okay, I can do this.

First I tried Isaac's birthday, then his first name and middle name, which was Chester—who could forget that?—his last name, and some combination of the three.

Nope. Too obvious.

Einstein?

No.

Newton?

No again.

I tried my name, middle name, which is Irene—Thanks, Mom and Dad, for the initials A.I.R. No big stretch to kids calling me Airhead there—last name and birthday.

Nothing. An irrational pang of disappointment stung me, but it was worth a shot.

Think. Like. Isaac.

Mendeleev? Becquerel?

Did I spell that right?

Galileo? Galileo Galilei?

There weren't enough spaces for the full name, but every time I tried a name or number shorter than the space allowed, the cursor kept blinking at me like an intolerable, sadistic eye. There was no Enter button, so I could only assume something would happen when I figured out the right numbers or letters.

"Ugh." If it could be a combination of letters and numbers, it could be anything.

I laid my arm across the door and dropped my head against it.

That stupid Apple Pi.

Wait a minute. I lifted my head and smiled. What a perfectly Isaac-y thing to do.

I typed in 314. The cursor kept flashing. Of course it wouldn't be something so short. I had no idea what came after four, but there had to be a book around here that could help. I combed the shelves, my finger tracing along the various titles: Quantum Physics—naturally, Advanced Chemistry—cheater, Ancient Alchemy—really?

I jumped to another shelf.

Mathematical Theory. Here we go. I checked the index. There were several listings for pi. The first one said, "a mathematical constant, the ratio of a circle's circumference to its diameter..."

Blah blah blah. Not helpful.

Then: "...for any circle, you can divide the circumference..."

Yeah, yeah, what's next?

One listed pi to roughly a hundred places. Ah-ha.

I carried it back to the keypad and began typing, 1592653. I was ten places in. Still nothing happened. I had space for two more digits. Carefully I typed 58 and waited, afraid to breathe.

Click.

Yes.

I shut the book and dropped it with a thud on the floor. Taking a deep breath, I pushed.

Several fluorescent lights buzzed to life overhead.

My jaw dropped.

Across from me in the narrow, rectangular room, a long skinny table held test tubes and flasks of different shapes and sizes. They were filled with liquids of various shades of blue, pink, green, and yellow, connected by a roller coaster of clear plastic tubing. Next to the table, neatly arranged on a rack of shelves were evaporating dishes, clamps, pipettes, beakers, and graduated cylinders, as well as dozens of plastic containers of chemicals grouped by like-colored labels.

When and how had Isaac accumulated all this? For a moment I considered he'd been stealing it, piece by piece from the school, but I shook the thought away. That wasn't Isaac. Still, if his parents bought it for him, he wouldn't be hiding it.

To the right of the door was a table holding a glass box with built-in thick rubber gloves for handling chemicals of a more delicate nature. The walls and base were streaked with black scorch marks as though something had blown up in there.

Beyond the glass box was a dented, rust-tinged refrigerator. Curiosity battled fear. I surprised myself with each step I took, afraid to see what was inside, but also *needing* to see what was inside. Cringing, I grasped the handle and pulled.

The fridge was all but empty.

Phew.

No pickled baby pig or severed hand. Not even a smuggled case of beer, which would've surprised me almost as much as the other items. Instead, there were five glass vials. Three contained substances of various shades of gray. These were labeled in Isaac's strange secret language I'd seen him forever using in his omnipresent notebooks. But the other two held a tiny amount of red liquid and were labeled with English characters: "E" and "AR."

I closed the refrigerator and spotted a granite mortar and pestle on the table. Inside was a gray and yellow powder with a large red circle in the center. Without thinking, I touched my finger to the crimson dot and pulled it out to examine closer. It looked like coagulated blood. My mouth twisted, and I scraped it off my finger with a shudder. I should've known better than to stick my finger into an unknown substance in Isaac's lab.

When I stepped back, I bumped into a trash can but spun to catch it before it fell. Something familiar was inside—a white rag with faint red stains. I stood, my eyes unfocused as I tried to remember. Was it toward the end of last week? Thursday? Maybe Friday? As usual, I was in the basement with Isaac, who was scrapping an old vacuum for parts. He asked me to hand him a particular gear, but it sliced my fingers when I picked it up. I dropped the gear and was about to put my bleeding fingers in my mouth when he pressed a rag to them instead. His voice was pained as he apologized.

When the bleeding slowed, he handed me three Band-Aids and took the rag. I didn't see what he did with it, but now I knew where it ended up—in this trash can.

I opened the refrigerator and looked again at the vial marked "AR." Those were my initials, on the container with my blood. I gagged and swallowed hard. The mortar and pestle had my blood inside.

Then it dawned on me. This was where Isaac had made the invisibility pill just for me. The formula needed my blood, so only my relatives could see me. The "E" on the other vial must stand for Einstein, but why wasn't there one labeled "IM" for Isaac? Why didn't he make his own pill? Did he have something against needles? Afraid to draw his own blood? That seemed unlikely. Then why create the pill for me? Was he planning to make me his human guinea pig all along?

Or did he somehow know I'd need it?

No. That was impossible, even for Isaac. But what about those gray vials? Could they be an antidote? I reached inside the refrigerator, then jerked my hand back and slammed the door.

Don't even think about it.

What if there were trace amounts of someone else's blood in there? My whole body shuddered. But blood was probably the least concerning part. They could be poison for all I knew.

I turned to leave when a piece of paper poking out from under a wooden test tube holder caught my eye. Isaac had written three words on it: "Immune—blood, Love."

Whatever that means.

I took one final look around before stepping out, tugging on the door until it swung shut with a click behind me. I put away the math book and shoved the heavy metal cabinet back into place. Then I pulled out the suitcase with Isaac's notebooks. Sitting on the floor, I paged through them. They all looked the same: worn around the edges, every page completely filled, except in one book. It must be Isaac's latest. Maybe his formula was somewhere in there. I flipped through it but could make no sense of the weird letters. Holding it upside down was no help. I sighed. There was probably only one key to what the words meant, and it was locked inside Isaac's brain.

I returned the notebooks and suitcase to their cabinet and left the house through the back door, locking it behind me. I hid the key under a small frog statue on the porch. Isaac would kill me if he knew, but it seemed a little late for safety-consciousness.

I made the slow journey back to the car, donned my protective clothing, and drove the rest of the way home. As I approached, a shot of panic hit me, but it soon faded. Mom wasn't home. She'd probably be out shopping for hours. I went to my room and laid down, pulling my pillow over my face and screaming into it. I'd tried to do *something* to help Isaac and had failed miserably. The worst part—what if he was counting on me? What if he expected me to figure out where he was and save him? What if he needed me to?

What if I couldn't?

Tears chased each other down my cheeks.

I didn't know I'd fallen asleep until I was awakened by a foot tapping and an all-too-familiar throat clearing. I looked up bleary-eyed to find Mom standing over me wearing a black and white vertical striped dress I hadn't seen before, most likely a new conquest.

"Well, hello there. So nice of you to wake up." She laid the sarcasm on thick. "I'm sorry to disturb you on your day off."

"My wha...?" I propped myself up on an elbow. "What time is it?"

"It's 3:30. Just in time for you to be leaving school, but clearly you're already here. If you're sick, Ana, you'd better tell me now."

"I'm not sick." Or was I? What was the smart play here? Too late. I'd already said it. "Um, I'm just really tired."

"You were tired when you got home yesterday too." Her eyes narrowed. "Do you have mono? I thought you and Isaac were just friends."

"We are, Mom. I don't have mono, and neither does Isaac, not that we'd be kissing anyway." My nose wrinkled. I gave my head a little shake to clear the thought.

"Taking a mental health day then, are we?"

"Yeah, I guess you'd call it that. Or a mental half-day?" I hedged. If she'd just gotten home, she'd have no idea how much school I'd missed.

"I got a call from the secretary."

Crud.

"She said you were absent from all your classes. I covered for you, of course, like any good mother would. I told her you were sick, and I apologized for not calling in for you."

"Thank you, Mom." I wished I'd said it with greater enthusiasm. It could've earned me some points.

"The secretary also happened to mention Isaac wasn't in school today, either. Now isn't that interesting? What have you and he been up to? Hmm?" Her toe began tapping again, in double time. The sound burrowed into my skull.

I let out a sigh and pressed my fingers against my forehead. "Yes, Mom, you got me. Isaac and I were up all night making out and now I'm totally worn out."

So much for earning points.

She pinched the bridge of her nose. "I don't care much for sarcasm, Ana. Instead, why don't you tell me what's really going on?"

I flopped my arm across my eyes. "You wouldn't believe me anyway."

She lifted my arm. "Why don't you try me?" Her tone was cool and low.

I breathed in, then exhaled slowly.

Screw it.

Maybe I was still disoriented from the midday nap, or maybe I just wanted to tell somebody. Or maybe I hoped it would get her off my back. Whatever the reason, I ignored Isaac's warning and told her. Everything.

First, it was the disappearing rabbit food. She snorted in disbelief.

Then masked men breaking into the house and kidnapping Isaac. Her eyes grew wide then narrowed.

Next came me swallowing the pill and escaping. She rolled her eyes.

The invisible drive home? She just shook her head.

Finally, I relayed the events of today. She stood looking at me with her hands on her hips.

When I finished, I felt better. At least I wasn't the only one, other than Isaac and his captors, who knew about all this insanity.

Not that Mom believed a word.

"Honestly, Ana, you've come up with some real doozies in the past, but this is your most creative story yet. Disappearing rabbits. Bad guys in masks kidnapping your friend." She raised her arms and dropped them. "It's great stuff. You should enter this into your next writing contest. You'd win for sure." She turned on her heel and left.

At least it made her leave me alone. I rolled over.

Half an hour later, I got up and took a shower. It was more just standing in the stream than actual showering. I thought the warm water washing over me would make me feel better, but it didn't. I was hopeless and back to square one. If Isaac needed me to figure this out, we were both in trouble.

I returned to my bedroom in a bathrobe with a towel on my head when the doorbell rang.

The front door opened, and Mom said, "What is it now?" in an acid tone.

I opened my door a crack to see downstairs. The bald man standing in the doorway pulled his navy jacket away from his wide girth to reveal his badge.

Oh no. Not again. I was wearing the hat and jacket. I even kept the gloves on to be sure.

"Pardon me, ma'am?" the man said.

She sighed. "I'm sorry, officer."

"It's Detective O'Hare."

"I'm sorry, *Detective.* It's just there was another policeman here last night. Surely my daughter wasn't driving hunched down in her seat again today?"

"No, Mrs. Roberts, this has nothing to do with that, but I do need to speak with her. Is she home?"

This must be about Isaac. Great. The police are on the case. But what do they want with me?

Probably to ask you questions, dummy. I gasped. *How are they going to do that?*

"She might be home. Why do you need to know?" Mom didn't try to hide her irritation.

Detective O'Hare regarded her coolly as he reached into his jacket pocket and pulled out a folded piece of paper. "This is a warrant to search the premises for your daughter and any evidence that would help us with our investigation." He stepped into the house. Three officers followed him. The last to enter was Ben Cody.

I hung my head. *Why does it have to be him again?*

"Barnes, Cody, you check upstairs. Halloway, you take down."

Mom gaped at him. "What investigation?" She put her arms out in vain to stop the officers from walking by her. "Wait a minute."

Ben, *of course,* was headed straight to my room.

Mom came after him, the detective following her.

"What's this all about?" she demanded, halfway up the stairs.

"It's regarding your daughter's friend, Isaac Mason," Detective O'Hare said.

Ben reached my room. I cringed back against the wall and turned my head to the side as he pushed the door open.

"What about Isaac?" Mom said as she entered the room. Ben reached around her to slide open my closet.

"He's missing. Please stay out of the way, ma'am," the detective said.

She stepped back toward the wall and spotted me behind the door. Her eyes widened as she took in my robe and towel.

I shook my head.

She cleared her throat. "What do you mean missing? And what does this have to do with Ana?" She shifted over to further block their view of me. The idea of me being seen by outsiders, let alone police officers, in a bathrobe and towel, saved me. She would consider it a major breach of decorum.

I peered over her shoulder. Ben pushed aside the clothes in my closet and inspected the shelves, which contained little more than shoe boxes filled with oil pastels, watercolors, paint brushes, and other supplies for when I was feeling creative in a medium other than writing.

Detective O'Hare didn't answer her. He walked to my desk and picked up a framed picture of Isaac and me at a county fair, touching our pink cotton candy together as if we were clinking wine glasses.

"Is this the two of them here?" he asked.

"Yes, that's them."

"I'd like to take this with me."

She hesitated. "Okay."

Must they? I love that picture.

Mom lifted her hands and shook them toward the detective. "You still haven't told me what this is about."

Detective O'Hare shifted his weight and stared at her for a moment. Meanwhile, Ben checked under the bed skirt. The dust bunnies weren't hiding me there. Then he headed toward my bathroom. I prayed I hadn't left it too dirty.

"As I mentioned, Isaac Mason is missing. When we investigated the Mason home, we found signs suggesting a struggle."

What? How? The place was scrubbed clean.

Ben returned from the bathroom with my cell phone and tossed it to O'Hare. With horror I realized I'd left it on the back of the toilet.

"We'll need to take a look at this," the detective said. Mom regarded the phone with a blank stare like she'd forgotten what the thing was.

Losing my phone didn't matter much since I'd already lost Isaac. Who was left for me to text? Remembering that I hadn't sent "omw" when I headed to Isaac's yesterday, gave me some relief. The cops would have no proof I'd been there. They couldn't force me to reveal Isaac's secret and break his trust.

"Moreover, your daughter's fingerprints were at the scene," O'Hare continued.

Ummm...

"Of course they were. Ana's there all the time," Mom said.

Obviously.

"They were found in a place that raises concerns," the detective said in a grim voice.

I put my hand over my mouth. The fire extinguisher. I'd forgotten about that.

"Wait. Did you say a struggle? At Isaac's house? And how do you have my daughter's prints?"

"When she got her driver's license, she was required to leave a thumb print with the DMV. Since she's Isaac's only known associate, it was a quick match. Now I need to question her. It would save us all a lot of time if you just told us where she is."

Though I didn't think it possible, the detective's tone had become even more serious. Just like this situation. I didn't like where it was headed. Would Mom rat me out? Even if just to clear my name?

"This is ridiculous, Detective," she said. "I can't believe you would suspect Ana. She'd never do anything to hurt Isaac."

Exactly.

"We'll determine that, ma'am."

Ben riffled through my desk drawers. The shock of this invasion of privacy made my fists clench. Looking around my room and bathroom was one thing, but this?

When he pulled my thick leather-bound diary from a drawer, I gasped. Mom shot me a warning look. I couldn't help it. My diary contained my deepest thoughts since freshman year. He flipped through several pages toward the end. No doubt he saw Isaac's name multiple times. He shut the book with a snap and nodded to O'Hare.

"We'll have to take that with us too," O'Hare said.

Mom lifted her hands and let them fall in defeat. "Whatever."

I poked her shoulder. She ignored me.

"Clear down here," Halloway called from downstairs.

I poked Mom again.

"Here too," said Barnes as she walked past my door.

I poked Mom again and again.

Detective O'Hare nodded to Ben and left the room. Ben started to follow him.

After the next jab, Mom looked at me.

"Not the diary," I mouthed, shaking my head. "No. No. No."

She gave the tiniest of shrugs, as if to say, "What can I do?"

Our exchange did not go unnoticed.

"Ma'am, please step away from the door."

CHAPTER 4

Mom stared at Ben, her mouth agape. I glanced down at myself. I'd just showered. Would Ben see a floating bathrobe and towel?

Fear caused an instant heat in my armpits.

Oh good. I'm sweating.

But would it be enough to make the towel invisible too?

Mom's face twisted into an apologetic grimace as she moved out of the way.

Ben's fingers curled around the edge of the door.

Oh no.

I grasped the corner of the towel and thrust it in my mouth. I shut my eyes tight then opened them, one after the other.

Ben was facing me. Something inside of me did a somersault. I stared into his eyes, which, this close, were a darker blue than I remembered.

As usual, he looked right through me.

"Never mind, ma'am," he said and stepped away.

Mom ducked her face behind the door and cocked her head to the side. Her eyebrows pressed so close together they were almost touching.

Ben headed downstairs. After a moment, Mom followed, clutching the railing for support. The three officers went outside, but Detective O'Hare turned to her.

"We'll need to speak to your daughter at some point. Maybe you could bring her to the station tomorrow so we don't have to come looking for her again."

Mom nodded, her face pale. She'd been shocked into silence.

So that's what it takes.

The detective closed the door behind him.

It was like déjà vu. Mom leaned her back against the door, just as she had the day before, only this time she slid to the floor. With a blank expression, she stared at her feet sprawled out in front of her.

"Mom?" I said in a low voice as I walked downstairs.

"He didn't see you." She wheezed as though the wind had been knocked out of her. "How did he not see you?" She looked up at me. "Why couldn't he see you, Ana?"

"I told you, Mom. Isaac made me invisible." I kept my tone gentle.

She shook her head. "It's not possible."

"I wouldn't have thought so either."

"But... how?"

"I don't know, Mom. He tried to explain it, but—" I shrugged. "Anyway, here I am." I gestured to myself.

"What does it," she stopped, apparently having a hard time finding the right words. "Feel like?" she finally said.

"It doesn't feel like anything. I mean, I feel the same, physically." Never mind the emotional and potential future mental implications.

"Good," she said with a long exhale. "But wait, *I* can see you." She furrowed her brow at me.

"That's because you're my mom. Only my relatives can see me."

"Ooo-kay." She splayed her fingers across her face and closed her eyes. They blinked open again. "Wait, do you mean only *blood* relatives can see you?"

I nodded.

She stared off into the distance for a moment then forced herself to her feet. Her eyes took on a wild cast as she pushed past me, up the stairs and into her bedroom. The door shut.

It was a lot to process. She needed time. I understood, and I was glad I'd purposely failed to mention the seven-day ticking time bomb to permanent invisibility, insanity, and death. No way she could handle that. I could hardly handle it.

I returned to my room to get dressed and consider this new development. I was a suspect. Correction: I was *the* suspect, which was crazy. Did they have no other leads? Then again, how would they with that sterile basement and the kidnappers wearing ski masks and gloves? If only I could give them some clue as to what really happened, but how? Frustrated, I turned my thoughts to Ben taking my diary. My fists balled up again as I paced the room. How dare he? Being ridiculously hot was no excuse. Couldn't he have seen it in my drawer and just ignored it? Would he actually read it? A high-pitched "Eeep" escaped my lips, and my cheeks flamed.

My fingers relaxed. I had an idea.

I rushed to Mom's room and knocked on the door.

No answer.

"Mom, can I come in?"

Still nothing.

"Mom?"

After a moment, I made out the word, "Okay."

I pushed the door open and found her sitting on the edge of her bed, hands clasped, eyes downcast.

"This is so incredible," she said. "I just can't believe it."

"I know, Mom. I'm sorry." I eased myself onto the bed next to her.

"What do we do? How can we get you back to normal again, and fast?" Her eyes were insistent as she grasped my hands.

"I've got a plan, but I need you to drive me to the police station."

"What? Why? You're not turning yourself in, are you?"

"Of course not. Besides, how could I?"

"Right." She looked at the carpet again, then up at me. "What are you going to do?"

"Just trust me, okay?"

She drew in a faltering breath. "Fine," she said, defeated.

"First, I need to borrow your fancy white gloves. My winter ones are too bulky."

"Huh?" She squinted at me, but then lifted and dropped her hands. "Whatever you say." With effort, she got up and went to her walk-in closet, returning with the long white satin gloves she often wore to fundraisers.

I tugged them on and flexed my fingers. These felt good. The winter ones were too loose. I couldn't risk one slipping off and falling to the floor, appearing out of nowhere in a room full of cops. "All right, let's go."

When we left the house, Mrs. Granville across the street was peering between her curtains. No doubt the arrival of the police had piqued her interested. It probably made her day.

"Open your car door and pretend to search for something in your purse while I get in," I said.

"Okay." She still sounded mystified.

"Don't talk, just do it. No need to make the neighbors think you're crazy."

She laughed nervously, which didn't help her cause.

As she rooted in her purse, I slid across to the passenger seat. She got in after me, moving like a marionette on strings.

When we pulled up across the street from the police station, I turned to her. "Give me fifteen minutes inside. Just drop me off and go buy eyeliner or something at the store."

"I'd rather wait."

"You shouldn't. What if they see you? It might look suspicious."

"I wish you'd tell me what you're up to."

"Don't worry about me. Store. Please."

She looked like she was about to protest but then muttered something about needing mascara.

We repeated our routine of Mom getting out of the car and checking her purse while I slipped out.

"You're sure you'll be okay in there, sweetie?" she said through her open window.

She never called me sweetie.

"I'll be fine, Mom. You can go. I promise I won't be seen."

She closed her eyes and sighed heavily. My attempt at lightening the mood had failed.

After she pulled away from the curb, I waited for a car to pass then jay-walked across the street to the station. The front door was propped open. That was one hurdle overcome, but the next challenge became obvious as soon as I stepped inside.

A wooden half door separated the waiting area from the offices beyond. Flush against the door was a raised platform with a desk. It was manned by a police officer typing on a computer. The only other person in the room was a woman with spiky pink hair, a low-cut shirt, short skirt, and black leather high-heeled boots. She was sitting in a chair against the wall, biting her red fingernails.

I walked to the swinging door and considered it. The tall desk on one side and an even higher partial wall on the other made the space too narrow for me to just sit down and swing my legs over. If I jumped, I could probably get one leg over, but then I'd have to hop away from the door to clear the second leg. I could just imagine someone coming through as I was stuck straddling the door. It was too risky.

Could I pull myself up onto the wall? Probably not since I had the upper body strength of a hamster. Plus, I wouldn't be able to hide the sound of my feet scrambling against the wall. The low volume of the television in the corner near the ceiling would do little to mask the sound of my efforts.

My irritation mounted as the minutes passed with me, arms crossed, staring at that stupid door.

A middle-aged policeman came down the hallway and up to the door. He hit a button on the other side of the wall. A buzzer sounded, and I leaped back as the door swung out. He held it open.

"Christina Marken, you can come back now," he said.

Spiky pink hair stepped forward. I got right behind her, careful not to run into her as she strutted through the door. I was almost through when it swung shut with a click and bumped my butt.

I followed the cop and Spiky down the hallway until they walked past a large open room with twenty desks in four neat rows. I broke away and scanned the room. Normally, from behind, it would be difficult to pick out one particular policeman, but I'd been studying Ben Cody from multiple angles for years.

He was on the left, three desks in. I stepped around one officer and hugged the wall, keeping my back to it as I slid around the corner, pausing and holding my breath when a cop walked by. Finally, I was next to Ben. I relaxed my shoulders and soaked in his soft brown curls, his deep blue eyes. My gosh, he was beautiful.

Remember what you came for.

Sure enough, as I'd both hoped and feared, he was reading my diary. He sat back in his chair and rested the book against the edge of the desk. He curled his fingers over his mouth and chin, his index finger across his cheek. A smile tugged on the corners of his lips.

Oh, no. What is he reading?

I edged closer. The entry was from freshman year:

Today a sophomore girl's backpack zipper broke while she was walking down the hallway. Everything spilled out. Books and notebooks splayed. Folders fell open with papers spewing out. Pens and pencils rolled across the floor. I was so embarrassed for her and then wanted to be her as I saw Ben Cody step forward gallantly. He corralled all her writing utensils and helped collect her books and notebooks. She smiled at him appreciatively. He returned a gleaming smile back. I suddenly hated that girl.

Ben chuckled.

I felt like my entire body had turned bright red.

He scanned a few pages and stopped again when he saw his name. It didn't take long. The page was dated October 20th of the same year.

I saw Ben today at the grocery store. He was picking out golden delicious apples. I like that kind too! Suddenly, he looked in my direction, so I ducked behind a Halloween display. I don't think he saw me.

Now Ben was shaking his head, his smile broadened.

O.M.G. How many such entries had he read before I got here? I knew there were about a hundred. I wanted to crumble into ash and blow away.

"Hey, rookie, you find anything useful in there?" another officer called.

"Uh, not yet. Still checking." He flipped to the more recent entries in the back.

"Come over here a minute and take a look at this."

Ben got up, leaving my diary on his desk. Several nearby cops followed him and gathered around the officer's computer screen. Here was my chance. I made sure no one was watching as I lowered the diary onto Ben's chair and leafed through the pages. Finally, I spotted an entry mentioning Isaac's online chat group, Inventor's Haven. I checked again that no one was looking and grabbed a pen from the mug on Ben's desk. Kneeling next to the chair, I circled "InventorsHaven.com," drew a line to the margin, and wrote "Apple Pi," underlining it several times.

The group of officers around the computer laughed and began returning to their desks. I put the diary back but was still holding the pen. Ben was two steps away. I dropped the pen on the floor and hopped back.

When Ben sat down and pushed his chair in, he stepped on the pen. His forehead creased as he scooted back to retrieve it and return it to the mug. When he turned back to the diary, my scribbled notation was impossible to miss. He swiveled to his computer, opened a new window, and typed inventorshaven.com in the navigation bar. A page opened with images of a cotton gin and printing press around the title in the banner. Ben clicked a button labeled, "Join the discussion." He was forced to register, so he filled in bogus information. Then he wrote, "Hey, everyone. I invented…" His fingers paused as he stared at the screen. "A hovercraft."

I stifled a laugh. Isaac had called hovercraft elementary.

"Let's see it," wrote JuniorEinstein3.0.

"Who cares," wrote Parrafinwax1.

"Who hasn't?" chimed in Gearsncheers.

We waited. Several more comments popped up in quick succession, most of them uncomplimentary.

Ben and I leaned closer to the computer, though I kept my distance from him, with difficulty. He smelled like chai tea, and I suddenly had a craving. For chai tea, also.

"Haven't you got anything else?" appeared on the screen.

It was from Apple Pi.

I lurched back as Ben sat up straight. "Gaines," he called, "I'm going to snag an IP address from a chat room user. We can get a physical address from there, right?"

"Sure," the officer two desks away said. "Once we have the IP, we can contact the internet company who provided it, and get the physical address from them."

"Good," Ben said.

Great. They're on their way. Now to get out of here.

I checked the time on Ben's computer. My fifteen minutes were almost up. Mom would be outside waiting for me soon. I hated leaving my diary behind, but there was no hope for it. I stood and hugged the wall, walking sideways around the room and retraced my steps to the waiting room.

Next came the problem of the electronic wooden door. I waited for someone to come through. The policewoman at the desk was telling a man how to get his car out of impound. Another man sat with his arms crossed, staring at the TV.

I kept waiting.

Through the open front door, I watched Mom pull up across the street. Two minutes later she got out and looked toward the station. I was still trapped behind the door, hearing the policewoman repeat her instructions for the third time.

Mom checked her watch. According to the clock on the wall, I was seven minutes late.

Don't come in, Mom. What will you say? "Excuse me, have you seen my invisible daughter around here?"

She walked to the other side of her car.

I bounced on my toes. *Think. Think.*

Mom looked left and right, ready to cross the street.

Spotting the policewoman's pen cup, I reached in front of her and tipped it over, making her stop mid-sentence. She and the man stared at the blue and white pens spilled on the floor on the other side of the wall.

"I'm sorry. Did I bump that?" the man said.

"It's okay," the policewoman said as she hopped off her stool and buzzed the door open. I rushed through ahead of her and out the front door just as Mom was coming in.

"What happ—"

I put an index finger to my lips and spun her around. "It's done," I whispered and led her back to the car.

On the way home, I told her what I'd done. She seemed far less interested in the method than in the possible result.

"Good. They'll find Isaac and get you back to normal right away," she said.

I didn't know if Isaac had an antidote for me. Most likely not. And what if it took days to prepare? More days than I had left? "Yea. At least, I hope so," I said.

She made an indelicate noise in her throat.

"No need to worry, though. This is Isaac we're talking about. If he can make people invisible, he can make them visible again, but it may take a little time."

She nodded, slowly. "You're okay, though, right? You're don't feel sick or anything?"

"No, Mom. I'm fine. But thank you for asking." Probably best to leave it at that.

She pursed her lips and said nothing for a minute. When she finally spoke, she seemed to be concentrating on each word.

"Okay, listen, Ana. There's something I need to tell you before tomorrow."

We turned onto our street. I waited for her to continue. "What is it?" I said when she didn't.

"This isn't going to be easy." She hesitated. "And you aren't going to like it, but I need you to hear me out."

"What, Mom?" Her uncertain tone was out of character and freaked me out a little.

"Well..."

I could see our house. An Uber was parked in front. A tall, thin man with salt in his pepper hair was getting bags out of the trunk.

"Look. Dad's home early."

She slammed on the brakes. The tires squealed. I was thrown forward then jerked back by my seatbelt.

"Mom!"

"Sorry, honey, I—thought I saw a squirrel."

A total lie. What had gotten into her?

Dad shut the trunk of the car and tapped it. The Uber drove away. We pulled into the driveway and Mom got out of the car, leaving her door open for me to slide out.

"Was that you squealing your tires?" Dad asked as he walked up to her.

"Yes, I saw a squirrel," she said.

"Be careful, Ronnie. What if there'd been a car behind you?"

"I know. I checked the rearview mirror before I hit the brakes."

Sure you did.

"Well, hey, sweetheart, I'm back early." He dropped his bags, threw his arms around her, and gave her a long, lingering kiss that made me feel the need to look away. When he stepped back, she was frowning.

"Don't worry. The golf outing was called off because some yahoo at one of the branches screwed up royally. The CEO had to get back and clean up the mess. It wasn't because of anything I did that he canceled, so cheer up." He smiled. "I'm just glad I'm not that other guy." He picked up his bags and headed toward the front door.

"Hi, Dad—" I began, but Mom spoke over me.

"I'm sorry to hear that, but it's nice to have you home." She shut the car door and followed him.

I jogged to catch up. I put my arms out, ready to give him a hug, but Mom stepped in front of me. I was confused, but then remembered we were outside. A man hugging empty air would be an odd sight. I returned Mom's gaze and nodded.

Right you are.

I followed Dad into the foyer as he set his bags down. "Good to see you," I said, but at the same moment Mom kicked his suitcase over and slammed the door.

Dad spun around. "What happened?"

"Oops," Mom said with an innocent shrug. "I guess I don't know my own strength."

"Well, take it easy," he said with a smirk. "And did you say something?"

"I just wondered if you were hungry. Can I get you something?"

"I could use a beer."

He still hadn't so much as acknowledged me. Fine, if he needed a drink, I wouldn't get in his way, but still.

Then he turned to Mom and said two words that almost knocked me over.

"Where's Ana?"

CHAPTER 5

The blood drained from my face.

"Oh, she's out with a friend," Mom said as she ushered Dad to the kitchen.

"Isaac, I assume?" he said with a laugh since there were no other options.

"Yes, Isaac." She glanced over her shoulder at me. In that single look were multiple emotions: sorrow, regret, fear. And pleading.

How long I stood there listening to the droning of their voices from the kitchen, I wasn't sure. When I realized my legs could move again, I forced them to drag me upstairs. As if in a daze, my eyes unfocused, I entered my room and gave the door a shove behind me. Though it was dark, I didn't bother with the light. I went to my bed, shoes and all, and curled into a ball under the covers. I stared into the dimness.

He's not my dad.

The thought hung in my mind for several heartbeats, finally replaced by: *Who is he then? And does he know I'm not his?*

Judging by his affection toward Mom, I guessed she'd lied to him too. Was she going to tell him, or was she afraid he might leave her once he knew the truth? If she didn't tell him, how would she keep it from him now? Would she make me stay hidden in my room, telling him I had a horrible virus, and he should stay away? Then he might never have to know what was really going on. No wonder she was so eager for Isaac to get back. It wasn't out of concern for his safety. All she could talk about was getting me back to normal. She wouldn't want to keep up this act for long.

And then came the real question: Who *was* my dad? Mom seemed so by-the-book. Did she have some sort of wild past?

Their raised voices drifted up to me from downstairs. I tilted my head toward the door and realized I hadn't shut it all the way. I winced, not wanting to get up.

"Why did you tell her?" Dad said. "We had an agreement."

He knows?

"I didn't tell her," Mom said. "She found out on her own."

"How is that even possible?"

"Well, it certainly wasn't *my* idea."

There was a pause.

"What happened here, Ronnie?"

I couldn't make out her response, but it was followed by silence.

"Have you been sampling the cooking sherry?"

"It's true, John. I didn't believe it myself until the police came."

"The police came?" His voice had risen several octaves.

I pulled the blankets over my head.

Roughly fifteen minutes later there was a knock on my door. I knew she would come, but I said nothing. After a second knock went unanswered, she pushed the door open and turned on the light. Slowly, she closed the door behind her and sat at the foot of my bed.

After a moment, she said, "I explained things to your father as best I could." Her voice was low and trembly.

"Now explain things to me." My voice was rock solid.

"Ana." She touched my leg, but I pulled it away. It was childish, but I couldn't help myself. It was like I hardly knew this woman.

She sighed. "Listen, I was going to tell you, eventually. I certainly never *dreamed* you'd find out this way."

"What was it, Mom? An affair? Or were you married before and figured I'd never do the math because I'm not good with numbers? How long were you planning to keep this up?"

"Well." She rubbed her fingertips across the smooth finish of her polished thumbnails. "We thought we'd wait until after you graduated college. You'd be more grounded then. Teenagers tend to be a little more... emotional."

"Emotional?" I pushed myself upright. "Did you think I would *ever* take this well? You've lied to me, Mom. My whole life I thought he was my dad, but instead my dad is, is what? A one-night stand? Some crazy fling because you got bored or drunk at some point? What?"

She took a deep breath. It was too long.

"Explain yourself!"

She put her hands up. "All right. All right. As I said, we were going to tell you. Your father and I—"

"Clearly he's *not* my father." I stopped, tears welling up from words I never thought would come from my mouth. But I'd have to dwell on that later. Right now, the best defense for keeping it together was anger. I swatted away the tears and pulled my shoulders back. "So, who is he really?"

She tilted her forehead toward me and exhaled through her nose. "For all intents and purposes, he is your father. This was a decision we made together." She drew in a faltering breath and stared again at her fingernails. "You were conceived through a, a donor."

My mouth fell open. I had *not* considered this possibility. When I found my voice, "Why?" was all I could manage to choke out.

"We tried for," she raised and dropped her hands, "seven years. And still, I couldn't get pregnant. We both got tested and discovered it had something to do with your father. We considered doing in vitro fertilization, but it was really expensive and doesn't have a great success rate. At the time, this was the best option."

"You really wanted a baby that badly?" My tone thawed. Maybe I could give her some credit.

"Well, we needed one. At your father's accounting firm, it was frowned upon to not have a family."

She said it as though this explained everything. She might as well have added, "Duh."

I gaped at her. Then I closed my eyes and shook my head. "I'm not hearing this. I can't *truly* be hearing this. You're joking, Mom. Please tell me you're joking."

"Oh, but we love you, Ana. We love you very much. Having you was the best decision we ever made." She rubbed my leg again. I didn't move away this time, but only because my legs, and the rest of me, felt like iron.

"Honestly, I don't know why you're taking this so hard. I mean, I knew it would be a shock, but why are you so upset? True, your father isn't your *biological* father, but he's still your dad. If we hadn't done this, you wouldn't even exist. Aren't you happy to be alive?"

Now it was my turn to fume through my nostrils like an angered bull. "So, you're telling me you *made* me. You…" I cast my eyes about the room, searching for the word. "You *manufactured* me just so Dad could get ahead in his business?"

"We did sort of want a child already, but that was what finally put it over the edge for us. We were starting to feel uncomfortable at company picnics. People were making comments, asking questions. It was awful." She gave me a pitiful expression as though I was supposed to feel sorry for her.

"I still can't believe what I'm hearing. You 'sort of' wanted a child?" I searched her face, waiting for an expression of concern, a word of comfort. When neither came, my voice dropped to a whisper. "How could you do this to me?"

"What do you mean, 'do this to you'?" Her forehead wrinkled. "We made you."

I stared at her for a moment. "You made me because it was too inconvenient not to. You made me to impress your friends and to keep up your image. Have you ever noticed that it's always about you? The beauty pageants and dance recitals when I was a kid? I hated those. But you insisted I do them because you needed something to 'tell the ladies about me.' It was never about me." I pointed to the door. "Leave," I said. "Please," I added through gritted teeth.

She opened her mouth to speak, but I had heard enough. "You can go now," I said, struggling to keep my voice steady.

She lifted her chin and left the room, pulling the door shut behind her.

I sank into my bed, putting the pillow over my head, hoping in vain to drown out everything: light, noise from the cars on the street, my parents' voices in the hallway. Instead, they all felt magnified, pounding into my brain.

The realization that the man I knew my whole life as my father was anything but was a jab to my gut. How was I supposed to feel about him now? What was I supposed to call him? Was he still my dad? Guilt curled its smoky tendrils around my heart when, for a flickering moment, I considered him an imposter.

I pressed the base of my hands against my eyes. This couldn't be real. Being invisible was bad enough, but this? This was far worse. Was my whole life a sham? I thought I knew them, but now my parents were strangers to me, and I a trespasser in their home. *I* was the imposter. I longed to leave but where would I go? Normally it would be to Isaac's house, but he was gone.

"Isaac," I called faintly to no one.

Aching for him, I squeezed the blankets around me, trying to suck out whatever comfort I could, but it wasn't nearly enough. How badly I wanted Isaac.

I crammed my eyelids shut but couldn't hold back the tears. One after the other rolled down my face until the sheet beneath me grew soggy.

My parents never really wanted me. They never *really* wanted me. And Isaac was nowhere to be found.

I'd never felt more alone in my life.

After what felt like hours, a wave of sleep crashed over me, carrying me along as it rolled back out across the dark, endless sea. My last thoughts were of Isaac, wondering if he, wherever he was, was calling my name too.

5 Days

Morning arrived stubbornly against my wishes. Light through the partially open blinds sent stripes of black shadow across the room like prison bars.

Only five days left to get an antidote from Isaac, but what did it matter? I dropped my clothes in a crumpled heap on the bathroom floor and turned on the shower. As I sat with my forehead on my knees, the water became burning hot. When that ran out, it turned icy cold. I dried off haphazardly before throwing the towel on my pile of rumpled clothes.

Waiting for me on my desk were a stack of pancakes with a large pat of butter melting on top, a mini carafe of syrup, and a tall glass of orange juice. Mom used to get on my case about putting butter on my pancakes, telling me it would make me fat. I shook my head at her weak attempt at a peace offering. I pulled on some clothes and let my hair fall damp and lifeless around my shoulders.

Today was Friday. Isaac had been gone for a day and a half. I knew it was unlikely the police would have any concrete answers yet, but I stayed hopeful they'd find him. I refused to think otherwise.

I grabbed my mom's white gloves and headed downstairs. She heard me and came running.

What good is being invisible if you can't even hide from your own mother?

"Ana, are you okay?" Her hands took turns clasping one in the other.

I didn't answer. Her husband came up behind her, looking in my general direction.

"Where are you going?" Mom asked.

"Isaac's," I said simply and yanked the front door shut behind me, Mrs. Granville be darned. I cut through back alleys and shady parts of town where I wouldn't normally go but, hey, I was invisible. Plus, if anything else bad happened to me, I wouldn't care.

About a mile from Isaac's house, a blue city bus pulled up to the curb near me. Brad from school hopped off. I raised an amused eyebrow. It seemed I wasn't the only one playing hooky. Brad was wearing different shoes than the ones Isaac had gotten with his goo. Maybe he'd had to throw them away.

Seeing Brad gave me an idea. Isaac's house could wait. I hadn't found anything useful in his basement, but maybe there'd be a clue in his locker. As soon as the last person stepped off the bus, I slipped on and took a seat in the back row next to a snoring man in serious need of a shower. It was a safe bet no one else would want this seat. I checked the line map. Four stops would bring me within a few blocks of school.

As the bus started forward, I watched Brad stride away to who knows where and kicked myself for missing a prime opportunity. I should've tripped him. He would've never seen it coming.

At each stop, passengers got on and off the bus. I cringed closer to the sleeping man when a woman looked ready to take my seat, but she shuttered, gripped her nose, and turned away.

As the bus drew nearer my stop, I waited for someone to pull the cord, but no one did. I stood and looked down the road. No one was waiting on the bench to get on, either. The driver checked his overhead mirror to see if anyone rose to get off. No one did, other than me. The bus sped up. It was nearly upon the stop.

I lunged for the cord. The driver hit the brakes, making me fall against the seat ahead of me. The people occupying it turned and looked through me.

"Cutting it close," the driver called in irritation as he swung the door open.

I rushed up the aisle as quickly as I could on tiptoes.

"Anyone getting off?" he said, searching his mirror.

I swept past him as he shook his head and yanked the door handle, muttering to himself. Turning sideways, I leaped. The door nipped the heel of my shoe as it slammed shut. My hip crashed onto the sidewalk. The hem of my shirt tore, and my elbow was scraped raw but not bleeding. It stung as I wiped off the bits of dirt and gravel. I exhaled slowly, stood, and limped away.

My stride was back to normal by the time I reached school. I didn't know Isaac's locker combination, but I'd try to guess it anyway. I doubted he'd use pi again, but who was I kidding? I still only remembered the 3.14. Maybe I'd get lucky with a birthday. If it came to it, I could put my ear up to the lock and try to hear it click when I reached the correct number. It was worth a try.

With a gloved hand, I opened the door just wide enough to slip inside. The hallway was teeming with students. *In between classes. Great.*

Everywhere I heard Isaac's and my name being whispered. Apparently, it took our disappearance for people to care about us.

Weaving between bodies was no easy task. One kid jogged past me and clipped my shoulder.

"Sorry," he called. Looking back, but seeing no offended faces, he shrugged and kept going.

When I turned around again, I hopped back just in time to avoid smacking into another kid. I spotted a math and a P.E. teacher and dodged students to catch up to them. Everyone steered clear of teachers, making walking behind them an easier path.

I listened to their conversation without *entirely* meaning to.

"I can understand needing to check things out, but couldn't they have waited for school to end first?" Coach Weaver said. "Surely that would've been a better time for the police to arrive."

"What?" I clasped my hand over my mouth.

The teachers stopped and turned, looking through me to a group of female students gathered nearby. The girls looked at them, said nothing, and went back to talking. The teachers exchanged a glance and kept going.

I leaned forward to hear the coach better.

"I'm just saying, couldn't they have come after hours? It's so hard to get my students engaged with all this commotion."

"Why do you care? You teach gym. Try holding their interest through trigonometry on a day like this," Mr. Rusket said.

"Still, it's more fun when they all participate. Not that Mason and Roberts ever did. The girl had real potential, though. She just didn't care."

Whoa. That had to be the nicest thing the coach had ever said about me. Usually, he was yelling at me to hustle and move my feet. He'd given up on Isaac long ago.

"I wish I could say the same about her in math," Mr. Rusket said.

Fair point.

"How was Mason?" Coach asked.

"How do you think? He took trig as a sophomore. My greatest challenge was not letting on that he could probably teach it better than I could."

I smiled. *That's my Isaac.*

Around the corner a crowd had formed right where I wanted to go—Isaac's locker. I broke away from the teachers and threaded my way closer.

"Stay back everyone, please," Principal Meyers said in an exasperated tone. She and a guidance counselor were holding the curious onlookers at bay. I slipped between the kids and ducked under the adults' outstretched arms.

Isaac's locker hung open. I wouldn't be playing safe cracker after all. Part of me was disappointed.

In front of the locker stood two police officers. I didn't recognize either of them and frowned despite myself. No Ben.

One officer was flipping through the stack of crisp notebooks neatly piled on the top shelf.

"Another one empty," he said.

"And look at this," said the other policeman. "A full box of pre-sharpened pencils. This kid must be a real hit with the ladies."

The first cop snickered. "Have you ever seen such a clean locker? Especially for a dude? And not a single picture hanging up." He picked up Isaac's Calculus II book and paged through it. Stuck inside were folded sheets of notebook paper covered with neatly printed math problems. "What do you make of this?" he said, showing it to the other officer.

"Looks like he's done his homework for the rest of the year."

The first cop shook his head. "Poor kid has no life."

He has me. My shoulders drooped. *Sort of.*

The other officer picked up Isaac's chemistry book. "Hello, what's this?" Tucked under the back flap of the book cover was a copy of the periodic table. It had been folded and unfolded so many times it was cracked at the seams. He held it out for the two of them to study. I balanced on my toes and peered over their shoulders.

A dozen or so elements had been circled in black marker. Some had angry red Xs through them, while others were highlighted in yellow.

"Probably for some sort of science fair project," one of them said.

I stifled a snort. What an understatement. That must be the key to his formula—or the antidote. But there was no way I could get it. I'd have to memorize it.

Hydrogen, Carbon, Iron, Iodine, Sodium... What's Ba? Maybe try a mnemonic. HIC-Fe-NaBa...

Too late. The cop was folding the table back up before I could catch the rest of the elements. He tucked it into the book and dropped it on the floor of the locker. I bit the corner of my lip, wondering how I could sneak in and grab it. Then I realized it didn't matter. Even if those highlighted elements were the key ingredients for invisibility, I didn't know their proportions or how or when to combine them. The table would be of no use to me.

The second cop dropped another book on the pile and said, "Let's go. This was a dead end." He swung the door shut.

I slunk away in agreement. A waste of time.

The bell rang and kids scattered like roaches when a light turns on. After a few bumps into confused students, I worked my way to a row of lockers and flattened myself against it. When the hallway cleared, my heart lurched as I realized I was standing in front of my freshman locker. The memory of that first day four years ago flooded back to me. I looked to the left, almost able to see Jennifer at her locker next to mine.

"Have you seen that new kid, Isaac, yet?" she asked, her eyes aglow with fresh news. "He just moved here from Florida. I hear he's a total brainiac. Shh. Here he comes." She nodded in his direction then turned to her locker, pretending not to watch.

Isaac walked down the hall, talking with another boy, who looked as comfortable as though his clothes were made of sandpaper.

"No, no, no. Water has the capacity to warm you very quickly because it has a high specific heat," Isaac said. "Clay is only 920 joules per kilogram per degree Celsius, but water is 4,190 joules..." The boy waved him off and hurried away. Isaac slowed to a stop, looking after him and frowning. The other students in the hallway snickered or rolled their eyes. In my mind a huge jar appeared around Isaac, trapping him inside like a helpless insect. He pressed his hands around the edges, pushed at the gold-colored lid, and pounded his fists on the glass. He looked at me, wide-eyed and desperate, shouting something unheard.

"Ana. Hello. Ana."

"Huh?" I said when Jennifer grabbed my arm.

"You better get a move on. Bell's gonna ring," she said as she jogged away.

I looked around and blinked. Isaac was gone and so was everyone else. I rushed down the hall to physical science, making it just as the bell rang. All the chairs at the double tables were taken except for one. I was about to sit when Jeremy jumped up from another table and slid into the empty seat. He gave me a smug look. I turned to the spot he'd left. It was next to Isaac.

"No problem," I said to Jeremy. "I'll be partners with the smart one."

The self-satisfied expression melted from Jeremy's face.

I sat down and gave Isaac what I hoped was a confident-looking smile. I wondered how long it would take him to figure out I was clueless in this subject.

He nodded to me and turned his attention to the teacher. After a few minutes, he pulled out a notebook and pen. I peeked at his writing, but it was gibberish to me.

When Mr. Winestone placed a stack of cards between each student pair and instructed us to arrange them as they'd be in the periodic table, Isaac kept scribbling. I picked up the cards and laid them out. They represented about a third of the elements.

Which one is the atomic number again? Right, the smaller one.

I thought I was making progress when Isaac, without looking up, said, "You've got an alkali metal in with the noble gases."

I stared at the cards.

He pointed to sodium with his pen. "This one. It goes on the other side."

"Well, he doesn't like it over there. Those other metals are too stuffy. He prefers it here with the old farts."

Isaac closed his eyes and shook his head for a moment. "And why is it partially covering argon?" He separated the cards.

"Because," I thought fast, "when you cover the 'r' in argon, together they spell my name. See, ANa."

He shook his head again, this time with a sigh, and turned back to his notebook.

I waited a minute. Then, with the eraser end of my pencil, I slid sodium back into place on top of argon.

"I see that," Isaac said.

I put the card back where it belonged and set my pencil down. I peeked at him from the corner of my eye. He was still looking down, but he was smiling.

After class, I wandered to the cafeteria. Isaac was next to me. Whether I was walking with him or he with me, I wasn't sure. We bought our food, and I sat at the long rectangular table in the corner. Though it was the first day of freshman year in a new school and a new cafeteria, I knew my place.

Isaac took the seat across from me. I was a little surprised but figured he hadn't made any friends yet. I felt bad for him, and I understood. Though I'd been with these people for years, my situation wasn't much better. By association with me or not, Isaac would've ended up here eventually. Even the nerd table gave him the stink eye, no doubt rejecting him because he made them feel as dumb as the jock table. Sure, it was a stereotype, but the muscleheads in our year easily qualified.

After a moment he said, "Traveling through the space-time continuum can, in fact, be achieved if all the necessary conditions are met."

The computer geeks at the other end of our table looked at us, then at each other and shook their heads.

"You know, L'Engle was onto something with her tesseract theory."

"You like *A Wrinkle in Time* then," I said.

"Naturally. That was the first book I read in kindergarten."

Of course. For me it was second grade.

"Using the fifth dimension to bend time is a remarkable theorem. Undoubtedly L'Engle was familiar with Einstein's Special Theory of Relativity," Isaac said.

As he continued, I glanced again at the kids at our table. They scooted farther and farther away.

By the end of the week, we'll have this table to ourselves.

A group of boys walked by, one pausing long enough to say, "Earth to Ana. Are you in there?" He and his friends laughed as they strode away.

"What was that all about?"

I shrugged. "I have a reputation here. Sometimes they call me 'weirdo' or 'space cadet.' That one was pretty old. They're running out of original material."

"You seem perfectly normal to me."

"*You* would think so." I smirked then pushed the food around my plate. "My mind wanders a lot. I've been told I have an active imagination. It means I'm not great at talking with people."

"I hope I'm not boring you."

"No." I met his eyes. "What you're saying is entertaining and totally out there."

"But you're not laughing. That's a first for me."

I speared a chicken nugget with my fork. "Not zoning out, for me, is a real accomplishment."

"For both of us then."

We smiled at each other.

"How long do you think before I get a nickname?" he asked.

I pretended to consider it. "I'd say you have until fifth period."

This time we smiled even brighter.

Less than two hours later, Isaac was called Beaker Brain for the first time.

I wiped a tear from the corner of my eye. Poor Isaac. My heart stabbed with a pang for how much I missed him. I cringed to think of what horribleness he must be enduring. And what was I doing for him besides chasing wild geese? Was there anything else I could do?

My mind came up empty like a freshly robbed vault. I slid to the floor and banged my head against the locker several times. The hollow metallic rattle echoed down the hallway. The nearest classroom door opened and Mrs. Milliger, my eleventh-grade history teacher, poked her head out, looking both ways. Her brow furrowed as she pushed her glasses higher up her nose.

"Is somebody trapped in a locker?" she asked.

Several kids snickered in the classroom behind her.

"It's okay. I'll let you out," she said, looking again left and right. After a moment she said, "Last chance," and paused before stepping back into the room and shutting the door. Outright laughter erupted behind it.

"Okay, you guys. Settle down," she said as I passed her room for the nearest exit.

I had no way of knowing I was walking out of my high school for the last time.

I meandered back to the bus stop and dropped onto the bench. For half an hour, I watched the road. When the bus finally neared, I stood, ready to leap aboard, but it didn't stop.

With a heavy sigh I sank back onto the bench and into a dark place.

What if he's already done it? I couldn't deny the thought. *And if not yet, what will happen once he does make another pill, or several? Will he need to make a lot, or just give up the formula so another scientist already on payroll can take over?*

I didn't want to allow the next logical conclusion to take form in my mind, but there was no stopping it.

Why would they keep him alive once they had what they wanted?

The question hung in my brain, spinning around and around like a lighthouse beacon, refusing to burn out.

A shadow fell across me that had nothing to do with my mood. My eyes widened. A forty-something-year-old woman was about to sit on me. Though I slid away, she caught my hand under her thigh. I bit my lip. Her forehead crinkled. When she stood to check the bench, I pulled my hand away.

"Hmmph," she said and sat down again, wiggling back and forth. She folded her hands on her lap with a pleasant smile.

For the next fifteen minutes, I sat as still as possible for fear of making a sound. At one point I crept several yards away to muffle a cough against my arm. The woman's brow creased as she turned toward the sound but looked forward again a moment later. I warily returned to the bench.

When the next bus arrived, a few passengers got off, and the woman got on, with me close on her heels. She chose an empty row near the front. Since the bus was sparsely populated, I figured passengers would spread out relatively evenly, like gas molecules filling a closed container. I took the seat next to her, feeling it was a safe bet.

Until the woman dropped her heavy purse on my lap.

I pressed my lips together to hold back a yelp.

"What on earth?" She lifted the bag and peered at the chair. I hopped up before she touched the seat, rubbing her hand across the burgundy fabric. She set the purse down again. "Weird." She closed her eyes and popped them open again, then reached into her bag for a bottle of pills, shook one out, and swallowed it with a large gulp from a water bottle.

As the ride continued, so did the flow of passengers. I was forced to spend the next twenty minutes seat hopping and dodging commuters, accidentally brushing against a few, who looked around, bewildered. Once I had to climb over a seat to get out of the way. As my stop neared, I scuttled up the aisle before anyone else, and swooped out the door as soon as it opened.

In the clear at last, I wiped the sweat from my forehead.

When I reached Isaac's, I let myself in through the back door and headed to the basement. The fire extinguisher was gone from the bottom of the stairs—probably in evidence lock-up at the police station.

In addition to the oily smell of dissected machine parts, a pungent rabbit odor permeated the air. I stooped next to Einstein's cage on the floor, pulled out the empty water bottle, and refilled it from the sink next to the washer and dryer in the corner. The food dish had nothing but crumbs left, I noted with relief. Losing his marbles or dying were no longer in Einstein's immediate future. The antidote must not have tasted bad, like Isaac feared. That, or Einstein was too hungry not to eat it.

Knowing he'd be visible now, I checked under the table and in all potential hiding places in the room but couldn't find him. Maybe he'd hopped his way to freedom. To be on the safe side, I poured more food into the dish.

Isaac's parents probably ignored the cage, thinking Einstein had escaped. Or maybe they thought I'd stolen Isaac's rabbit, too, when I'd bashed him on the head and dragged him out of the house. As if that were even possible.

The tray below Einstein's cage needed to be emptied. Several times when visiting, I'd noticed this and tried to take care of it, but Isaac always stopped me, insisting he'd do it himself later. When I'd return the next day, the tray would be clean, so I didn't make an issue of it. I just never understood why he wouldn't let me help.

Since he wasn't there to stop me, I slid the tray out.

That's when I saw it.

Hidden beneath the tray was a white envelope with one word written on it: Ana.

I left the tray on the floor and sat down. The enclosed letter, in Isaac's stunted scrawl, was dated November 3rd, five months ago.

Ana, I'm afraid this is one of those 'If you're reading this,' letters that you hate in movies. But unfortunately, this does indeed mean something bad has happened to me. I could even be dead, and that's a shame because I never got a chance to tell you how I really feel about you.

When we moved here and I started at your school, I knew it would be hard, as it's always been, for me to make friends. But then you came along. You were so terrible in our physical science class, but you meant well. You were so cute and sweet and a little bizarre, that I liked you right away. I was amazed you actually liked hanging out with me too.

We've only become better friends. <u>Really</u> good friends. Now, when I'm thinking of you and pouring hydrochloric acid, I have to stop because my hands shake.

I've wanted to say something for two years now but was afraid I'd push you away. I couldn't handle that. I'd be lost without you.

What I really want you to know, now at least, since it no longer matters, is that I love you. I love you so much, Ana. I hope you're able to find someone else to entertain with your funny stories—someone else who can appreciate how great you are.

Be happy.

~ Isaac

P.S. Thanks for taking care of Einstein. I knew you would.

CHAPTER 6

I reread the letter and read it once more, allowing each word to sink in but not knowing how to feel, other than surprised. Finally, I refolded the letter, tucking it and the envelope separately into the back of my jeans, feeling them scrape against my back, turning invisible. I stared at my feet, wondering what to make of this new development. I was flattered of course, but...

I looked up and sighed, imagining him standing in his usual spot, screwdriver in hand. I could almost hear the '90s grunge music—archaic to me—that Isaac was so fond of thanks to his parents. It typically played low in the background, except for what Isaac considered the really good parts, for which he'd crank the volume, bopping his head, hair flopping wildly to the beat. This always made me laugh. Somewhat defensive, Isaac told me this was how his parents danced in the living room to bands like Alice in Chains, Stone Temple Pilots, and Pearl Jam.

Isaac once proclaimed he remembered hearing Nirvana while in utero. Then he chuckled at a joke I didn't get until he explained *In Utero* was one of their albums. But because his adopted parents didn't like grunge, he could only do this when they weren't home.

Next, I looked to my chair and pictured me swiveling back and forth, spinning a tale about one of his creations coming to life and demolishing everything in our town. But not the donut shop, Isaac had insisted, and I had agreed. We both liked that place too much to have it destroyed, even hypothetically.

The memory afforded me a weak smile. I missed Isaac. I worried about Isaac. I cared deeply for Isaac. But did I love Isaac?

I had to admit he'd filled out nicely since freshman year, transforming from the stereotypical nerd into kind of a hottie. Maybe the real reason classmates still picked on him was not so much out of habit but resentment that he'd overcome his former awkwardness. I'd always been proud to hang out with him, regardless, but perhaps lately my street cred had improved by association.

A sudden thought brought me up short. Had I totally misread the stink eye so many girls had given me? I assumed that was just their low-impact way of bullying me for being abnormal, but could they actually be jealous of me, thinking Isaac and I were dating since we were always together?

"Huh," I said with a self-satisfied smile and my hands on my hips.

But I let my arms fall. Would we ever be together again? He'd worried about losing me by telling me how he felt, but now I really had lost him. Tears pooled in my eyes at the thought of my best friend being gone forever.

No.

I couldn't think that way. How could I go on if I believed he'd never return? And what about this letter? Would it change things? I considered putting it back in its hiding place and pretending I'd never found it. But is that what I wanted? It would never work anyway. For one thing, I'd torn it open. I could still act like this never happened, that everything would be life as usual once he was rescued and I was myself again. But I knew that even if—when—Isaac returned home safely, things would never be the same.

I sighed, emptied and replaced the tray under the rabbit cage, and lumbered up the stairs.

Two car doors slammed shut. I rushed to the living room window. Isaac's parents were making their way up the front walk.

I ran to the back door and out. The view through the window panel in the door told me I was just in time. The front door was opening as I closed the back.

Isaac's dad must've heard me. His head jerked up. He walked with purpose to the back door. My eyes widened in horror. I hadn't locked the door yet. I only managed a half step back when he opened it. He stood inches from me as I leaned away.

Almost afraid to breathe, I remained frozen. His breath, smelling of sour cream and onion potato chips, touched my face with a slow, steady pat. A strand of my hair tickled my cheek as he inhaled and exhaled, forcing me to fight an intense urge to scratch my face.

Finally, he shut the door, clicking the lock into place. My lungs set their captive air free. I stepped back and stumbled over a terracotta potted plant. It fell to the next cement step and crashed open in a mess of dirt, leaves, and roots.

I bolted. The door opened again, but I was gone, not slowing until I was two houses away.

Even though I knew he couldn't see me, both Isaac's dad and mom had always made me uncomfortable. They never seemed happy with me hanging out with Isaac, though they didn't say it. They hardly said anything. They were even less outgoing than Isaac. Not that I was outgoing, but still, as adults you'd think they'd have better social skills.

My mind wandered back to the one time I had dinner with them. It was earlier this school year. Isaac and I were so caught up in his lab that we hadn't noticed his parents had come home.

Mrs. Mason ambled down the stairs in a black skirt, her white blouse hanging loose around her waist.

"Isaac," she called in a pleasant tone, but her voice cut off when she saw me. "Oh, hello, Ana. I didn't know you were here. What a nice surprise." Her smile was unconvincing.

"Hi, Mrs. Mason," I said. "Sorry, I didn't realize the time."

"Well," she hurried to push her shirt back into her skirt. "So long as you're here and dinner's ready, you might as well join us."

I looked at Isaac. He shrugged.

"Okay." I turned back to Mrs. Mason. "I'll just call my mom and let her know."

"Excellent idea." Her lips pulled up at the corners for a half second before she went back upstairs.

I checked Isaac for signs that I was making a mistake, but he gestured for me to follow her. I was hungry after all. Maybe this wouldn't be so bad. I trudged upstairs.

After a quick call home, I sat at the table next to Isaac. Mrs. Mason lifted on her toes to pull another plate from the cupboard, and again to get a glass for me. She was on the short side but didn't need to go on her toes. I wondered if she did so for exercise, or if she was afraid keeping her heels on the floor would invite a mouse to bite her.

A little furry brown body appeared from under the sink, its head lifted, nose twitching. The mouse's nostrils led it toward Mrs. Mason's feet. Red eyes zeroed in, it charged full ahead, teeth bared.

"Ana." Isaac swatted my arm with the back of his hand. I squinted at him, trying to focus on his face. "My dad asked you a question."

I shook the image away and turned to Isaac's former teacher. Now he and his wife were science professors at the local college. He, too, was still in his work clothes, but his paisley green tie was loosened and hanging over his shoulder. His forehead crinkled all the way to his receding red hairline. He frowned at me under his glasses.

"Oh. Sorry, Mr. Mason. What was it?"

"I was just wondering if you like shepherd's pie?"

"Yeah. My mom makes it sometimes. It's great."

"Well, what my wife makes isn't quite like that."

I laughed, thinking this was a joke, but he wasn't smiling. "Oh." I cleared my throat. "I'm sure it will still be good."

What Mrs. Mason placed before us was instant mashed potatoes, ground beef in a strange creamy gray sauce, topped with canned mixed vegetables. My mom would turn her nose up at this, but I dug in with a polite smile. Extended time in his lab was probably not the only contributing factor to Isaac's thin frame. If my imaginary mouse friend was too slow to feast on Mrs. Mason's heels, I'd gladly let him glut on the non-shepherd's pie, if he'd have it.

Since the Masons weren't a chatty bunch, I tried to fill the awkward silence.

"Moving to Ohio from Florida must've been quite the change for you all," I began.

"We wanted a fresh start as a new family," Mrs. Mason said. "Here's as good as anywhere." She went back to eating.

I tried again with Mr. Mason. "Isaac mentioned you're an inventor."

"Oh." Mr. Mason frowned. "He shouldn't have told you that. I've tried a few things in the past, but nothing worked out. I wouldn't call myself an inventor."

"That's for sure," Mrs. Mason muttered. She tapped her fork on her plate and stared at him. "You promised me when we got married that we'd make millions from your inventions. Yet not a one of them amounted to anything."

He met her gaze with narrowed eyes. His face brightened when he turned to Isaac. "You'll invent something great, though, won't you, Isaac?"

Isaac shrugged. "I don't know," he mumbled.

"What are you working on now?" Mr. Mason said.

"Nothing really," Isaac said.

"I'm sure it's not nothing."

Isaac shrugged again.

"It isn't nothing." I chimed in. "It's a robot, right, Isaac?"

He gave me a mournful look I didn't understand until his father said, "*Another* robot?"

"Oh," I said quietly and sank lower in my seat.

"Surely you have enough of those already," Mr. Mason said.

"What about some of your old projects?" Mrs. Mason said. "Have you picked one of those back up?"

"No."

"Hmm." She and Mr. Mason exchanged a look. "Perhaps it would be a good idea to complete one task before you begin another. I'm sure you've got some good ones that maybe you gave up on too soon."

"I don't know," Isaac said.

His parents exchanged another look but said nothing.

Having only chewing noises to break the silence was unsettling. I imagined the sound of me sipping from my glass echoing across the Grand Canyon. I ate as fast and as quietly as I could. Isaac, not needing to be a genius to sense my discomfort, rushed to finish only two bites after me.

"Thanks for dinner, Mom." He wiped his face with his napkin. "I'll walk you to your car, Ana."

"Okay. Thank you for a nice dinner, Mrs. Mason." I figured politeness overruled honesty in this case.

"You're welcome," she said without looking up.

"Good night, Ana," Mr. Mason said with no emotion.

Once outside I shivered. "Brrr. I'm guessing neither of them won 'most congenial' for their senior superlatives."

"Yeah, sorry. They're not great with outsiders."

"Is it outsiders or just me?"

"Hard to say. You're the only outsider we've had."

"Don't they have any friends?"

"Not that I know of."

"I'm sorry."

"Don't be. We all like it quiet, I guess." He stared at his feet. "I miss the music, though." Then he grinned up at me. "Sometimes my parents would have to shout above the songs. Then one or the other would say something like, 'Hey, quit interrupting Eddie.'" He stared into the night, smiling at the memory. Then his face fell, and he looked at me again. "Sorry. Eddie Vedder. The singer of Pearl Jam," he explained.

"Yes, I remember." Isaac had been instructing me in the ways of grunge music, like his parents had done for him. It was growing on me.

"The Masons. I mean, Mom and Dad," Isaac corrected himself, "just talk about work and lab stuff, if they talk much at all."

"I'm sorry for messing up the routine."

"No, that was nice. I like when you're here."

"Thanks, but maybe I'll just go home for dinner from now on."

He smiled. "That might be best."

"See you tomorrow."

He stood on the sidewalk and waved as I drove away.

From then on, whenever Isaac's parents came home, I left soon after. I was grateful they took Isaac in, and he was glad they let him do as he pleased. I just wished they didn't both have the personality of a cardboard box. At least when Isaac came to my house for dinner, my dad kept him actively engaged. Even though Dad was a money person, not a science guy, he was always asking Isaac questions about his lab work. As terrible as it felt to admit, Isaac's crazy stilted family life made my own seem great by comparison.

A skateboarder came soaring down the sidewalk and almost crashed into me. I dove onto the nearest lawn and decided to stick to grass for the rest of the way home. I was far too preoccupied to dodge pedestrians. When my thoughts landed back on the issue with my own parents, I realized the gloom of that situation had been hanging over me the whole time. Bringing it back to the surface overwhelmed me.

I sat on the cement base of a light pole and stretched my legs out onto the yard in front of me. I felt wrung out like a soggy sponge. My emotions were raw and cracked, my body running on fumes. I hadn't eaten since yesterday, and I was worn out by the human version of whack-a-mole from students and bus commuters. I tapped my head in time against the pole: *What—am I going—to do?* My will power to keep from crying was fraying.

A car pulled into the driveway of the house I faced. A young boy and girl ran out the front door.

"Daddy!"

"There's my monkeys." The man scooped his children up, squeezing them in a bear hug and swinging them back and forth. They laughed as their short legs swished through the air.

The corner of my mouth curled up. I acted the same way as a kid. I'd run to my dad, and he'd pick me up, sometimes spinning me around in a circle, other times smothering me with kisses. Mom would lean against the doorway, cross her arms, and say, "Now don't eat her. We have perfectly good food for dinner inside." He'd release me saying, "Oh, all right. But there'd better be dessert, although nothing's sweeter than Ana." He'd wink at me, and I'd giggle behind my hands.

I sighed. I had a good childhood on the whole. There were vacations to water parks and national monuments. The memory of one failed attempt at camping brought me a weary smile. Dad and I had just finished pitching the tent when Mom shrieked. She'd spotted a bug. It was just a millipede, but no matter. The tent came down and we were in hotels for the rest of the trip.

Sure, my parents loved me. Their ultimate reason for having me still made me steam, and keeping my unusual conception from me for so long was inexcusable. Though I knew they loved me, my feelings for them were shaken. Our relationship had permanently been altered at the worst possible time.

The sun was advancing on the western horizon, transforming stripes of yellow, orange, and red into purple, dark blue, and black. Invisible or not, walking home in the dark would be creepy. I struggled to my feet and plodded along.

Isaac's letter was sticking to my back. It reminded me that Isaac and I drew together because we were both looking for a friend. We didn't want to be alone. My parents had me because they wanted to fit in. For them it was a social reason too. But out of it came genuine love. Isaac and I loved each other too, though in different ways. The idea of being more than friends had never even crossed my mind.

I felt differently about Ben Cody, however, and Isaac knew it. How painful it must have been for him to listen to me gush about Ben. I cringed as I remembered going on and on about Ben being valedictorian and how great I was sure his speech was. How sad I was not to hear it. How anguished that he was going away to the University of Michigan. How far away that seemed. How I looked forward to holidays and summers when he'd be home again, and I might have a chance of seeing him.

My gosh, I'd been an idiot.

But there was more. Me sharing local articles about Ben graduating with honors. Ben being among less than 1% of applicants chosen to attend Police Academy. Ben excelling in aptitude and physical training tests. Ben, at twenty-one, being the youngest recruit to join the force. Ben adding on to the long line of cops in the Cody family who came before him.

Idiot wasn't a strong enough word to describe me. I went on and on about a man to whom I was already invisible. I was a fool, filled with shame.

Yet despite all, Isaac loved me.

A sudden warmth filled me. Isaac loved me, and not just as a friend. He loved me romantically. This was a new experience for me.

"Whoa." I stopped in my tracks. Something monumental dawned on me. That scrap of paper in Isaac's secret lab. He'd written "Immune—blood, Love." Now I got it. My mom was immune to the invisibility because we were related by blood. That was obvious. Just as clear was my dad couldn't see me because we weren't blood relatives. Sure. But the love thing? Didn't my dad love me? Of course he did. Was Isaac saying…

He *was* saying it—those who are *in* love with you can still see you. Not just your run of the mill, "I love you, man," type of thing, not even daddy-daughter love. That's why he'd written it as capital-L love. He meant the big kind. I *knew* it. I *did* see him look right at me in the basement when he told me to make a run for it. This letter confirmed it.

Something else made it all perfectly sensible in a weird science-y sort of way. Isaac said he'd included oxytocin in his formula. That was the hormone that makes people in love bond with one another. My memory floated back to that horrible day last year when I made the mistake of going to the grocery store the day before Thanksgiving. The check-out lines stretched into the aisles, but I'd promised Mom I'd pick up a few things for her while she was busy with Turkey Day preparations. To pass the time, the woman in line behind me started up a conversation. She told me that if a man ever tells me he loves me, I should have his blood tested. She said when a person is in love, his blood contains more than the usual amount of a certain chemical. She didn't say which, but I was willing to bet that chemical was the hormone oxytocin.

I was this close to patting myself on the back. Isaac hadn't told me this part, most likely to protect his secret, but he probably didn't count on me figuring it out on my own.

Last night, curled up in bed, I ached for Isaac to comfort me, and felt all the more lost knowing he was nowhere to be found. And yet, here, with his letter, he'd managed to wrap his arms around me and squeeze.

My eyes filled with tears. Isaac was there for me even when he wasn't. How could I have spent all this time hung up on Ben?

As twilight faded, I made it home. Through the kitchen window I saw Mom hand my dad a plate of food. I pushed the door open. Dad's barstool fell over when he jolted upright.

"Not eating at the table tonight?" I said, whipping my gloves off and flinging them over my shoulder.

Dad's eyes widened. His hair wasn't neatly combed like normal. And was the man wearing sweatpants? I didn't even know he owned a pair.

"Ana, you're really there? Does it hurt at all? Are you okay?" he said.

"Yeah, I'm fine." My glance flicked away from him.

"Oh, Ana." Mom rushed to me, arms out.

I lifted a hand. "Wait."

Her arms fell.

"First, I have questions, like who my real dad is."

They looked at each other uneasily before Mom spoke in a faltering voice. "We don't know. It was an anonymous donation."

I let that sink in, trying not to grind my teeth in frustration. With effort, I kept my voice level. "Do we know *anything* about him?"

"He's Caucasian and college-educated," my dad said. He seemed to be having trouble standing his barstool back up.

I shut my eyes and took a deep breath. "So, you're telling me there's no way I can ever meet him. No way I'll ever know what he's like, or what he looks like. No way," my voice rose despite myself, "to know if I have any half-siblings. No way to know if anyone else in this world, besides my anonymous dad and you, Mom, carries half my genetic code. What if I have a sibling living nearby? What if I didn't need to spend half my life lonely in my own home wishing I had a brother or sister to play with?"

"We never knew you felt that way, Ana," Mom said. "Why didn't you say something?"

I glanced at my dad, who still seemed bewildered, then back at her. "Would you have listened?"

She looked to him for support, but his expression showed he had nothing to offer. I didn't wait for an answer. I didn't need to.

Because I was on the verge of collapse, I grabbed my dad's plate and fork, to his stunned amazement, took them to my room, and set them on my desk. My stomach growled, pleading, as I stared at the plate, but all I could taste were salty tears.

My stomach lurched upward. I tried but failed to swallow it back down as it crawled its way up my esophagus and, starfish-like, out my mouth, spreading itself before me, oozing, dripping fluids onto my carpet. It zeroed in on its prey. Jerking my body forward, it leaped onto the plate, sucking it clean with a sickening suction noise.

A knock on the front door, and the revolting image was gone.

I stumbled backward onto the bed and felt my mouth, my throat, my stomach. I ran my hands along my body to be sure it was still intact. It was, but was my mind?

My heart pounded to the point of being painful.

"I was only imagining it," I said out loud, though quietly, somehow afraid of my own voice. "It's okay. It's over." I swallowed hard. "It's okay," I told myself again. "It was just your imagination. You've had worse," I lied to myself. Then, "Stop talking to yourself or you really are going to be crazy."

Another knock.

Get it together. It was nothing. You're fine.

Still breathing hard, I pushed myself up from the bed and turned off my light just before the front door opened.

"Frank. How are you?" my dad said with surprise.

"Good, John. Thanks. May I come in?"

I assumed my usual position, peering through the crack in the doorway. It was Frank Wallace, one of my dad's oldest friends. They got together for bi-monthly poker games and the occasional pint when Frank wasn't on duty. Frank was a police lieutenant. And he wasn't alone. He was followed in by Ben Cody.

Seriously? Are there no other cops on the force?

When Ben entered, he looked up at my room.

"Is your daughter home?" Wallace asked my dad.

By now Mom had joined him. She put a hand on his arm. It looked like affection, but I knew it was a warning.

Dad hesitated before answering, "No."

Wallace turned to my mom. "Hello, Veronica."

"Hi, Frank. What brings you here?"

"We're still trying to locate your daughter."

"Oh, I'm sure she didn't go far. She just had a little spring fever and senioritis to contend with. I'm certain she'll be back soon," Mom said.

"So, you're not surprised by her disappearance?"

"No. She and Isaac like to go off for a few days now and then to get away from the other students. They don't really fit in well, you know. I think they just need a break sometimes. Normally a mom would be concerned, but Isaac's a good boy. Plus, they both get excellent grades, so where's the harm, really?"

When did Mom become such a good liar? Besides lying about my dad.

"Do you know where they went?" Wallace asked.

"Oh, no. I don't want to pry, so I never ask. All I know is Ana is always happy and refreshed when she returns, so..." She shrugged.

Ben shifted uncomfortably. He glanced my way again.

"That's odd," Wallace said. "Isaac's parents say he never leaves home except for school or the library and occasionally to come here."

"Did they? Well, it's been at least a year since their last outing. I think during that time Isaac's parents taught a lot of night classes. They probably hardly noticed he was gone. Maybe they've forgotten."

She was good, but Wallace didn't look fooled.

"I see," he said and turned to my dad. "Is it all right if I send Officer Cody here up to your daughter's room to have a look around?"

I could almost see my mom's nails digging into my dad's arm. She talked a good game, but she was scared.

"Oh. Sure," Dad said.

Wallace gestured to Ben, who took the stairs two at a time. I flattened against the wall as he pushed the door open. He found the light switch and spotted the food on my desk. I willed my stomach to stay quiet.

Ben called over the balcony, "You might want to come look at this, Lieutenant."

Wallace started up the stairs. Mom stared at Dad, wide-eyed, before they followed him. When they reached my room, Mom spotted me half hidden behind the door and quickly looked away.

Wallace walked to my desk and turned to my parents. "Can you explain this?"

"Well—" my dad began.

"We just wanted to have it ready in case she gets home late and is hungry," Mom said. "If I don't leave it here for her, she might not eat at all. She's so skinny, she doesn't really care about food. Hot, cold, whatever. If I don't give it to her, she won't bother eating." Mom forced a little laugh. "She's been gone for two days, and this is typically the time she gets back."

I continued to marvel at her quick thinking, but it was thin. Ben looked at Wallace who nodded. Ben pulled out a pair of white latex gloves and a clear plastic bag from his pocket.

"You say Ana hasn't been here to touch her food?" Wallace asked.

"That's right," Mom said.

My teeth sank into a thumbnail as Ben put my fork and plate into the bag. They'd find my prints on the dishes and know Mom was lying.

Wallace walked into my bathroom while the four of us stood silently in my room. Ben held my dinner hostage. Mom clung to Dad's arm. The bathroom light went off and Wallace returned. I stepped back as he opened the closet door, pushed aside the hangers, then closed the door.

"Could I trouble you for a glass of water?" he asked.

"Of course, Frank. Come with me." Dad led him from the room. Mom followed.

Ben lingered, looking at my belongings. He didn't appear to be searching for anything, he just seemed interested.

Good thing I didn't have any cat posters on the walls—anymore.

He stared for a while at the framed picture on my desk of me with my parents. Then he studied the certificates and awards from the various writing contests I'd entered over the years. One was a plaque from a state essay contest I won my junior year.

Why do I still have those up? Tomorrow, I'll take them down.

Mom wandered back into the room. "Is there anything else I can help you with, officer?" Her tone was light, but she shot me a quick look of concern.

"No, thanks, Mrs. Roberts. I was just admiring your daughter's impressive collection of awards here."

Never mind. They can stay.

"Yes, she's quite talented. We're very proud."

"I remember hearing her name a lot during morning announcements when I was a senior. The school was clearly pleased with her accomplishments."

He remembers hearing my name?

"I also remember reading her poetry in the school paper. It was really inspired."

This was too much. Almost.

"That's nice," Mom said. "Her poetry really is some of her best work."

This was also a shock. Was Mom just keeping up her act, or was she being serious? I only remembered her saying something positive about my poetry once. Usually, she'd read a poem and say, "Yes, Ana, but you can't build a career on poetry, you know." Without Isaac, and sometimes my dad, cheering me on, I might've given up writing altogether.

"Well," Ben said. He looked around one last time, nodded to my mom and left the room.

She followed, and I trailed along as they went downstairs. Dad and Wallace walked toward us from the kitchen, the lieutenant carrying a glass of water.

"I'm friends with Richard and Helen Mason. I know how much they care for their son. He's practically all they ever talk about. I, for one, am quite interested in Isaac's skills." He said the last part more to himself. "If Ana happens to get in touch with you while she's away, please let me know. She has something we need."

'She has something we need'? That was the exact phrase one of the kidnappers used. How odd.

"What do you mean?" Mom asked.

"Information," he said, "about where they are." He turned to my dad. "John, we've known each other for a long time. I trust you, and I need you to be straight with me. Do you know where Ana is?"

My eyes widened. Mom's expression mirrored mine.

"I can honestly say I don't know where she is. I haven't seen her once since I returned from my business trip. You'd think she'd come home to greet me, but so far, she's been a no-show."

I grinned. Mom tucked in her lips.

"All right, John. Thanks for your time." Wallace handed him the glass. "I'm sure we'll get this all sorted out soon enough." He turned to Mom. "Good night, Veronica."

"Good night, Frank. We'll see you again soon, I'm sure."

Wallace walked to the door. When Ben turned to follow, I quickly stepped out of his way. He stopped and jerked back, squinting at the space I'd just left. His forehead wrinkled. Finally, he shook his head and left, closing the door behind him.

I turned to Mom. "What just happened?" we both said at once.

CHAPTER 7

"I think my stomach growled," I said and swallowed hard again while feeling my midsection to confirm everything was where it should be. "Did you hear it growl?"

Mom shook her head. Dad was looking about a foot to my left, shaking his head too.

"Maybe you just couldn't hear it from there. That must've been weird for him, but he'll probably shake it off."

Mom nodded.

"I can't believe they took my food," I said.

"You mean *my* food," Dad said with a smile.

I put a hand on his arm. He jumped.

"Sorry." I pulled my hand away. "I guess I should warn you before I touch you."

"No, it wasn't that. Well, it wasn't just that. My shirt disappeared for a second." He stared at his arm. "Whoa."

"Then I'm sorry for that too." I put my hands behind my back. "And by the way, you were terrific, Dad."

"Thanks." He smiled crookedly.

"And you, Mom, quick on your feet there."

"I know." She fluffed her hair. "Now how about we eat?"

"Sounds good to me," Dad said. He was trying to keep his tone casual, and it showed.

Mom smiled at him then looked at me, one eyebrow raised.

My stomach growled for certain now. How could I still have an appetite after what I'd seen in my room? My hands were shaky. Was it from hunger? The cops showing up again? The Incident proclaiming my pending insanity? Probably D) All of the above. But I needed my strength to keep my wits about me.

"Lead the way," I told Mom, who looked both pleased and relieved.

Still, I lingered in the foyer, letting them go ahead of me. I wasn't keen on being with them, but hoped their presence would keep me grounded in reality.

Though grateful for their performance with Lieutenant Wallace, the fallout from the donor bomb was still causing me radiation poisoning. Maybe that's what gave my normally mild science fiction daydreams a nudge into the horror realm. Regardless, I steeled myself and plodded after them.

The dishwasher was hanging open, nearly full. Mom pulled out three clean plates and loaded them with food.

"I hope it's still warm," she said.

"Who cares?" I said.

"I'm with Ana," Dad said.

We settled at the table and into an understood truce.

Dad stared in my direction as I ate my meatloaf. "It's incredible. Your food just floats through the air. Then it disappears."

"I could put the gloves back on if you'd like, but that would only help you see the fork."

He shook his head. "That's okay."

Though he appeared to be trying not to watch me, his eyes still flickered up each time I took a bite. "Isaac really did it," he said, seemingly to himself. "So many possibilities."

"Don't get used to it," I told him, hopeful I spoke the truth.

"But why not stay this way? Think of all the things you could do," Dad said with a light in his eyes.

"Errm," I uttered.

"Well, I mean," he floundered. "I'm not entirely sure what the practical, *legal* ramifications would be, but still, from a business standpoint…"

I just looked at him, though he didn't know it, unsure how to respond, and not wanting to go into the whole permanent-until-death-do-me-part aspect of my invisibility.

Mom stared at her plate, not having touched her food. "Do you want to talk more about, you know?" she asked.

"No, I'd rather not," I said in a flat tone. Then, eager to change the subject: "Shouldn't we be worried about them taking my plate? They'll find my prints on it for sure and know you were lying."

"Yes, and they'll find mine and your mom's, too. What will that prove?" Dad said.

"Maybe you're right." But I was still uneasy. "And why haven't they found Isaac yet? Instead of looking for me, they should be looking for him." I dropped my fork in irritation. It clattered against my plate. Dad gaped at the fork's sudden appearance.

"I'm sure they're doing their best with what they have," Mom said. "But, I know. It's frustrating." Her lips pulled into a frown. She reached out to clasp my hand.

"Aaaah," Dad yelled, falling back in his chair.

"What?" Mom and I both yelled back.

"Please stop doing that," he panted, clutching his chest.

Mom and I stared blankly at him.

"You flickered out of existence when you touched her," he said to Mom.

"Oh," she looked ashen faced. "Sorry."

"Me too," I said in a quiet voice.

"It's okay." He sat upright again. "This will take some getting used to."

After a moment, we all resumed eating, though in silence.

How much longer will this take? How long can we hold up? How long can Isaac hold up?

Or could my mind hold up? The time bomb to my insanity was ticking, almost palpable and menacing, behind my eardrums.

"But what if Isaac is in serious trouble?" I surprised myself by blurting out loud.

"Don't think that way, sweetie," Mom said. "You know they didn't take him to hurt him."

"But what if they *are* hurting him?"

She couldn't answer that. "John," she said, as in, "Say something."

"I'm sure he's fine," he said. "They don't need to harm him."

"If only we knew for sure," I said. "I wish you could've asked them about the case. But I guess that's out now that you've made up that story about the two of us going away somewhere."

"Sorry." Mom's shoulders drooped. "It just came out."

"I'd be interested to know if the police have anything, too," Dad said, "but I don't know what else you could've done to explain her disappearance. They'd never believe you if you told them the truth."

I slumped against the back of my chair. He was right, of course. At least now the cops had some explanation for my whereabouts, whether they believed it or not. My vote was not.

Was there any way I could further help them? Maybe slip an officer a note that said, "Isaac Mason was kidnapped!" But then they'd spend time trying to find out where the note came from. If they somehow traced it back to me, they'd want to know how I knew. They'd waste even more time on their stupid search for me, pulling resources away from the search they should be conducting for Isaac. I dropped my head into my hand.

"Uh, honey," Mom said, tentative.

I tilted my face toward her.

"Mrs. Mason called while you were out."

Further complications. Perfect.

"She sounded pretty upset. She asked me to have you call her, or better yet, to come to their house and talk to them."

I straightened. "And what did you say?"

"I told her I didn't know where you were or when you'd be back. What more could I say? Though I wanted to tell her the whole story. They need to know what happened to their son."

"I know, Mom, but let's not tell them yet. Not unless we have to." I shuddered at the thought of why we, rather than Isaac, would have to explain it to them.

"If you say so."

I stabbed at my meatloaf. Keeping the Masons in the dark was hard, but I needed to hold onto hope that the police would find Isaac soon. Then all would be resolved without me revealing his secret. After his emphatic plea to keep quiet, which I'd already ruined, I decided I'd just keep it within my family. Already more people knew than Isaac wanted.

"What did you do today?" Dad said, his tone cautious, like he was unsure he was allowed to ask.

"I went to Isaac's to refill Einstein's food and water and clean his cage. And..."

"And what?" Mom said.

I hesitated. "And I found a note from Isaac under the cage. He... He told me he loved me."

Why was I telling them this? But also, I needed to tell someone, and who else did I have? I looked up, expecting them to be startled, but they weren't.

"Of course he loves you, Ana. How did you miss that?" Mom said.

Dad nodded his agreement.

I stared, slack-jawed, from one to the other.

"He's been head over heels for you since freshman year," Mom said. "Surely you're not shocked to hear it, are you?"

I knitted my brow. "Well, yeah."

"Think about it, Ana. Why else would he let himself be tethered to you in science labs year after year after year? Wouldn't someone with his brain capacity rather work with someone who knew what they were doing, at least slightly?" Mom said.

"A little harsh, but I get where you're going with this." I thought it was just because we were good friends, if I thought about it at all.

"And the star stickers on your ceiling? No boy would do that for a girl unless he really liked her," Dad said.

My forehead wrinkled. "I guess you're right. We've just never been that way. He never acted like *that* in the slightest toward me. I had no idea."

Mom looked at me like she pitied me for only now discovering I was an idiot.

How could I have been so blind? My heart filled with a sudden warmth but cooled quickly at the thought of never seeing Isaac again.

I choked on a sob that turned into a ragged cough. When I took a drink from my glass, Dad gasped.

"The water moves on its own and pours into nothingness." He turned to Mom. "Isn't that incredible, Ronnie?"

She scrunched her lips to one side. "I don't see it. Everything about her looks perfectly ordinary to me."

"That's too bad," he said. "It's really remarkable."

"Once Isaac is rescued, he'll get me back to normal," I said.

So long as it happens soon enough.

"Let's hope so," Mom said. "I'm not sure I can handle more police visits."

Her and me both.

Dad said nothing. I asked about his trip, but he gave vague answers, which didn't tell me anything. "It's boring. You wouldn't want to hear about it," he said.

"Fine." I didn't press it. "I think I'll head to my room now." I'd eaten most of my food and was impressed I'd lasted that long.

"All right," Mom said with a trace of disappointment.

"If you get hungry again later, I picked up banana split ice cream at the store today," Dad said. His voice grew louder as he spoke, as though I was walking away.

I was still standing by the table. "Thanks, Dad. I'll keep that in mind."

"Oh," he said, startled.

Mom rubbed his shoulder. She looked at me and opened and closed her mouth, as though wanting to say something but not knowing if she should.

"What is it, Mom?"

"Well." She half shrugged. "I was just wondering. If we were to think hypothetically. *Not* that I think this will happen." She raised a hand toward me to emphasize the point. Then the last words tumbled out of her. "But what if Isaac can't make you visible again?"

I met her gaze, not sure what to tell her.

She stumbled onward. "I mean, how will I explain it to my friends that you're gone? When you're supposed to be away at college, that will be easy.

But what will they think if you never come home for Christmas or for the summer? What will I tell them? They'll think we've had a falling out. That I can't get along with my own daughter and so she never wants to come home again."

I stared at her, my expression flat. "Tell them I've died."

"Oh, Ana, no. I can't do that. I'd have to make up a story. Then there'd be a funeral to arrange. How would I explain the closed casket?"

I drew in a breath and held it, watching her expression turn from concern to wonder to irritation that I wasn't answering her.

"Don't worry about it, Mom. You won't have to lie to your friends or do a closed casket. If we don't find Isaac in the next five days, there's a good chance I'll die from this anyway."

She blinked at me. Dad dropped his fork. "You mean," he said, "someone could actually die from Isaac's invisibility pill?"

"Without taking an antidote within a week, yes. It's that or going insane. Maybe both."

He leaned back in his chair. "Huh. That changes things," he said quietly.

"Ana, no," Mom cried. She shook her head, causing welled-up tears to spill. She grabbed Dad's wrist, but he was typing something into his phone.

"They'll find Isaac, though," I said to her, as much as to myself. "We have nothing to worry about." It was the second time I'd lied to her in two days.

She nodded fiercely and the tears fell faster. Both hands gripped Dad's arm now. He looked up at her and around toward me, having lost the tone of the conversation. Seeing his wife bobbing her head up and down, he nodded too.

"Good night," I said, offering Mom the best smile I could muster.

"Mmmhmm," she uttered back, apparently not trusting herself to speak.

I turned, and with sluggish feet, headed for the front staircase, wondering why I had told them. Then again, maybe it was good that they were warned now. Ease the blow, should it come to that.

I made it as far as the first step when I had to sit down. With the backdrop of Mom's sobs and the murmur of Dad's comforting words, I considered new possibilities. Would I turn visible again if I died? If not, what if I keeled over invisible on the sidewalk, only to have poor, unsuspecting pedestrians trip over me?

Or would I feel the end coming? Would it be painful? Should I go into the woods to die alone under a tree like a dog, maybe never to be found? Would my decomposing body finally turn visible? Should I take a shovel and literally dig my own grave?

Or would I simply disappear from the world without a trace, having never seen Isaac again?

With that thought, my energy began to drain from me. Before I lost the will to move, I pulled myself up and plodded along to my room.

On my desk, a small white rectangle waited for me. Ben's business card. He'd somehow put it there without me noticing. I flipped it over and found a hand-written phone number. Since the number on the front included an extension, this must be his cell. I'm sorry, but did he actually want me to *call* him? Pfft. Not likely. I wasn't crazy. Yet.

I shoved the card in a drawer. After a moment, I took it back out and gazed at his name: Officer Ben Cody. I traced my finger over the letters. A light smile touched my lips.

Ugh. Knock it off. I threw the card back in the drawer.

I'd always idolized Ben, but at least Isaac and I were friends. Ben and I had never even spoken to each other. How could I be hung up on a stranger when this awesome guy had been right in front of me all these years?

I couldn't think about this anymore. I changed into pajamas. Though it was still early, I was ready for bed. I brushed my teeth, going through the motions. It was the least I could do to hang on to some degree of normalcy. Besides, when was the last time I'd done this? Or taken a real shower, for that matter? It seemed the last two times I'd set foot in that little glass box was for a hose off and nothing more. For whatever it was worth, and to keep some sense of control, I'd make a point of correcting that in the morning. For now, I just wanted to collapse.

I didn't know if Isaac would be saved, or if there was anything I could do to help him. I didn't know if or when I'd go completely crazy and die. I didn't know if I'd ever see my best friend again. Or if anyone other than Mom would ever see *me* again.

An exasperated glance upward led my eyes to the ceiling. The star stickers mocked me. Isaac had spent at least an hour painstakingly displaying them for me. What had I done for him that even came close to this level of devotion?

Let's see. When he was being abducted, I literally disappeared on him and saved myself.

What a great friend. I rolled over and pulled the pillow over my head.

4 Days

A dull light fought its way into my room. I dragged myself out of bed to squint through the slit in the window blinds. The sun was near the eastern horizon. Finally, I'd woken up early.

I tried not to think about only having four days left. Or that I'd never gone this long without seeing Isaac. The closest I'd come was when he had the flu and was absent from school for three days. Mom had forbidden me from visiting him, worried I'd get sick too, but on the third day, she couldn't hold me back. Knowing I was going with or without her permission, she packed me some hearty soup. After my visit, Isaac was well enough for school the next day. Mom was sure her revitalizing fluids had done the trick. I knew better. It was the bearer, not the gift.

Remembering my promise from the night before, I stepped into the shower. The shampoo bubbles gliding down my wet back were delightful, but I quickly rinsed them off, feeling guilty for finding any enjoyment while Isaac was still missing. As I watched soap slide down the shower wall, I considered how it would leave scum that I'd have to wash off with yet another cleaner. Soap needing to be cleaned was pretty messed up. Kinda like me.

I tried a deep, calming breath. *It's almost over.*

Despite myself, I laughed. What I'd called my homestretch mantra for getting through senior year had been repurposed with a much more sinister meaning. One way or another, my life, as I currently knew it, was coming to an end.

Or, I reminded myself, it could mean Isaac's captivity was almost over. Perhaps the only way to stay sane was to stay positive. As well as I could, I'd make that my game plan.

I hadn't combed my hair in days. Yanking the brush through my wet, tangled snarls sent shots of pain to my scalp, which felt good because it felt real. The bags under my eyes, too large to qualify as carry-on luggage, were the result of waking at odd hours, swearing I'd heard Isaac calling my name.

Enough was enough. I needed answers.

It was time to spy on some cops.

Apparently, I was getting better at being unheard as well as unseen. I slipped downstairs and out the front door without any parental interference. But it was Saturday morning. Lawn mowers were running. Someone was washing her car. Driving unnoticed wasn't an option. I buried my hands in my pockets and set off for the police station on foot.

When I find Isaac, I'll have to thank him for the extra cardio.

Along the way, I thought through how I might get over the electronic door and into the room with the cops. I couldn't wait forever for someone to be called through the door like last time. Should I have brought a stepstool and then used it barefoot? But once I stepped off the stool, could I reach over and grab it with my hand before it turned visible again? I'd probably end up leaning too far and falling back over. Maybe I'd have to try scaling the wall like a ninja after all.

Even then, to find the right cop, I'd need to wander around the room, listening to conversations or reading over shoulders. What if this case was top secret and details were only discussed in a private office? I couldn't put an ear to a door without making it disappear. I also might overhear more than I intended to, more than I was supposed to, about other cases. This plan was getting uglier by the minute, but I was getting more desperate by that same measure of time.

When I reached the police station parking lot, a mere two cars were in it. My pace slowed as my concern grew. Where was everyone? With my gloved hand, I gave the front door handle a tug, but it didn't budge. That's when I noticed a sign on the glass.

Station Hours

Monday-Friday 8:30 a.m. - 7:30 p.m.

Closed Saturday and Sunday.

If you need immediate assistance after hours, use the red phone to call inside. An officer will be dispatched to you.

In case of an emergency, call 911.

To the left of the door, a red old-school phone enclosed in a clear plastic box was attached to the wall. Not bothering to think it through, I opened the box and picked up the phone. Someone responded immediately.

"Hinckley Police Department. How can I help you?" a man asked.

"Hi, uh. I'd like to speak with Lieutenant Wallace, please." I winced.

What am I doing?

"I'm sorry, miss, but the lieutenant isn't in today. Is there something I can help you with?"

"Uhm, sure. Can I come inside to talk?"

Seriously, what am I doing?

After a pause, his tone changed from friendly to concerned. "Yes, one moment."

The phone disconnected and I hung up. My heart pounded as I waited. *Now what?*

Less than a minute later, a female officer came to the door, unlocked it, and pushed it open. She stood in the doorway, looking out, her brow furrowed.

Come on. Come on.

She stepped out farther, one hand on the door jamb, making a tunnel with her arm. I was just about to slip underneath it, when she shook her head with a scowl and stepped back inside. The door nearly shut on my foot—all I was able to get through. She reengaged the lock, and her form retreated into the darkened depths of the station.

!!!

Calling and trying again did not seem like a viable option. I waited, hoping someone else would come along.

And waited.

To pass the time I read all the fliers posted in a glass-cased bulletin board on the wall: information about a new stop light being added on Sydney

Street, safety tips for driving in snow and rain, community news, and my favorite: a missing persons notice with Isaac's face next to a "person of interest" page featuring my senior photo. I stared back at myself, the canned, forced smile, the impatience and boredom: the face of a former "typical teen."

After sitting with my back against the wall for an hour, I called it a bust. One foot in front of the other, I told myself, and not just for the long walk home.

When I arrived, Mom was pacing in the kitchen.

"A bathrobe? At 11:00?" I was too surprised not to comment. And was I mistaken, or was her hair unbrushed? "Did you sleep in?"

"No, not really," she said. "I just felt like taking it easy today."

"Okay," I said, slightly mystified. On a normal Saturday she'd be shopping for a new Gucci handbag by now, hoping, and expecting, to run into a few friends.

She stopped tracing a path in the oak flooring long enough to stick a fingernail in her mouth.

My eyes widened. "Are you biting your nails?"

She examined her index finger, bewildered. "I guess I was," she said in a quiet voice.

I gave her a moment to recover before asking, "Is the polish okay?" though I could tell it wasn't.

"Ohhh," she said sadly, staring at the nail, but appearing not to see it.

"Mom." I waited for her eyes to find my face. "It's going to be okay." I hoped she'd view my whisper voice as comforting. The truth was, I didn't have the strength to say it with conviction.

She stuck her hand behind her back and offered me a tight-lipped smile. Straightening her shoulders, she said, "Of course it will, honey. I have every confidence in the police and in Isaac. Everything's going to be fine. Now then. Your dad and I have already eaten, but would you like me to fix you some eggs?"

I returned her gaze for a few seconds then sank onto my usual seat at the counter. "Might as well." My voice sounded hollow, like my body was an empty shell, and I was watching and hearing myself from the outside.

Mom soon had a frying pan on the stove, butter sizzling. She spun around from the refrigerator, a brown egg in each hand.

"One or two?" she asked, her smile returning somewhat to normal. Cooking had that effect on her.

"Two," I said without thinking. Could I force them both down?

She cracked each, one handed, into the pan.

"You're really good at this."

"I know," she said.

That made my lip curl a centimeter. "And humble too."

She grinned, then dropped shredded cheese, both cheddar and Colby, into the pan. "Why not?"

"Sure, load it up," I said, though with no emotion.

In the silence that followed, a heavy gray fog I'd been fighting back for days strove to overwhelm and smother me. The weight of it pressed me into my seat as though I'd instantly gained a hundred pounds. It was like old-timey black and white projector films where the edges of the screen are black and fuzzy. I imagined a slow fade out with a circle of light in the center that gets smaller and smaller before the darkness overtakes it.

Since Isaac's abduction I felt like half my brainpower went toward keeping that scratchy charcoal blanket from enveloping me. Every day he was gone made it harder and harder to hold it back. Now the circle of darkness hung on my shoulders like a metal coat. The hole was tightening itself around my neck, strangling me.

"So, spring break is this coming week, right?" Mom said, jerking me into focus. The cloud took a half-step back. Mom's voice seemed a little shaky, like the cloud was encroaching upon her too.

"Yes. I'd completely forgotten." At least I wouldn't be missing more school, as though that was my greatest concern.

"What were your plans for the week?" She added a splash of milk to the eggs and scrambled them with a spatula.

I tried to think back while the storm cloud, waiting in the background, growled for my attention. Isaac and I had talked about this weeks ago—felt like years. "Isaac wanted to have a picnic in the park," I remembered, "and he said he found a place where we could go horseback riding."

She cocked an eyebrow at me. I pushed my lips to one side. I got it now. Those were classic romantic boyfriend/girlfriend things to do.

"I guess those are out, at least for the time being," I said.

"Do you think you'd like to do them once Isaac returns?"

Once Isaac returns. I clung to those words. The gray cloud was angry now, barking at me to succumb to it. "I don't know," I said. Sorting out my feelings for Isaac would have to wait. My emotional capacity had already reached critical mass.

"Well, anyway, I was thinking of going shopping today."

Apparently, we were going with a "business as usual" attitude.

She let it hang, as though I'd take her cue. When I didn't, she added, "Maybe you can come with me?"

I raised an eyebrow.

"Why shouldn't you come? I could use your help picking out a new dress. You could just nod or shake your head."

I gave her a blank look.

"It would be nice to spend some time together. I…" She cast her eyes downward. "I do enjoy spending time with you, Ana." She looked back up at me with a hopeful expression. "Maybe we'll find a dress for you too."

I was about to object. For starters, why did I need one? And she knew I was never one to get excited over dress shopping. But most of all, this normalcy felt out of place. Chit-chatting, shopping, eating, breathing.

The phone rang. Instinctively, I went to answer it.

"Ana, no."

"Oh, right." I stopped myself short as she grabbed the phone off the wall.

"Hello." Her cheerful greeting sounded fake. "Hi, Frank. I didn't expect to hear from you again so soon… That's an odd question," she said with a small laugh, "but, yes, I was grabbing dishes directly from the dishwasher last night. I don't usually do that, you see, but I guess I got a little behind on my housework, and I suppose that saved time… The one for Ana? Yes, I think I did."

Lieutenant Wallace had gone to the kitchen last night for a glass of water. He'd seen the open dishwasher and the missing plate. Alarm bells started going off in my head, but Mom was too comfortable with this old friend of the family to recognize what was coming next.

"Yes, I'm certain," she said.

I grabbed the phone from her and hit the speaker button, laying the phone on the counter.

"I called in a favor with the weekend lab tech, who rushed the order for me. The plate and fork we picked up yesterday had fresh, clear prints from your daughter on them."

"Well, so?" Mom said.

"You used vinegar in your dishwasher, didn't you? I detected a whiff of it."

"Yeeees."

"If the dishes had been freshly washed, particularly with vinegar, since your daughter's alleged outing, why would her prints be so pronounced on them?"

My eyes widened. Mom gawked at the phone. Dad came in carrying a coffee mug and had a newspaper tucked under his arm. His forehead creased as he looked at his wife, then down at the phone.

"I wanted you and John to hear this from me first. A lot of speculation has been going around the station regarding Isaac Mason's disappearance and your daughter's involvement," Wallace said. "She's still the prime suspect, you realize. The working theory is they had a lover's quarrel. Then she knocked him out and stashed him somewhere."

I couldn't help but roll my eyes. *Idiots.*

"Surely you realize that's ridiculous, don't you, Frank? For one thing, they're not even dating."

"I know, Veronica. My top rookie and I don't believe it either."

Did he mean Ben?

"But personal feelings aside, we have to do our jobs. And right now, it looks like you and John are protecting her. As such, you could be charged with obstruction of justice. If she's innocent, why don't you let her come forward and make a statement? She may be our best chance of finding this boy. The longer you keep Ana hidden, the guiltier she looks and the greater trouble you're putting yourselves in."

The blood drained from Mom's face. Speechless, she looked at Dad, who stared back at her. My eyes darted from one to the other.

Say something. Anything.

"She's invisible," Mom blurted and immediately covered her mouth with her hands.

Anything but that!

"Mom," I mouthed, gaping at her.

Dad looked at her with his arms spread wide, eyes bulging.

"Uh, come again?" Wallace said.

"It's true." Mom rushed on. "Isaac made a pill that turned Ana invisible and then he was kidnapped. We haven't seen or heard from him since. And, yes, Ana is right here with us. I can see her. I'm the only one who can. Say something, Ana."

I closed my lips tight and backed away, shaking my head.

The other end of the line was quiet. Finally, Wallace said, "It sounds like I'm on speaker phone. John, are you there too?"

"Yes, Frank, I'm here." Dad's voice was sober.

"And can you see your daughter?"

"No, I don't see her."

Another pause. "Well." The lieutenant seemed to be at a loss. "Let's not worry about these lab results right now. Maybe your dishwasher isn't very thorough. You folks take care of yourselves over there."

"Thank you, Frank. We will," Dad said and pushed the off button.

For a moment, we stood in silence.

"What just happened?" I said, looking at Dad. He was staring at Mom. I looked at Mom. She was staring back at him. Then she turned to me and— smirked.

"Mom?"

She grinned.

"Why did you tell him that? You sounded completely nuts."

"I know, but it threw him off. Did you hear that? He didn't know how to react. This should buy us some time."

"But now he thinks you're crazy, Ronnie," Dad said.

"It's true," I added. "What if he mentions this to his wife? What if word gets out? You'd be a laughingstock among your friends." This wasn't a fear of mine, of course, but I was shocked she was willing to take the risk.

"Oh, who cares," she said as she put an arm around me. "I did what I had to do to protect our daughter." She kissed the side of my head. We ignored Dad's small leap. "And now I think I need to start over on your breakfast."

Acrid smoke rose from the blackened edges of the eggs.

"Besides," Mom continued as she dumped them in the trash. "We need someone on our side. Frank's a lieutenant. He's a good person to have in our corner."

"What corner, Mom?"

"Eventually the truth has to come out."

"Would you want it to?" I said. "Do you want people knowing your daughter is invisible? That she's a freak?" I mean, more so than I already was, according to kids at school.

"So what?" she said with a passion she normally reserved for a new pair of shoes. "It's not fair that the cops are after you. You did nothing wrong. I need to defend you by letting everyone know the truth, no matter how strange and crazy it may sound, or that it makes me sound." She lifted her chin. "Somebody has to know what really happened and what Isaac has done to you."

"But, Mom," I kept my tone gentle, "don't you see it's because someone found out what Isaac can do that this whole thing started? We have to keep it a secret as much as we can to protect him."

"Oh," she said, pursing her lips. "Yes, there's that, but I also need to protect you. And now us." She pointed to Dad and herself.

"All the more reason we need to find Isaac quickly," I said, "though I don't know how." At that my voice cracked and my eyes stung.

Mom gripped my arm. She bit the side of her lip as though grasping for something reassuring to say but coming up short.

The suffocating cloud smiled in triumph as it rushed forward.

"Let me make you an omelet." Mom opened the fridge to get the eggs out again.

"Forget it, Mom. I've lost my appetite. Why don't you just go shopping." It wasn't a question.

"I don't," she began, studying my face as though trying to gauge what I wanted. "Or you could come?"

"No, just go, please." Shopping wasn't a mood boost for me like it was for her.

Her face fell a little. She turned to Dad. "John, do you want to come with me?"

He hesitated. I willed him to agree. "Okay," he said, finally.

"I'll go get ready," she said.

With Mom out of the room, I turned on the kitchen television and flipped through the channels until I found the local news station. I didn't have to wait long before my fears were confirmed. There was Isaac's picture on the screen. To my surprise and dismay, my school photo soon appeared next to his.

"Isaac Mason was last seen talking with fellow senior Anastasia Roberts before leaving school early on Wednesday. Both students were absent Thursday and Friday. Police report that Anastasia's parents don't know where she is, though they say it's not unusual for her to leave for days at a time without warning."

"Great, now I'm a delinquent," I said. "That or you guys get the parents of the year award."

"Mr. and Mrs. Roberts declined to comment further on the matter," the newscaster said.

"What?" I looked at Dad. "Did they call you?"

He nodded, still looking at the TV. "Earlier this morning."

Just when I thought things couldn't get more out of hand. Then Isaac's parents appeared on screen, Mrs. Mason crying, Mr. Mason holding her and looking grim.

"Where are you, Ana? Why won't you come talk to us? Tell us what you know about where Isaac is," she sobbed.

"I don't believe it. This is insane." I wanted to tell them. But could I? Should I? How far was far enough in honoring Isaac's wishes? Would he want me to stay quiet, even now?

"Ana Roberts, and her parents, are still refusing to cooperate with police in their missing person's investigation," the reporter said.

Now Isaac's father spoke up. "Don't you care, Ana?" he said, emphatically looking into the camera. "Don't you care about our son? Why won't you help us?"

I couldn't jab the off button fast enough. I didn't know if I should be angry or sad or... I gripped my hair by the roots. "Aaaaah," I growled in frustration.

"You don't need to tell your mom about this. It will only upset her," Dad said.

Ya think? is what I wanted to say in my irritation, but instead I just said, "I won't."

Mom came back downstairs, eyes sparkling, though with a shine of something different, like tears she was trying to pass off as excitement. "Ready?" she said to Dad.

"As I'll ever be." In my direction, he threw an exhausted look, which Mom always pretended to miss.

Before she followed Dad out the front door, she sent a smile back to me that was both sympathetic and encouraging.

An emotional shock wave hit me as the door shut. I thought I was the clever one, lying to Mom for her sake. Being brave and strong. Keeping up the pretense that I wasn't worried.

But she was the one lying to me. The one trying to hide how scared she was, so that I could keep it together.

I fumbled for the barstool and slid slowly onto it.

Okay, if Mom was going to be as tough as the acrylic nails she sometimes wore, I could be too.

I considered the situation. There were only a couple of cops at the station, but did detectives work weekends? Was anyone looking for Isaac now, or did they figure it could keep till Monday? The idea made my nostrils flare. *I* couldn't wait that long. I needed answers. But, how? Who could I ask?

I grimaced and shut my eyes, trying to push out the thought that occurred to me.

Isn't there another way?

I searched for a better option but couldn't think of one. I'd have to do something I'd only fantasized about but would never dream of doing in real life.

"Gah." I threw my head back and stared at the ceiling.

It's the only way.

But...

No buts.

"Fine," I shot back to myself.

Like it or not, it was time to face my biggest fear: *talking* to Ben Cody.

CHAPTER 8

I flipped Ben's business card back and forth across my fingers as I stared at the phone. My hand trembled as I reached for it.

I dropped my hand. I couldn't do it. Not after what he had read in my diary. It was too humiliating.

But I *had* to. Before I could talk myself out of it, I grabbed the phone and stabbed in the numbers.

Part of me hoped he wouldn't answer. I was nearly hyperventilating. My heart thumped against my chest, and my hands were so sweaty I had to switch the phone back and forth to dry my palms on my jeans. After the third ring I was rooting for voice mail.

What am I thinking? I can't call him.

I was about to hang up when—

"Hello."

I panicked and almost hung up anyway.

"Hello?" Ben said again.

Even his phone voice was hot.

"Hi," I faltered. "Is this Officer Benjamin Cody?"

Why am I being so formal? I know it's him.

"Yes, it is. May I ask who's calling?"

"It's Anastasia Roberts." I was fully in it now.

A book fell on the other end of the line.

"Ana," he said. "I'm glad you called. Where are you?"

Why, so you can come arrest me? Fat chance.

"It doesn't matter. I was just calling to ask if there's any progress locating Isaac Mason." The words were stilted but I somehow managed to get them out.

"I'm not really supposed to discuss the case with you, Ana."

Hearing him say my name made my stomach pirouette.

"I, I realize that, but could you just tell me if you've had any luck getting an address for Apple Pi?"

"How did you...?" There was a long pause followed by a sigh. "It's not as easy as I originally thought. This Apple Pi person is using a proxy server, which makes tracking him down a lot more difficult. It's going to take some time."

"I see." My heart sank. "How much time?"

"A couple more days maybe. Look, Ana. Where are you? Why don't you come in and talk to us?"

"And be thrown in jail? I don't think so."

"I know this wasn't a lover's quarrel. And Lieutenant Wallace believes me. For one thing..." He took a slow breath. "I showed him your journal."

My face went up in flames. Scratch that. My entire body was an inferno.

"I know you and Isaac aren't like that," he continued. "That is, unless something's changed?"

Is it my imagination, or did his question sound like more than police business?

"No, nothing's changed."

"Good," he said.

Was that relief in his voice?

"But I may have a harder time convincing the rest of the police force," he added.

"I should go."

"Ana, wait."

But I pressed the off button and thrust the phone back on the wall. I bent over, hands at my knees, breathing deeply for a minute, mostly in relief that it was over. I put a hand over my eyes. How many more cops were planning to read my diary? Were they sending out excerpts in memos? Printing copies for the entire precinct?

Could the humiliation get any worse?

I walked circles around the island, replaying the conversation in my mind. Ben believed I was innocent of harming Isaac. That was good, but of course he believed me. He knew I was a foolish girl who had a four-year mad crush on a man whom I had, before now, never even spoken to.

He must think I'm such an idiot. I mean who does that? I'd never be able to speak to him again. It was a sad thought, but facing him would be too mortifying.

Shoving that aside, there were other matters to attend to. Proxy server? Who were we dealing with? That sounded serious. And a couple more days to track down Apple Pi?

"Are you kidding me?" I yelled to no one. "Now what?" I buried my face in my hands, fighting the urge to pull out every dish in the kitchen and smash it into unrecognizable bits.

The black cloud loomed closer, poised and ready to pound me flat into the ground.

Nope, nope, nope, I told both it and myself as I resumed my loop around the kitchen island. *I will not give in.*

My feet stopped moving.

Not yet anyway.

I needed to do something to keep my mind off everything. But what?

Then I knew. It was the last thing I wanted to do, but it was exactly the thing I should do: my homework. It seemed like an activity from another life, one lived years ago, but it might have a sobering, calming effect, which was just what I needed. I went to my room and did every subject except chemistry. That book I refused to touch.

In the midst of this, the phone rang several times. Journalists from news programs or websites left messages requesting statements from my parents. Each call irritated me more than the last. When the doorbell rang, I was ready to lose it, or at the very least, snap another pencil in half.

Don't tell me they're showing up at the house now, too.

When the bell was followed by a thundering knock, curiosity got the better of me. Were reporters really that aggressive? Or were the police here to arrest my parents?

I rushed downstairs and looked through the window. My heart stopped. It was worse than I'd feared. The Masons were on my doorstep.

"Ana, are you in there?" Mrs. Mason called. Her voice sounded neutral, but the desperate look in her eyes was not. She thumped on the door again. After a moment she said to her husband, "We need to find her. Look for another door."

I followed him through the house, watching out windows as he ran to the left and found the kitchen door. The knob shook as he failed to open the locked door. He ran around the back of the house, looking for more doors. Not finding any, he rejoined his wife in the front.

"The other side's locked too," he said.

"She's probably in there hiding from us and her guilt."

"Should we break in?"

My eyes went wide, and I took a step back.

"No, we can't do that," Mrs. Mason said. I relaxed my shoulders somewhat. "Besides, I think I see a neighbor watching."

I followed her gaze across the street. Sure enough, there lurked Mrs. Granville, half her face visible behind the curtain.

Bless her.

"Come on. Let's go," Mrs. Mason said, defeated.

I sat on the stairs and pressed my knuckles against my forehead, then pounded them on my knees. I hated the Masons thinking I had hurt Isaac. I knew they weren't fond of me to begin with, and there was nothing I could do about that, but to be blamed for something awful that I would never do...

Their hatred for me was probably growing with each passing day. This made me all the more frustrated waiting for Isaac to be found and everything to be explained. I wanted to tell them he'd been kidnapped, but how could I without explaining why? Without betraying Isaac?

His face appeared in my mind as his words returned to me. "Listen, Ana. No one can know. Do you understand? You're the only person I trust with this. Promise me you'll keep it a secret."

A promise I'd already broken. But if he wasn't found in the next few days, the Masons might not be able to take it anymore. Neither could I. I'd have to tell them everything.

After deleting the reporters' phone messages, I returned to my room and the convenient, though annoying, distraction that was my economics book.

Sometime later, the front door opened. Someone was sniffling. From the balcony I watched Dad lead Mom inside to a foyer chair. He stepped back out and returned with several large shopping bags. Evidently, the retail therapy hadn't done much good. Mom was dabbing her eyes with a tissue.

"What's wrong?" I asked as I came downstairs.

Mom straightened. "Oh, nothing, really. It's just I ran into an old friend, Peggy. She's Frank Wallace's sister-in-law. She came up to me at Macy's and asked how I was feeling. She wanted to know if I'd like to set up an appointment with her husband, a psychiatrist."

Dad shook his head. "I'm shocked Frank told his wife. That's unprofessional."

"Oh, he didn't," Mom said. "I'm sure that shrew was listening in on his phone call. She does it all the time and hears everything that happens in this town."

"Well, that needs to stop," I said, cringing at the possibility of her eavesdropping while Lieutenant Wallace was telling others about my diary.

"I'll mention it to him," Dad promised.

"Are you going to be all right, Mom?"

"What does it matter, really? Let them think what they want." She crumpled the tissue in her hand. "I know the truth."

"Okay, but just in case, maybe some of that banana split ice cream would help," I said. "In fact, I could use some too."

But there wasn't enough comfort food in the world to prepare us for what came next.

Car doors slammed shut, followed by loud voices. We looked at each other with mirrored expressions of confusion and alarm before stepping to the window. Roughly two dozen students from my high school, most of whom I knew by name, poured from haphazardly parked cars. Either they lacked parallel parking skills, or they felt their task too important to be bothered by DMV curb-distance regulations. They clustered in front of the house and, once all in place, held up neon poster board signs that read "Free Isaac," or "Save Isaac." Someone with artistic skill had drawn a picture of Isaac's face, crying.

The ridiculousness and absurdity of it all made me want to laugh despite the shock. "Do they think I have him chained up in the basement?"

A bright pink sign held by a cheerleader, in uniform, lest anyone forget, popped into view. The sign screamed, "ANA IS A KILLER!"

I froze. Mom's startled cry sent her into a coughing fit. The knot that formed in my stomach was beyond the skill of the most accomplished sailor to untie. Bile burned my throat.

Then someone sent up a cry of, "Let Isaac go," which turned into a group chant that grew louder with each repetition until the words were chiseled into my eardrums.

Mom looked from Dad's clenched fists to his face. "What do we do?" she said between coughs.

"First we call the police," he said.

He left for an inner, quieter part of the house. When he returned a minute later, he said, "They'll send someone over as soon as they can."

After several more rounds of chanting, a football player shouted over the others, "You suck, Ana."

This must have been a signal. They all dropped their signs and ran to their cars. The tension in my shoulders eased, but only for a moment. The next onslaught was about to begin.

Grins and laughter replaced the earlier shouts and chants as the thwack of dozens of eggs pelted the front of our house. The three of us reflexively took a step back.

"I'm going out there," Dad said.

"Don't," I told him. "They'll just target you."

As if to punctuate my words, an egg crashed against the window. Someone pointed at my parents and laughed. More eggs followed until the glass was a dripping tapestry of oozing yolk and shattered shell fragments.

Dad remained where he was. Mom took refuge behind him. "Where are those police?" she said.

Someone did come, but it wasn't a cop. A van emblazoned with the local news station's insignia parked in the middle of the street. A pretty female reporter hopped out, tugging her skirt straight. The driver joined her on the sidewalk as soon as he'd retrieved his camera from the back of the van.

The cheerleader dropped her egg carton in favor of her inflammatory hot pink sign. Brandishing it for the young camera man, she smiled and bent a knee for an upwards side kick like she'd just completed a cheer.

Dad cracked the window open.

"What's your name?" the reporter asked the girl.

She leaned toward the microphone. "My name is Emma Delorio, and I'm here to tell you that Ana Roberts is a psychopath. She kidnapped our friend Isaac Mason and may have murdered him by now. We all know it." She nodded to her cohorts until they rumbled their agreement.

"Wow," I murmured. "Our friend?" My brain, torn between laughing and crying, settled on neither. Instead, I seethed. My hands reflexively formed tight balls.

"Yeah," the football player shouted, elbowing Emma out of the way. The dirty look she threw him was an incomplete pass. "Ana sucks. Isaac rules."

"Really?" the reporter said with an arched brow. "You're a friend of Isaac Mason?"

"Sure. We all are," he shrugged.

By now the rest of the kids had picked up their signs, having tossed their empty cartons into the bushes. The cameraman panned across the disjointed rainbow of clashing colors.

Emma edged her way in front of the microphone again. "There was always something screwy about Ana, you know what I mean?"

"I'm afraid I don't," the reporter said. "How do you mean?"

"Just a little out there, you know? Like, off, or something."

"Yeah, we call her space cadet," another kid, Gunner, shouted. I knew his name but didn't have any classes with him. He was in remedial everything.

The "whoop whoop" of a police siren stopped the reporter's next question. With so many cars and the news van in the way, the officer parked at the end of someone else's driveway. On both sides of the street, neighbors had left their houses to gawk at the spectacle on our front lawn.

Mom must've noticed this for the first time too. She gasped, shut the window and the curtains, and stormed off to the kitchen.

Dad reopened the curtains on a stream of students running to their vehicles as Lieutenant Wallace got out of his car. The reporter tried to engage him with her microphone in his face, but he responded with a "get out of here" jerk of his thumb. He shook his head at the fleeing kids. More than one drove a tire over the curb in their haste to leave.

Wallace stormed across our lawn, stepping on signs left strewn on the grass. Dad let him in before he needed to knock.

"Thanks for coming, Frank," Dad said.

"You all right, John?" he said. Mom peeked her head out of the kitchen. "Veronica, you okay?" She waved him off and disappeared back into the kitchen.

"You wanna press charges on those kids?"

Dad hesitated, looking around for me, as though for guidance, but that proving useless, said, "No. They're just being dumb."

Wallace nodded and stared for a moment at the floor. The memory of the morning's phone conversation seemed to descend like a heavy blanket of awkwardness. Wallace cleared his throat then peered through an egg-free patch of window.

"Let me get that reporter out of here for you. If she, or anyone else comes back, you let me know, all right?"

"I will. Thank you." They shook hands in what appeared to be a particularly manly grasp before the lieutenant left. The news crew tried once more to get a comment from him, but he shooed them back to their van.

As soon as Wallace walked past them, the reporter touched the cameraman's arm and pointed toward our door. They'd only gotten two steps before Wallace turned around and laid into them. With the window now closed, the words were indistinct, but his tone wasn't. Whatever ultimatum he'd delivered was enough to make the news team's heads turtle between their shoulders. They left quickly.

Wallace stomped the rest of the way to his car. After he drove off, Dad and I stood in silence for a moment.

"Are you all right?" he asked quietly as though unsure I was still there and not wanting to be caught talking to himself.

I swallowed the acidic juices that had crawled up my throat. "Yes," I said, my voice feebler than I would have liked.

Dad nodded then went to comfort Mom. I stood in the foyer, mindlessly watching the last of the egg splatters race each other to the bottom of the window. The one I'd been rooting for lost. I headed for my room. Mom came out of hiding for me, but I told her I was fine without looking at her.

My best friend was missing, and idiots were using the occasion to smear my name and gain attention for themselves. I gripped my pillow with both hands and yanked. Being unable to tear it only added to my frustration. If I just ran away, my parents wouldn't have to deal with this. They could honestly say I was gone, that they didn't know where I was.

But neither would Isaac. More than anything, I wanted to get out of there, but I knew I'd have to return. I slipped out of my room and out the front door undetected.

I ran. Through my neighborhood and into the next and the next. Street after street, some well maintained, others cracked and weedy, disappeared behind me. Chilly wind whipped my eyes until they stung and teared up. Telephone poles with pictures of Isaac's and my face sprang up at nearly every block, haunting me, chasing me. Ironic that I was everywhere and yet nowhere. I didn't stop until I finally outran the faces, my lungs burning and my legs threatening to fold beneath me. I let them and toppled into a yard, panting. My hand landed in a tangled rose bush. Thorns poked and scratched me in retaliation for my intrusion.

How long I lay there, I wasn't sure. Clouds ambled by, carefree, looking down on the world without a milliliter of concern for its inhabitants.

"I'm trying, Isaac," I whispered. "Really, I'm trying, but I don't know how to do this without you."

I knew it was only my imagination when the next cloud came along, looking uncannily like Isaac's face.

"What should I do?" I said to it.

A puff of wind blew its mouth open.

"You suck, Ana," came Isaac's voice.

"No," I yelled back, unsure if I was actually making any sound.

"You killed me. I'm dead now because of you," he accused.

The Isaac cloud formed eyebrows that arched like the tops of triangles.

"It's all your fault I'm gone. You're a murderer." Another cloud in the shape of a forked tongue blew through the face's mouth. A chorus of high school students shouted at me at once. "You're the worst, you freak. How could you kill our friend, Isaac? You should be in jail. You should be dead."

"No, no, no." I clamped my hands over my ears and shook my head then shoved it between my knees, squeezing my brain to make the deafening noises stop. I crossed my arms over my head, rocking back and forth.

"Stop," I cried, tears streaming down my face. "I'm sorry, Isaac. Please. Stop."

Silence.

I fell over and looked up, squinting in the brightness of a steady blue. I pushed myself upright and examined the sky. No clouds anywhere to be seen.

I took a deep breath, letting it out slowly in stutters and wiped my face with my sleeves.

I didn't want to think about what another false vision meant. I refused to let the thought form concrete words in my mind. Not yet. My mind wasn't completely lost yet.

I clambered to my feet and examined my surroundings. I wasn't sure if I was still in Hinckley or if I'd strayed into the next town over. I jogged back the way I'd come, relieved when I finally reached familiar streets. When I arrived home, Dad was near the garage, rinsing out a rag and bucket. A ladder leaned against the front of the house. The egg mess was gone. I considered thanking him but feared my voice coming out of nowhere might give him a heart attack. Sending someone into cardiac arrest wasn't the best way to show gratitude.

I crept inside and upstairs to my bed.

It was definitely another sleep in your clothes sort of night.

My defenses against the demented cloud of sorrow that had been tormenting me all day crumbled. Without flinching, I let it crash into me like a wrecking ball through a brick building. I bawled my eyes out, clutching a box of tissues.

Where was Isaac, and how would I find him? Maybe I should just give up and resort to a life of crime. It would be so easy. I didn't even cast a shadow.

I rolled to face the wall. As though there wasn't chaos-a-plenty filling my life, another inescapable frustration crept up within me: I hated being invisible not only to the father who raised me, but also to the one who had no interest in ever knowing me.

What did he get, anyway? A hundred bucks and freedom from responsibility? He didn't know or likely even care I existed. That stung almost more than I could bear.

Giving him the benefit of the doubt, I decided he was a struggling writer in need of money. My writing bug came from somewhere, and it wasn't from my mom. Perhaps he wanted to travel the country like Jack Kerouac or John Steinbeck and write fabulous tales about his journeys.

Locking out the pain, I filled my mind with travel stories I'd read. I eventually fell asleep picturing cross-country drives with my real dad: fields of wildflowers in spring, butterflies fluttering along the highway through the Great Plains. In Yellowstone a curious burro came up to my car window and sniffed at the glass. A click and a flash told me my dad had taken a picture. I turned, but his face was obscured by a Polaroid camera. When the picture slid out, I held it, watching the image slowly come into view. I could see the burro and window frame, but where my face belonged, the film Remained blank.

3 Days

The next morning, a minefield of tissues littered my bedroom floor. I resolved to stay in bed all day. Mom came in to check on me, but I rolled over and wouldn't speak to her. I saw no reason to talk or get out of bed again, ever. What good could I do? For Isaac, myself, or anyone?

A half hour later, Mom carried a tray of food to my desk. It would've been more appropriate to slide the tray across the floor into my room like it was a prison cell.

"Ana, honey, are you all right?"

I stared at the stars on my ceiling and wouldn't look at her.

"Ana, talk to me." After a moment she sighed. "Please hang in there," she said and left the room.

Roughly an hour later the phone rang. Dad answered it, said "no" a couple of times and, "I'm telling you she's not here."

Must be the fuzz after me again. Good luck with that.

Ten minutes later there was a knock on the front door. Mom's heels clattered across the foyer floor. She was back to dressing up, probably to compensate for yesterday's fiasco. Or maybe she was trying to maintain some measure of normal for my sake just as much as for her own.

"Oh, it's you again," she said, her voice alarmed.

I sat up. *Who is it?*

"I want to talk with Ana. I know she's here."

My eyes widened. *Ben. What is he doing here?*

"Look, officer, please. We've had enough police visits," Dad said. "And I already told you, you won't find Ana here."

"Today is my day off," Ben said. "I'm not here as an officer. I'm just here as a friend who would really like to talk to your daughter." His voice was insistent.

"Well, hey, you're welcome to try." It was Mom this time.

Footsteps on the stairs.

Oh no. What's happening?

I flung the covers from me and grabbed my slippers off the floor. I shoved them on my bare feet to keep my sheets from disappearing and lunged back to the corner of my bed. I held my knees to me and checked to be sure I wasn't pressing down on the corner of my pillow or anything that might give me away.

There was a gentle knock on my door. After a moment, it opened slowly. Ben came in, wearing blue jeans and a pale gray T-shirt. He stared at the tissues scattered across the floor, then to the right at the rumpled bed. He crossed the room to the desk and glanced at the latest untouched meal. Finally, he sat down on the edge of the bed.

I pulled my legs in closer, careful not to make a sound.

He ran his fingers through his glorious mass of brown curls and sighed.

Mom leaned against the doorway, arms crossed. Dad stood behind her.

"I told you she wasn't here," Mom said, ignoring the tissue-strewn carpet and unmade bed that proved I at least had been.

Ben stared at the floor. "The next time you *see* her..." His tone indicated he was no fool. They were seeing me plenty. At least, my mom was. "Please ask her if she wouldn't mind calling me again. There's more I'd like to talk with her about."

My parents straightened and exchanged a glance. I hadn't told them about the brief phone conversation yesterday.

Mom nodded. "Okay." It sounded more like a question than a statement.

Ben stood and took two steps toward the door. He froze.

I held my breath. *Oh no. Do I smell?*

He was directly in front of me. If he raised his left arm and leaned sideways, he could touch me. He stood there, unmoving.

What is he waiting for? Why isn't he leaving?

After half a minute he left, gently pulling the door closed behind him.

When the front door shut, I shivered and crawled under my blankets, slippers and all.

What did he want to say to me? Or rather, what did he want to 'talk about' with me? Was there a new lead? There probably wouldn't be on a Sunday. He said he wasn't here on official business. Did he want to discuss other matters? He probably planned to scold me for my stupid overtures of love and devotion in my diary. Maybe he was taking it upon himself to tell me to move on and get a life. What would a police officer want with a screwy, love-sick high school girl anyway?

I sank deeper into my bed and stayed there, waiting, hoping, and praying for night, and sleep, to overtake me.

2 Days

When Monday morning arrived, Isaac had been gone for four and a half days. I had until Wednesday afternoon to get the antidote. The panic of losing him, and myself in the process, was clawing its way into every nerve and blood vessel in my body. Hopelessness threatened to suffocate me. But today, at least, there was one productive thing I could do, and the one thing Isaac, in his letter, had asked me to do: take care of Einstein.

I ducked out the front door before Mom could stop and question me. Heading to Isaac's brought mixed emotions. His was a place I'd so often been comfortable and free to be myself, but knowing he wouldn't be there made me feel all the more empty inside.

Although the morning started cool, it warmed up by the time I was halfway there. Despite my overall feeling of miserable uselessness, I grudgingly admitted that the sunshine felt nice. Little white, yellow, and violet heads of crocuses dotting various yards, heralding spring, also strove to boost my mood. I pulled up my sleeves and stretched out my arms, lifting my face to soak up the sun's warm, soothing rays. The gentle, refreshing breeze smelled of flowers and newness, giving me a small glimmer of hope that maybe, somehow, Isaac would be found in time.

I entered through the back door of his house, after returning the key to its frog statue guardian, and locked the door behind me out of habit. I headed down the basement stairs. When I reached the bottom step, I stopped just short of setting my foot on the floor. I pulled my foot back and leaned down for a closer look.

Every square inch of floor tile was covered in a white powder.

Flour? But why?

A noise on the stairs above me interrupted my thoughts.

My breath caught in my chest.

Isaac's dad was coming down, his face determined. I looked again at the flour-strewn floor. To step on it would mean discovery, and something in Mr. Mason's demeanor told me I did not want that. The stairway was too narrow for me to slip past him.

I was trapped.

He was two steps away. With my right hand I grasped the metal bracket supporting the handrail. With my foot at the edge of the last step, I held the rest of my body out into the room, supporting my left leg with my hand under the knee.

I stopped breathing.

Isaac's dad crouched on the bottom step and examined the floor. He rested his hand on the end of the railing, an inch from my forearm. Fearing his fingers might graze me, I lowered myself closer to the ground, curling my leg like a squatting warrior yoga position. My forehead beaded with sweat.

The seconds ticked away.

Just when I thought I might fall, Mr. Mason stood and took his hand away from the railing. I bit my lower lip as I pulled myself higher.

He reached an arm into the room, sweeping it from side to side. His fingertips passed within centimeters of my sucked in stomach.

After an agonizing moment, he turned and went upstairs.

I exhaled slowly and pulled myself to the security of the bottom step. I whipped my gloves off and dried my palms by gripping the sides of my shirt. The last thing I needed was my sweat to leak through the gloves, turning invisible anything I happened to touch. I put them back on and listened to Mr. Mason's footsteps above me.

Would he come back? Was he convinced I wasn't there?

One foot at a time, keeping against the wall where the floorboards didn't creak, I ascended the stairs, pausing after every step to listen. When I reached the top, I peered out, one way, then the other.

There was a rustling in one of the bedrooms, followed by the sound of a heavy box being set down on a dresser. I tiptoed down the hallway. Mr. Mason emerged from his room with something in his hand. A gun.

I clutched my chest. Was the beat of my pounding heart filling the entire house or was it just my ears?

Isaac's dad walked in a half-crouch to the dining room, the gun held confidently in his right hand. When he stepped out of view, I considered making a run for the back door. But it was locked. Unlocking it and throwing the door open would take too much time. I looked to the front door. Not only was it locked, it was dead bolted. I hung my head.

I took three quick silent steps toward the back door and slid around a curio cabinet.

Mr. Mason entered the kitchen. He paused to listen, then turned down the hallway toward me. He held his left hand out, sweeping it around corners and small nooks—hiding places like mine.

I put my back against the side of the cabinet and slid to the ground as Mr. Mason continued his slow, deliberate march down the hallway.

He stopped a foot from me, cocking his head to the side, listening, always listening. I held my breath. His arm felt the empty air where I'd just been standing. I scrunched lower to the ground and sucked my lips in to keep from screaming.

He moved on. At the end of the hallway, he turned right, heading toward the bedrooms. I pushed myself up and took several cautious steps toward the door. I was nearly there when he emerged from a bedroom.

I stood frozen in the middle of the entryway. If he came my way, he'd walk right into me.

He turned toward me. I thought my heart might stop. But he changed his mind and continued in the opposite direction.

I exhaled—slowly.

When he entered another bedroom, I stepped forward and put my hand to the lock. I gritted my teeth and turned it, oh so slowly, until it clicked faintly.

Sweat coated my forehead. I waited, watching. Nothing.

My hand was on the knob now. I rotated it an inch at a time while keeping an eye on the doorway to the bedroom.

The knob was fully turned. I pulled. The door didn't budge. I tried again harder, gritting my teeth.

The sound was gut-wrenching.

Mr. Mason flew from the bedroom, nostrils flaring. I flung the door wide and ran. A shot sounded and the bullet whizzed by my head.

He's seriously shooting at me?

I had to give him credit for his impressive aim, essentially shooting blind. He may have taken out a few strands of my hair. *Still, he nearly shot me!* I dropped to the ground in case he tried a second time. Worried I was leaving an impression in the grass, I scrambled to the house behind his, slinking into the shade.

I had moved just in time. Mr. Mason leaped down the back steps and examined the grass where I'd just been, probably checking for blood. I bumped the neighbor's aluminum siding as I backed farther into the shadows. Mr. Mason lifted his head and strode with purpose toward me.

What is he, part bat?

I almost screamed when the door next to me swung open and a man in his early thirties stepped out.

"Hey, was that a gunshot?" He looked at the weapon in Mr. Mason's hand. "Oh." He took a half-step back. "Everything okay, man?" His voice was unsteady.

To his credit, Mr. Mason looked remorseful. His shoulders slumped. "There was an intruder in my house. Did you hear anything?"

"Hear anything? Yeah, I heard a gunshot."

"I mean see anything." Mr. Mason wiped a weary hand across his forehead.

"Nah, man. I saw nothing. You want me to call the cops for you?"

"Don't bother. I already did." A woman in her mid-fifties had joined the party from her back porch next door. "They're on their way."

Mr. Mason grunted.

Since he was distracted, I slipped around the corner of the house to the front yard and took a different street home. After a block, I slid to the ground, clutching the grass, crushing the blades between my fingers, spilling their juices and staining my gloves. I pressed one to my chest as I gulped air.

I was almost shot in the head. How did this happen? How did he even know I was there?

I scanned my memory. The last time I was at the house, he saw me shut the back door just as he and Mrs. Mason entered through the front. He could've written that off as his imagination. But—the potted plant. I'd kicked it over and spilled the dirt. In my hasty departure, I'd probably stepped in it, leaving a tell-tale footprint. Isaac's dad had opened the door and looked right through me. The footprint was proof I'd been standing there, invisible.

I sucked in a breath. Isaac's parents must've noticed I was feeding Einstein. His food and water weren't refilling themselves, and who else would be doing that but me?

I couldn't blame them for hating me. If someone had taken, possibly killed, my son I'd hate them too, but shoot a gun at me? Maybe he hoped to wing me, slow me down so he could get some answers. Perhaps he wanted revenge. Fine. And yet I fed Einstein because—I felt guilty?

Whatever the motivation, one thing I knew for sure: Einstein was on his own. I would not be returning to that house again, not even to explain what had happened to Isaac. They'd have to find that out from the police or from Isaac himself.

I struggled to my feet, brushed the loose grass from my pant legs, and headed home.

As I neared my house, I was about to turn up the driveway but stopped. Something wasn't right.

I slowly turned my head. Across the road one house down was a dark blue sedan. It wasn't one of the usual cars parked on our street. It could belong to someone visiting a neighbor, but something about it made the hair on the back of my neck stand on end.

I cautiously stepped forward to get a closer look. Two men sat inside: one reading a book, the other eating a sandwich—and staring at my front door.

Cops. They weren't here to protect us from egg-wielding teens. That would be a waste of time, especially for two of them. That just left one explanation. My house was now the subject of a stakeout.

CHAPTER 9

It had only been a matter of time. The police didn't buy Mom's story that I was on a mini vacay, so now we were all in trouble. If I could turn myself in to protect my parents, I would, but how? Just walk into the precinct and start yelling, "Over here"?

The thought of all those officers knowing about an invisible girl and the boy who created invisibility made me uneasy. Could they be trusted? If word got out, even after Isaac was saved, would he be safe? Would I?

It was time I accepted an awful truth. Things would never be the same, even if Isaac was rescued and I got back to normal. Isaac wouldn't be safe here. People, governments even, would kill—or torture—for his knowledge. He'd have to disappear, with or without his parents. And I'd go with him. I was too intertwined in this. We'd change our identities, move far away, and leave our families behind. It would have to be done. Where we went from here, I'd let Isaac decide. No doubt he'd be the brains of the operation.

My mom and dad were not aware of Operation Descartes and that Isaac and I would disappear, not so literally, should he get into trouble. But the less they knew about Isaac's and my whereabouts, the better. Plausible deniability and all that.

I closed my eyes to fight back the sting of tears. Could I really leave everything and everyone behind?

I walked to the kitchen door at the side of the house. It didn't face the street and Mrs. Granville's window. It was still visible to the plain-clothed officers parked in their car, however. I couldn't just open the door and walk in without them noticing.

I peered under the curtains. Where was Mom? Why wasn't she in the kitchen, like always, concocting something? She couldn't have gone shopping. Her car was in the driveway. I was making a point to notice cars now since my sun-filled, wind-swept, flower-smelling brain had neglected to notice the tell-tale car in Isaac's driveway. Did no one use their garages anymore?

I tapped on the glass and waited. Nothing. I tapped again. Finally, she came down the back stairs, blowing on her freshly painted pink fingernails. I was glad to see she was at least attempting to keep things normal, for her sake. Or for mine.

She didn't notice me, so I knocked on the window. She jumped, then pressed a hand to her chest when she saw me. She grasped the door handle ever so carefully so as not to smudge her nail polish, but I pulled the door shut when it opened.

"Wait, Mom, first get the trash. We're being watched."

"What?" Her nose scrunched and she tried the handle again, but I gripped it tighter.

I spoke as loud as I dared, accentuating each word. "Grab the trash and bring it out."

Her eyebrows nearly touched, but, still trying to salvage her paint job, she lifted the half-empty bag out of the garbage can.

When she stepped outside, I looked at the cops. Sure enough, the one in the driver's seat hit the arm of the other. They both sat up straighter and watched.

"Don't look around," I said. "And don't speak."

She lifted the lid of the outdoor trash can and dropped the bag inside. The policemen went back to their snacking and reading. I slipped inside before Mom shut the door behind her.

"What's going on, Ana?" she said over the backdrop of loud swing dance music coming from her bedroom.

"Two men are watching the house from a car across the street," I said.

"What? Why?"

"They're cops, Mom. They're looking for me."

"Oh," she said with a frown. "But I suppose that makes sense. So, what does that mean for you?"

"It means I'll just have to lay low, I guess." I now had no place to go anyway.

Her face brightened. "That's not so bad. You and me." She touched my forearm with the back of her hand. "We can hang out."

"While we still can," was left unsaid.

When I didn't respond right away, she said, "Look, I'm sorry about those kids."

"Forget it." They were the least of my concerns.

"And the thing about your other dad."

That one hurt more.

"And this Isaac situation and you," she gestured toward my body, "is awful." The sorrow in her voice came close to matching how I felt. "What can I do to help?"

I gave her an exasperated, hopeless shrug.

"Why don't we go back to Isaac's house and look for something useful."

"I already tried that."

"We could go again. Maybe you missed something."

I closed my eyes and shivered at the idea of returning to the scene of this morning's crime.

"Or not if the memory of what happened to Isaac is too much for you."

I allowed the misinterpretation of my reaction.

"I'll call Frank and see if they know anything yet."

I grabbed her arm as she turned to leave. "You can't ask now. He thinks you're crazy, remember?"

She looked down. "Oh, right." Her face brightened. "So, we canvas the neighborhood. That's a thing, right? Knock on doors. Bang some heads together to get information out of people?"

"Mom, what?" I couldn't help but laugh.

She shrugged. "Desperate times."

I shook my head and smiled at her. "Thanks for trying. I appreciate it."

She chewed her lower lip. "I can show you my new clothes?"

I cocked an eyebrow. The last time she did a fashion show, she asked me to suggest purses and shoes to go with each outfit. After a few of my suggestions, she made comments like, "Huh, that's an interesting choice," or "I'll just keep that in mind." Clearly, I was no authority on these matters.

"I'm going to pass, Mom, but thanks."

Her face fell. "All right. Let me know if you change your mind. In the meantime, I'll try to think of something we can enjoy doing together."

Was she guilt-tripping me? And with clothes? Not that she knew this, but I'd nearly been shot. Clothes were the last thing on my mind.

With a final mournful glance at me from the stairs, she returned to her room and shut the door, muffling the trumpet and saxophone from her surround sound speakers. I exhaled slowly. No part of my life seemed normal right now.

I went to the den and opened the laptop. When I searched for the local news call letters, IGIA, what popped up after I typed the "I" was inventorshaven.com. Someone had been on this website recently. It wouldn't be Mom. Why would she care? It must've been Dad after Mom told him what I'd done in the police station. He was probably curious to see what sorts of things were on here, given his interest in Isaac's work.

I typed in the proper website and found live news coverage.

"Wow."

Mr. Mason was standing in front of his house with the same female reporter who had been at mine.

Already? The man must love the attention. Did he call the news station himself?

In the background, police officers wandered in and out of view. I tried to spot Ben. No luck.

"Just over an hour ago the Mason home was broken into, but Richard Mason was ready. Tell us what happened." The reporter shoved the microphone in his face.

"I was at home, just taking care of some things, when I heard someone come in through the back door."

"Was the back door locked?" she asked.

"I couldn't remember for sure if I had locked it."

She nodded.

"I tried to be real quiet as I eased my gun down from its hiding place." He looked at the camera and held up a hand. "Which I keep for protection. It's registered and perfectly legal," he explained. "This person was stealthy. He was somewhere in my house, walking like a cat."

"Then what happened?" the reporter asked, appearing nearly breathless.

"He made a break for the back door. I chased after him and fired a warning shot into the grass."

He was aiming a little high for the grass.

"What did the intruder look like?"

This should be interesting.

"I didn't get a good look."

Tell me about it.

"But he was wearing jeans and a sweatshirt with the hood pulled up."

If I'd been drinking something, it would be spewed all over the screen.

"Did you see anything else?"

"No," Mr. Mason said.

"And could you tell if the intruder was male or female?"

"I didn't see their face, and I couldn't tell from behind."

"Could it have been a woman?" she pressed.

He hesitated then nodded.

"Mr. Mason, do you think the person you saw could've been Ana Roberts, possibly coming back to get something belonging to your son, Isaac?"

I sucked in a breath. "Don't even."

"Well, it's hard to say for sure." He rubbed his chin. "But it could've been."

"Oh, no you didn't. Un-freaking-believable." I slammed the laptop shut and climbed the stairs to my room two at a time. When I touched my door handle, it turned on its own. I took a step back. An eye appeared in the slit of open door, staring at me, only not. Then a cloth-covered ear, before the door opened wider onto a man in a ski mask.

My heart leaped to my throat. I backed into the hallway railing. My shoe kicked against it. Mom's music didn't cover the sound. The man's eyes widened, turned toward me, and narrowed.

He took one step out and looked toward Mom's closed door.

I slid to the left.

He leaped to where I'd just been. His arms closed on empty space.

Chest heaving, I tiptoed backward. He spun his arms toward me and nearly grabbed my hair.

After another tentative swipe, "Are you here, little girl?" he said in a seductively sweet, low voice as he stepped toward me. "Come out, come out, wherever you are. I promise not to hurt you."

His tone indicated the exact opposite.

I matched him, step for step, as I backed down the hallway. At a crescendo in Mom's song, he launched toward me. I almost screamed as I stumbled backwards, nearly falling.

His dirt encrusted fingernails clutched the air in front of me.

I tasted blood from having bit my tongue. My eyes watered from pain, fear, both?

He stood before me, waiting, listening.

Another step and he'd walk into me.

Listening.

Waiting.

For me to make a move.

Mom's music was between songs. If I slid away, he might hear me.

Waiting.

Listening.

The beating in my chest matched the tempo of the drums kicking off the next song.

After one more arm sweep, which I limboed away from, the man spun to search the other direction, feeling the walls and the floor by the railing.

He stood. "Huh, maybe not," he muttered, then swung himself, one handed, over the railing.

I rushed forward to see him land on his feet and run toward the den. I dashed to a hallway window. The man ran through our back yard and disappeared into the trees. The shadows beneath now seemed darker.

My skin crawled when I returned to the den to shut and lock the window.

I was just in here a minute ago.

I made doubly sure the window was locked.

A shudder rippled from my head and down my legs. My stomach seized.

He was in my room.

Why *was he in my room?*

I went upstairs and, standing as far back as possible, eased my bedroom door the rest of the way open with my foot. But booby traps didn't appear to be the reason for his visit.

My room had been tossed. Everything I owned had been taken from my drawers and closet and thrown into the center of the room, and, by the looks of it, trampled upon. Books were strewn about, my mattress flipped over, pictures torn from their frames.

He'd come for that mysterious key, just like the kidnappers said they would. Having my face on the news next to Isaac's made identifying me easy enough. Finding out where I lived wouldn't be difficult after that. But did he find the key? Judging by the mess, he either found it in the last possible place to look, or eventually gave up. How was I to know the difference?

Now what? Tell Mom?

Nooo...

Talk about your epic freak-outs. She'd insist we pack up and move to Middle of Nowhere, Wyoming. I couldn't have that. I needed to stay here. Isaac had to be found. I'd be lost without him, in more ways than one.

What did that leave? Calling the cops? When I was trying to avoid them? No good. That would alert Mom, and it's back to Cow Patty County. Besides, these kidnappers were pros at covering their tracks. It seemed my best course of action would be cleaning this up before Mom saw it.

Forty minutes in, I was nearly done, and nothing seemed to be missing.

Unless it was all in my head.

My hands, as I stretched them out in front of me, faded in and out.

Not. Again.

My shallow breaths ramped up, louder and louder. The wheezing made my throat feel like it was being clawed by animals from the inside. My head ached.

Dizzy. About to pass out.

I flung myself toward the window, yanked it open, and smashed the screen from the frame, watching it tumble two stories, as I lunged forward, nearly falling myself.

I gripped the window frame, my nails scraping the paint.

Panting, panting.

Finally, I stumbled backward, tripped over something and fell. My head hit the bed frame. The pain shocked me into sucking in a full breath. I slowly released it as I felt my head. No blood on my fingers, which were fully there, on both hands.

My breathing semi-regulated, I looked around the room. It was still there, nearly complete. A cool breeze through the large rectangular gap in the wall met my face, and I considered the screen.

If I leap through the window to retrieve it, will I fly? Will I float to the ground? Is any of this real? Was that man even here? Did I trash the room myself, if it was ever trashed at all?

My throat threatened to seize again. I gripped the front of my shirt, as though that would help, and willed myself to calm down.

I grabbed a pencil from the floor, rolled it back and forth in my hands, and poked my finger with it. I clung to that pencil, then got up and set it on my desk, staring at it as a tangible reminder of something real.

Another rush of crisp air, and the curtain gently stroked my arm.

Isaac needs me to stay sane. If craziness is coming, I'll fight it as long as possible.

Ignoring the screen for now, I shut the window and finished putting the room back in order, all the while wondering what Isaac could have meant about me having a key. I had a key to his house, but that didn't matter to the kidnappers.

The last book to go back on my shelf was Edgar Allan Poe's *The Purloined Letter*. Isaac gave it to me for my birthday last year. I cracked a smile. The story was about people looking for something—a letter, hidden in plain sight, so obvious it was completely overlooked. My smile fell as I cocked my head to the side. I had a letter, one from Isaac that I'd just gotten, though it had been written half a year ago. No way he could've known when I'd find it.

Except he knew I wouldn't find it unless something happened to him.

I pulled open the top drawer and grabbed the love letter I'd taken from Einstein's cage. When I'd found it on the floor, it had been separated from its envelope, probably read. For some reason, that made me blush. Who cared if this guy knew how Isaac felt about me? Still, I resented the invasion of privacy, as though it wasn't bad enough he'd seen all my underwear.

I reread the letter that I'd read so many times before. There weren't any big letters that were supposed to be small or vice versa, as though Isaac would be that obvious. I looked closer for tiny dots in odd places, ink spills signifying something. I flipped it over and upside down like I'd done with his notebooks when trying to figure out how to comprehend the special writing. Was there a watermark that held significance? I ran my fingers over the paper, feeling for anything unusual. Maybe holding it up to the light... Nothing. To be sure, I took the lampshade off, a little surprised the intruder hadn't.

When I held the letter up to the bare lightbulb, small images came into focus. What was this? Invisible ink? I sniffed it. Lemon juice. Classic. Above one of each letter of the alphabet, plus each different punctuation mark, was one of Isaac's strange hieroglyphic letters. What about any unused letters? I flipped the paper over and held it again to the light. There were the letters J, Q, and X, as well as numbers 0-9 and various mathematical symbols like square root, long division, and some I couldn't name, with their corresponding glyph.

It was a cypher—the key to reading Isaac's notebooks.

A jolt shot through me. Did he even mean what he'd written in the letter? Did he love me? Or was this letter just a delivery device, one he could be fairly certain I wouldn't throw away after reading?

Part of me was saddened by the idea of that being his only motivation. Another part felt relief. I couldn't decide which side was heavier. My feelings were a perfectly balanced seesaw.

But why did they need the cypher when they had Isaac to translate? My heart sank as the rest of my body dropped into my chair. I raised a hand to my trembling lips. Unless... I dared not think they no longer had Isaac because he was... No. Not dead. No way he could be dead. Somehow, I would've known it, felt it, if he was no longer on this earth. If not dead, just uncooperative. A muffled cry escaped my lips as I dropped the letter to my lap. Was he... tortured?

Tears spilled over at the image of him being punched, kicked, dragged to a Medieval rack to be stretched. His screams echoed to me through the void. His anguished eyes met mine. He opened his mouth to scream again, but it came out as a ring.

The telephone was ringing. I shuddered and looked around my room to remind me where I was.

The phone rang again. It could be a reporter wanting a statement after that interview with Mr. Mason. I flung my door open, only now realizing Mom's music had stopped.

"Don't answer it, Mom," I shouted.

"Okay," she called back, her voice sounding confused. I took the stairs two at a time. If the machine picked up, Mom might hear the message being left, but I had no interest in her finding out about my morning.

I reached the kitchen, hoping to catch the phone before the last ring, but stopped short. I couldn't answer it. My voice sounded too young to pass for Mom's. Could I pull off a convincing deep male voice? Probably not.

Too late. The answering machine kicked on. I was about to pick up and hang up when—

"I thought Ana would like to know we managed to track down that address she was asking about," Ben said. "Some officers and I will be leaving the station soon to check it out. Thanks for passing this message along to her."

He hung up and the machine beeped.

I drew in an exhilarated breath before running to Mom's room.

"They've got an address for Apple Pi. You have to take me to the station, fast."

"Oh," Mom said, pulling herself away from the full-length mirror on her closet. She took in the clothes, shoes, and purses lying on the bed. It was against her moral principles to leave her room a mess.

"Ignore them. We gotta go."

"But." She reached her arm over the shoulder of her dress toward the dangling tag.

I yanked it off.

"Ana! You could've torn the fabric."

"Mom."

"Right, okay. I'm sure it's fine. Let's go."

I grabbed the now grass-stained gloves, and we left through the front door. Mom was careful to keep her eyes averted from the nondescript cop car across the street. She was becoming a master at casually opening and closing both the house and car doors, giving me time to go through. It helped that I was getting more skilled at crawling across the driver's seat, so she didn't have to stand for long, looking spacey like she may have forgotten something.

Finally, we were off. I could hardly believe it.

Truly? They found the house of Apple Pi? Where? Is it far?

I couldn't wait to see Isaac again. It'd been nearly a week since he'd been abducted—the longest week of my life. I felt like a kid on Christmas Eve. My legs were twitching. I bounced on the seat, wanting Mom to drive faster.

"I'm going. I'm going," she said, but with a smile.

"I just don't want the police to leave before I get there."

"How are you planning to do this exactly? Do you want me to follow them?"

"I don't think that would work. They would no doubt spot you and turn you back." I remembered all too well my lack of success tailing the van that carried off Isaac. "Plus, it's probably not kosher to have civilians at takedowns."

"Well, what about you?"

"I don't plan on being seen, Mom."

"Right."

When we arrived at the station, a dozen officers poured from the building. I spotted Ben among them.

"Pull over. Let me hop out."

"But, how? Should I get out first?"

I was already crawling to the back seat. I exited away from the view of the police station.

Mom looked through her window at me, her eyes wide and her face creased with worry.

"I know, Mom. I'll be careful. Thanks for the lift." I touched my fingertips to her window and was off, looking both ways before running across the street. I dodged a couple of officers and scanned for Ben.

There he was, opening his car door.

Now what?

"Cody, aren't you riding with me?" another officer called to him.

Ben took a step away from his car as I ran up to it. "No, Murphy's with you," he called back.

I seized the opportunity to grip the headrest with one hand and the steering wheel with the other. I launched myself across the driver's seat into the passenger side of Ben's car. When I landed, I couldn't help but be proud of myself.

Who knew I could do that? What a timesaver.

Ben got in next to me and fastened his seat belt. I'd have to do without. Hopefully this mission wouldn't involve any crazy car chases.

Ben turned the key.

We're on our way, Isaac.

The door next to me opened. I shrank back as a leg entered the car.

"Hold up, Murphy," Ben said, leaning across me toward the officer. I shied away and held my breath. He was inches from me. One of his curls brushed my cheek, which was steadily growing warmer.

Officer Murphy pulled his foot back and bent down. "What's up?"

"Captain said you're with Riley."

"Roger that." Murphy swung the door shut and jogged to Riley's car.

I almost sighed in relief but caught myself at the last second. I wanted so badly to ask Ben where we were going and how long it would take to get there, but of course I couldn't.

Please, God, don't let me have to sneeze, like, ever, on this trip.

We followed four cars out. Riley and Murphy brought up the rear.

Six cars. What were they expecting to find when we got there? Would there be gunfire? I shuddered, remembering my own near encounter with a gun that morning. How would Isaac feel if I told him what his dad had nearly done to me? And what exactly *was* he planning to do to me? I didn't like to think about it. All I cared about was retrieving Isaac, unharmed.

I held my curled fingers to my lips, thrilled I'd be there when Isaac was rescued. He'd want to see a familiar face, one other than Ben's. I frowned. He probably wouldn't be pleased to see Ben, particularly, but he'd be happy and *able* to see me. I smiled at the thought of his face lighting up when he spotted me.

My knee started to bounce. I pressed my hand against it to stop the motion. I took quick, quiet breaths to calm myself. I checked the clock on the dash. We'd been driving for seven minutes.

That's it?

To distract myself, I studied Ben. He was definitely distracting. I leaned against the headrest and soaked him in, so handsome and rugged but not proud. Such a good man, fighting crime. He looked sharp in his uniform, focused, determined. There was something more. Concern? Is that what I was seeing? I lifted my head for a better look. It was.

Awh, how sweet.

Snap out of it, Ana.

I pulled my eyes away.

But not for long.

I was in a car with Ben Cody! Of course, he had no idea I was there. It was like a half victory. I leaned closer and took a whiff of him.

Mmm. Such a manly scent.

His eyes narrowed as if in concentration, and he looked out his side window for a moment.

I straightened. I couldn't do this to myself. I had to move on. Ben would soon be in the past, where he belonged.

I stared out my window as evening fell. Dad would be home from work soon. I'd miss whatever scrumptious meal Mom was making. But I wasn't hungry. Just incredibly eager for this to be over.

I rested my head against the window and gazed up at the darkened sky. Out here in the country, it was easier to see the stars, little white pinpoints of light against endless black. I sat up. Where were we? This must be the outskirts of town. The back country road we bumped along could seriously use a repaving. A wall of pine trees sprang up on either side of us, obscuring any remaining signs of civilization. Where was Ben taking us?

I relaxed against my seat. The other police cars were indeed still ahead and behind us.

A voice scratched over the walkie-talkie strapped to Ben's shoulder.

"Approaching target. Shut off headlights," the voice instructed.

Ben obeyed. The wall of trees ended, and we emerged into a large clearing. In the center was a two-story log cabin.

My heart beat faster. We were here. It was almost over.

The police cars parked along the lane. Ben got out and joined the others who collected around their commander. I stayed in the car but slid to Ben's seat for a better view. When Isaac was brought out, I'd be ready to jump out and run to him. My muscles tensed, aching for that moment.

How much longer?

The cops fanned out around the cabin. Ben was sent to the back and out of sight. Hand signals were passed around. Two men positioned themselves by the front door.

I gripped the steering wheel. The nod was given, the front door kicked in. Kevlar-coated officers rushed in, weapons drawn.

For a moment there was shouting all around the house. Then silence.

No gunshots? Good, but still, why weren't bad guys pouring through the door like when stores open on Black Friday? And where was Isaac? Why wasn't anyone bringing him out yet? Did I need to go in and get him myself? What was the holdup? I leaned forward, craning to see better.

The police reemerged. Ben and the others conferred once more with their leader. I wished I could hear them, but it was soon clear I didn't need to. All of the officers except the one in charge were returning to their cars.

Isaac wasn't here.

No one was, apparently. I scooted back to my seat and sank into it, wishing it could swallow me whole. When Ben got in the car, I didn't look at him. I buried my face in my hands, trying not to cry.

Now what? Where was Isaac? Where had they moved him? He could be anywhere.

Ben drove in a circle through the grass and back out the way we'd come.

How would they find him? What other leads did they have? I gave them the only one I had, and it hadn't panned out. Maybe they could track down the owner of the cabin. They had to be able to find out who had recently been there.

I tried to cheer myself, but in truth, I was spiraling. It was back to my imprisonment where the entrances to my home were being watched. How much more could I take of this? I was useless before. Now I couldn't even help Isaac by looking after his pet bunny. I silently banged my fists against my forehead.

Back in town, Ben was last in the caravan this time. At a four-way stop, the police cars all turned right, toward the station. Straight ahead was the street leading to my house. When Ben pulled up to the stop sign, he waited. The other cars got farther and farther away. No one else was at the intersection. Why weren't we going?

Then he spoke.

"Would you like me to drive you home, Ana?"

CHAPTER 10

Everything in my body stopped: heart, lungs. Even my brain seemed to falter from the shock.

If not the effects of invisibility, the stress had truly made me lose it.

I just imagined that, right?

Right?

Slowly, eyes wary, I turned to face Ben. He was—looking at me.

"You can... see me?" I whispered.

He nodded. His smile was sad, though.

I didn't believe it. "Touch my nose," I commanded.

I expected him to tap it with his finger. Instead, he gently cupped the side of my face with his warm hand and touched my nose with his thumb. Then I understood. I shut my eyes and put the weight of my head into his hand, pressing it to my shoulder. After all the anxiety and poor sleep I'd been experiencing, this quiet car ride must've lulled me into a nap. I was dreaming, but what dream ever felt so sweet, especially after all the nightmares? A smile crept across my face.

"Ana."

"Mmm..." Hearing him say my name was always nice. This fantasy was only a temporary escape from my awful reality, but I was going to enjoy it for all it was worth until our journey came to an end.

"Ana?" he said again, but his tone was different this time, confused.

I opened my eyes. His eyebrows were scrunched together.

"Ohmygosh." I lifted my face, and he pulled his hand away. "I'm not dreaming?"

He smiled and shook his head.

"Ohmygosh," I said again. I had *sniffed* him. I floundered for the door handle and got one foot out of the car.

"Ana, wait."

He reached for my wrist. Could he feel my pulse throbbing as though trying to break free?

"You can see me? How?"

"Shut the door and let me explain."

My mind at war, I wanted to flee—spring from the car and keep going until I collapsed, but how could I run from *him?* Slowly, my eyes locked on his, I pulled the door shut.

"I'm not going to arrest you if that's what you're worried about."

My eyes widened. I hadn't considered that. I was still trying to figure out why he'd want to talk after I'd smelled him like a bouquet of freshly cut roses. Since I was too stunned to answer, he continued.

"I started to see you when Lieutenant Wallace and I were at your house. When I turned to leave, I saw a shiny white outline of you." He squinted as he looked through the windshield. "But then it was gone." He paused. "The second time was yesterday when I was in your room. I didn't see you on your bed at first, but then when I was leaving, I *could* see you." He looked at me with wide eyes. "You were shimmering. It was hard for me not to turn and stare. I wasn't sure if I was imagining it. The first time I just wrote it off as me not getting enough sleep. The second time I wondered if I was losing my mind. I watched the light fade around you from the corner of my eye. Then you were there, but indistinctly, like when you wipe something off a chalk board, but it's still sort of visible, you know?"

I nodded slowly. There was a short tentative honk. We both checked a mirror. A car was behind us, waiting. Who knew for how long? The driver probably felt uneasy honking at a police vehicle. Ben rolled down his window and waved the car past us. When it was gone, Ben drove through the intersection and pulled up to the curb.

"I'm glad you made it to the station in time after I called. I saw you run up to me." He smiled. "That was a nice leap you made into my car."

The right side of my mouth tilted up.

"But you still weren't fully there. More like a dull glow this time. But when I came back to the car from that cabin," his voice grew softer, "you were completely there." He tucked in his lower lip for a moment. "I'm dying to ask what happened to you, but I'm guessing this isn't the right time?"

As if I were able to speak at all. I merely shook my head.

"But it no doubt has something to do with Isaac?"

I nodded. *Is this conversation really happening?*

"I'm sorry he wasn't there, Ana." His tone was consoling. "I could tell how anxious you were."

"I'm sorry too," I managed to say, though quietly, as I stared out my window. Hoping he wouldn't notice, I pinched my arm, just to be sure I was indeed awake.

"I should take you home and get back to the station. They'll be calling me soon, but you and I need to talk about this at some point."

I looked back at him. "You sure you don't want to turn me in? Won't you get in trouble if someone knows you found me?"

"I don't intend for anyone to find out." He checked his mirrors and pulled back on to the road.

We drove the rest of the way in silence. I stared straight ahead, but I could see Ben look at me several times.

Could I trust him? How well did I even know him? To be honest, not well at all. Would he really keep me a secret, or did this new development put me in even greater danger?

When we parked in my driveway, he got out and held the door open. I slid out after him rather clumsily. It was much harder to be cool knowing he was watching.

The plain-clothed policemen ducked down in their seats. They probably didn't want Ben to blow their cover, but he didn't look at them.

I followed him to the front door. He knocked politely. A moment later Mom opened the door, with Dad behind her. She frowned when she saw Ben, but her eyes widened when she spotted me. She recovered and said, "Yes, what is it, officer?" She opened the door wider so I could slink in.

"I, uh, was just wondering if Ana has turned up yet," Ben said.

"No, she hasn't," Mom lied, with a touch of defiance in her voice.

"Okay," he said.

"Well, if that's all..." She started to close the door.

Ben looked at me and lifted his hand. He opened his mouth to say something, but the door shut.

After a brief silence, Mom pelted me with questions. "So? What happened? Did you find Isaac? Does he have the antidote? Is he home safe?"

Her voice seemed far away as I slowly turned toward her, squinting to make her out.

"Speak, Ana."

"He wasn't there," I said in monotone. "The house was empty."

Her face crumpled a little, but she pulled her chin up. "It's okay. There's still time."

"I'm sorry, Ana," Dad said. After a few tries, his hand found my shoulder and rubbed it.

"Do you want to talk about it?" Mom asked.

"No. I'd rather just go to bed."

"Would ice cream help?" Dad offered.

"I don't think so, but thanks." I headed to my room. By walking or floating, I wasn't sure. Some strange power was propelling my body forward. I could tell they were standing there, watching me go. Or rather, Mom was. Dad would be doing his best. Mom was no doubt dazzled by my newfound skill of levitating. But as I shut the door behind me, the full weight of reality sank in.

No. Isaac.

I wanted to slide to the floor right there, but I knew if I did, I wouldn't be able to get up again. I made it to my bed and, as I'd been doing so often lately, lay staring at the ceiling. I could probably draw all the constellations by heart. Isaac taught me their names too. Cassiopeia, Ursa Major and

Minor, Draco, Hercules, Scorpius, Libra, Bootes... A few of the others were on the tip of my tongue, but I gave up and rolled over to face the wall. This had been one of the craziest days of my life. I didn't think the day I turned invisible could be topped, and I'd certainly never forget the moment I learned the truth about my dad, but this day. Mr. Mason and his gun, then the man in my room, followed by the hugely disappointing police operation. It was a crushing blow. Isaac was still out there, who knows where, just waiting to be rescued. And I?

I... don't know what to do now, Isaac.

The textured wall grew blurry. I blinked against the tears and hiccupped a shuddering cry as I clutched my blanket to my chest. My fists balled around the fabric, trying to channel my frustration into the threads, the pattern imprinting onto my skin. The now-familiar images of Isaac being kicked and beaten formed in my mind until I shoved them back and locked the door behind them. I couldn't bear to think about that. The fear and worry made me want to explode.

I forced my brain down another path. The lightness I felt while coming upstairs drifted toward me again. My fingers relaxed their death grip on my unoffending blanket.

Ben Cody could see me.

But how? Could he actually be in love with me? That seemed seriously unlikely. I must've made a mistake. Or Isaac did.

Only Isaac never made mistakes.

I couldn't believe Ben loved me, but for the moment, I was going to allow myself to. After the day I'd had, I needed some happy thought to cling to, like his nearness in the car, or how I was able to study him closely without detection. Only it wasn't actually without detection. I decided to move on quickly. His startling revelation and the way he held my cheek in his hand. I lingered on this memory for a while. Then there was the concern on his face as Mom was closing the door.

I rolled into a ball. How could I think about Ben when Isaac was still missing?

My resolve from earlier took up residence at the forefront of my mind. Once Isaac was back, we'd leave town and probably be together the rest of our lives. I knew he'd take good care of me, and he was smart enough to get any work he wanted. Maybe we'd get married and start a family of half-geniuses who'd solve all the world's problems. Look out, global warming, here come the Masons.

I sighed. It wasn't such a bad plan. In fact, it was the best plan. It's what had to be done.

Then again, a few hours earlier I never wanted to see Ben Cody again let alone be seen *by* him. That had changed. I did see him, and I liked it. He saw me, and I liked that too.

He had never touched me before, let alone held my face so tenderly. I tried to touch him once, casually, in high school. In the hallway I planned to bump into him and maybe "accidentally" drop something. Our hands would "accidentally" touch as we both reached for it at the same time. But he deftly sidestepped around me. I almost tried again later, but I was afraid he'd catch on. After that, I just watched his movements from afar.

He was kind and outgoing. He had plenty of friends. Female ones, too, and when I began watching *them*, I could tell a few wanted to be more than friends. I would eye them suspiciously and imagine negative things about them. They were probably nice girls, but I saw them as competition in a race I was too chicken to enter.

I wondered back then why Ben didn't appear to be dating anyone, but I got my answer when I stood around the corner from his locker one day. He was talking to one of his football buddies. I knew eavesdropping was wrong, but I reasoned that I was simply overhearing, and that was a different thing entirely.

"Why haven't you gotten with Christa yet?" his friend asked.

I didn't know who Christa was, but I was already plotting her imminent demise.

"She's nice," Ben said, "but I'm not interested."

Christa was safe—for now.

"Why not? Have you *seen* her?"

"Of course I have, but I want to be a cop. You know that. I need to focus on my grades if I'm going to make it into the Academy. I don't need any distractions right now. Besides, senior year is a bad time to start dating.

Everyone will be going their separate ways soon—off to college, meeting new people. And who wants a long-distance relationship?"

"Who said anything about a *relationship*?" his friend asked. "I'm just talking about having a good time."

"That's fine for you, but like I said, I'm not interested."

"Suit yourself, man."

How many other men there were like Ben—interested in something real and not just a good time? I knew the answer was few to none. Isaac would be another, but when *he* thought about bases, it was how they reacted with acids. Before reading his hidden letter to me, I never even knew he thought of girls in that way.

When I went to football games to watch Ben play, Isaac was kind enough to go with me, but paid no attention to the game or the people around us. He just sat next to me, and as close as possible to the nearest light so he could write in his notebook.

Aside from these last several days, Isaac was almost always with me. And yet I was hung up on Ben Cody, a man I'd never before spoken to.

How can Isaac love me when I've been so terrible to him?

My stomach let out a low, sustained grumble. Sleep would be difficult if I didn't eat something first. I dragged myself from the bed.

The house was dark and quiet except for a dim light escaping from under my parents' door and the murmur of their TV. I didn't want to disturb them, or worse, inspire them to talk to me, so I left the hallway light off as I crept down the front stairs. I picked my way to the kitchen and opened the fridge.

A glass pan with layers of pasta stripes, red sauce, greasy cheese, and flecks of spinach greeted me. Lasagna. Mom had made one of my favorite meals. I eagerly pulled out the large pan. It was impossible to make a small lasagna, it seemed, even though there were only three of us, but no one complained about leftovers.

I peeled back the foil covering and inhaled deeply. The spicy aroma of Italian sausage filled my nostrils. Even cold, the stuff smelled delicious. I carved a generous portion out onto a plate and put it in the microwave. While that heated, I got myself a glass of water.

A knock on the kitchen door almost made me drop the glass. A pair of blue eyes peered at me below the scalloped edge of the white lace curtain.

This is what Mom must've felt. At least it was daylight when I'd startled her.

Ben was standing outside.

No use hiding from him now. I shook off my surprise and opened the door. Instead of his uniform, he wore khaki pants and a navy-blue T-shirt with a police academy logo in gold.

"I'm sorry I frightened you. I just wanted to stop by to be sure you're okay. I realize it's getting late, but I saw the kitchen light on, and thought maybe we could talk."

He wanted the details on Isaac. He may have been in civilian clothes, but he was still a cop.

"May I come in?" he asked.

"Right, of course." I opened the door wider. "Have a seat." I gestured to the bar stools. He sat in mine, which made me smile as I closed the door. Then I remembered my lasagna. "Um, are you hungry? There's leftover lasagna. My mom's a really good cook. I was just getting some for myself."

"Sure," he said. "I haven't eaten yet. Thanks."

I pulled the plate from the microwave and touched the lasagna. It was barely warm. I put it back in for 30 more seconds.

"Sorry, it's just microwaved," I said.

"That's pretty much how I eat all my meals, unless they're delivered by a pizza guy."

I grinned. Until I felt self-conscious.

Ben Cody is alone in my kitchen with me.

I turned to the fridge and removed the lasagna pan again. He was watching everything I did. I tried to act normal, but my limbs felt like they were being pulled by puppet strings. The microwave beeped. I retrieved the plate and set it in front of him with a fork.

"Would you like some water or milk maybe?"

"Water is fine. Thanks."

I handed him my glass. "I didn't drink out of it yet."

"I wouldn't mind if you had."

He said it in a casual "I'm not a germaphobe" way, but still, my cheeks burned. To cover, I took my time getting a new glass from the cupboard and filling it. "You can go ahead and start," I said half over my shoulder.

I cut another piece of lasagna for myself, a much smaller one, since my stomach suddenly felt the size of a chickpea, and waited for him to begin the inquiry.

"You were right about your mom's cooking," he said. "This is very good."

"I was sure it would be."

Enough with the chit-chat. Please, let's get this over with.

But instead, he asked, "How are you holding up? I'm really sorry things didn't work out today."

Still not the question I was expecting. "Yeah, that was a real bummer."

A bummer? What a stupid response.

"Look, there are still ways we can find him. We'll be able to figure out who owns that cabin, for starters."

"I know," I said, but my tone was glum.

"We'll track down if the owner was staying there or renting it to someone else."

I clattered my plate in the microwave and punched some numbers. When I turned around, he slid off the barstool and walked to me. My eyes widened. I froze. He put his arms around me.

Umm. What's happening?

Too stunned to react, I stood there, letting him hold me in his comforting arms.

No freaking way this is real.

But it sure feels nice.

Unbidden, a heavy sigh escaped my lips. I relaxed and hugged him back, resting my head against his shoulder.

When the microwave beeped several seconds later, we were still holding each other.

"It's going to be okay, Ana. We'll find Isaac for you."

"Uh-huh," I mumbled.

"He's a genius, right?"

"Yeah."

"There's a law against harming geniuses. I know because I'm a cop. It was on the final exam."

I giggled as I soaked in his warmth. I was thawing, relaxing, finally. He said something else in a reassuring tone, but I didn't catch it. Then—*Oh, no.* I couldn't help myself. This was too overwhelming. My emotions were so fragile there was no holding it back. I started crying. He held me tighter and my tears turned into sobs.

This is great. Just great. He finally sees me and maybe even loves me, and here I am blubbering into his shirt.

That and I needed a tissue, badly.

I let go of him and tore off a paper towel. I blew my nose as quietly as I could, but there's no way to sexy-up a good nose blow.

"I don't think I'm really hungry anymore," I said, keeping my back to him.

"That's all right. Maybe I should go. I'm sorry. I just..."

Now I made him feel bad. "No, thank you for coming. I needed that." And really, I did. I turned toward him. "It was kind of you to check on me." I looked around the floor, at his feet, at his legs, but not at his face. I didn't want him to see mine. My eyes and nose were probably red and puffy.

"Maybe I can pick you up for lunch tomorrow. I can fill you in on the progress of the case, and you can explain to me what happened to you. Would that be okay?"

I nodded, only glancing at him for a second before examining the floor by his feet again.

"All right. Goodnight, Ana." He walked past me to the door. He paused to look at me, but I refused to meet his eyes. I didn't want to start crying again. He closed the door gently behind him.

"Goodnight," I said quietly as the curtain swayed back into place.

He wasn't here about the case at all. He was here just for me.

CHAPTER 11

For a minute I stood with my eyes stuck staring at nothing. I blinked and wiped my nose again. I looked at my food for a while before forcing myself to eat, my tongue barely registering the taste.

My thoughts were muddled as I set the empty plates in the sink. When steam from the hot water hit my face, I remembered what I was doing and rinsed the dishes.

Isaac was indeed a genius. The kidnappers would be fools to hurt him. They should be treating him like royalty, even if just to exploit his abilities and milk his brain for all it was worth. If they wanted what he had, they'd have to work for it. Maybe things weren't as dire as I imagined. Isaac was probably doing fine. Why hadn't I considered this possibility before?

Because Ben wasn't here lifting my spirits before.

A smile spread across my face. Tomorrow *Ben Cody* was picking me up for lunch. I ran upstairs to my room.

My parents' door opened. "Everything okay, Ana?"

"Yes, Mom. I'm fine. Goodnight."

I shut my door and whipped open my closet. What was I going to wear? I felt like such a girl, for the first time ever. Even though it was late and I was tired, I wasn't going to be falling asleep anytime soon. I threw several clothing options onto my bed before narrowing them down. The finalists were carried to the bathroom so I could view them in the mirror. I settled on a purple scoop neck top. Next it was skirt, shorts, jeans? What to pair with the shirt?

An hour and a half later, after trying on a half dozen candidates, the outfit was perfected, and I knew what to do with my hair. I pulled out long forgotten makeup and practiced applying it for another half an hour. Then I remembered shoes. And should I wear a scarf?

It was 2:00 a.m. when I collapsed into bed. I fought hard to think about mundane things—anything but Ben. It wasn't easy. Mentally reviewing my economics notes finally did the trick. I fell into a dreamless sleep.

1 Day

I sprang awake at eight the next morning. Today was the sixth day. A mental brain scan brought back surprising results: my emotional state skewed heavily toward excitement.

Ben Cody.

My pulse spiked, then slowed.

But Isaac.

And the antidote.

The part of my mind filled with first-date jitters, which had fired up like I'd shot-gunned a Rockstar energy drink, now sank. Guilt, worry, fear, and dread swamped into the ensuing void.

The feelings settled there like a soggy old boot.

Then a fishhook yanked it back up.

"He's a genius, right?" Ben's voice floated back to me. "There's a law against harming geniuses. I know because I'm a cop. It was on the final exam."

But how did I *know* he was okay? How could I without finding him first?

Having lunch with a cop would help. He might have answers. It wasn't a date. It was a fact-finding mission, a collaboration.

With that frame of mind shoved firmly in place, my heart rate normalized. I showered and was about to get dressed when I thought better of it. I knew I should try to eat something, which meant going to the kitchen, which would involve Mom. I didn't want her to see me dressed like I suddenly cared. She'd start asking questions, especially since lately I'd been throwing on whatever wrinkly, questionably clean clothes I first laid eyes on.

I settled on going downstairs in my bathrobe. She'd understand. Isaac had been missing for almost a full week, and yesterday had been a huge letdown. Plus, I didn't want to take the chance of dropping food on the outfit I'd spent so long planning out the night before.

When I entered the kitchen, Mom sang out, "Morning, Anastasia."

Something was off. "Good morning, Mom." My tone was cautious. Did she somehow know what I was up to today?

"Would you like some waffles with boysenberries?" she asked.

"That's right, your ladies' brunch. Is that today?"

"Well, it was going to be, but apparently word got around I wasn't feeling well, so the women took it upon themselves to cancel the event on my behalf. I have four pints of boysenberries, so I hope you like them."

Even if I wasn't fooled by her overly pleasant tone, the way she slammed the lid on the waffle iron spoke volumes.

"I'm sorry, Mom."

She waved me off, but her façade was beginning to crack. She handed me a plate with a waffle and a generous pile of boysenberries. She lifted her chin. "Whipped cream?"

"All right."

I originally intended to eat maybe a quarter of a bagel, but I had no choice now. I nibbled at the waffle. "Mmm. The boysenberries were a good choice."

"You really think so?"

"They're okay," I admitted.

"Maybe we can mix them with ice cream later to get rid of them."

I smiled. "Good idea." But my smile faded. "I'm sorry this happened. You were just trying to protect me. You shouldn't be punished for it."

She smacked the counter. "That stinking Peggy and her sister Sarah Wallace." She picked up the whipped cream can and squirted some into her mouth. A lot of it hit her face instead.

"What are you doing?" I tried hard not to laugh.

"It looks so much more satisfying on TV," she complained after managing to get most of it down. She wiped her face with a napkin.

I hopped up and hugged her. "Oh, Mom. Forget about those women. Eventually it will all blow over."

"I hope so," she said. I started to let go, but she held me tighter. "Ana," she began.

"Yes," I said, mystified, when she didn't continue.

"I don't care about those women."

"Okay."

"I'm going through the motions of being upset with them, but I'm actually relieved. I didn't want them here. They're not the ones I care about. They're not the ones who matter."

I nodded, my chin tapping her shoulder. I didn't know what to say. The silence became awkward. "It's the boysenberries, isn't it? You're worried about them going bad before we can eat them all?"

"Oh, Ana," she laughed, released me, and wiped her eyes. She took a step back and looked at me. "How are you holding up?" she said, her tone serious.

"I'm okay," I told her. "Don't worry about me. I'm fine."

She looked at me sidelong. "You sure? You seem a little... different."

"Yeah. I'm good." I pulled out a smile for her.

"Okay," she looked me up and down with her eyebrows raised before turning her attention to the waffle iron that had just beeped.

I went back to nibbling my waffle. It was difficult to eat. Mom was being extra nice and concerned, which was cool, but still, the countdown to Ben continued. He didn't say when he was coming to get me, but I'd guess around noon. Would three hours be enough time to get ready for lunch with Ben? Correction: fact-finding mission with Ben? Still, my stomach felt inexplicably tight. After getting down a quarter of the waffle, I couldn't swallow another bite, but I didn't want Mom to feel bad.

"Do you mind if I take this back to my room? I should probably get dressed." It was a lame excuse, but it was the best I could do.

"Oh." Her disappointment was evident. "Sure, sweetie. Whatever you want."

"The waffle's delicious, by the way."

She gave me a weak smile. "Thanks."

I felt bad leaving her, but duty called. Back in my room it was time to prepare myself. I flossed the boysenberry seeds out of my teeth.

Horrible things. We'll be eating them forever.

I brushed my teeth and got dressed. Next it was the hair.

Ben and I are only comparing notes. Still, it won't hurt to look halfway decent for him.

I dusted off the rarely used torture devices Mom had given me ages ago: a hair straightener and a curling iron. I straightened the bulk of my hair and tried to curl the bottom out, but the curls were different heights and, incredibly, different sizes. To add injury to insult, I burned the back of my neck.

How can this be so complicated?

I tried over and over, but some curls ended up facing sideways. I attempted to fix it with my brush, but that left me with a frizzy puff of brown hair like I was wearing a bird's nest for a hat.

There was a definite downside to Ben being able to see me now. I slammed the brush down and blew out through my nostrils like a bull in the ring.

It's either me or you, hair. Only one of us can win.

I stopped myself short with a pang as I thought of Isaac and how I'd never gone to such lengths, or any, for that matter, when going to see him. Should I have? Did he mind what I looked like on a typical day? Would I ever have one with him again? Was there hope of me having a *normal* day, period?

There was a knock at the front door.

Ben can't be here already!

I checked the clock. It was only 9:30. I cracked my door open and peered down.

"How lovely," Mom said as she set a large colorful bouquet of mixed flowers on the foyer table and pulled out the card.

"For crying out loud." She tore the card into pieces and threw them on the table.

"What is it?" I said, stepping into the hallway.

"It's a get well soon message from Trisha Clarke."

"Oh, Mom."

She put her hands on her hips and shook her head at the floor.

Apparently, she still cared about them a little. I sighed. "Mom..."

What am I thinking? Should I do this?

"You want to come up and help me with something?"

Crud. I guess I'm doing it.

So, I told her. Eventually I'd have to anyway. The revelation that I was about to have lunch with a cop, and that I was good with that, hit my mom in stages. First, she was scared, then concerned, and with a bit of coaxing, pleased. I realized I'd overshot when she started bouncing up and down and clapping her hands. Finally, her tone turned serious.

"Is that what you're wearing?"

After a great deal of arguing and complaining, on both our parts, and several wardrobe changes, I wound up back in the original purple top.

"At least put a skirt on, Ana," she said in a disapproving tone.

"And crawl across Ben's car seat with my knees tangled up in it? I don't think so."

"Fine," she relented, "but maybe a different pair of pants."

And so it continued, with many muttered comments regarding my insufficient clothing selection.

"You really need to let me take you shopping," she complained.

Eventually we were equally satisfied with the shirt and a pair of white pants. But then she saw the utilitarian sandals I'd slipped on.

She tsked and shook her head. "Wait right here." She left the room and returned a moment later with a shoe box. "I bought you something when your dad and I went shopping the other day. I was planning to give you these when you turn 19 next month, but I think you need them now."

"You got me shoes for my birthday?" I took the box from her.

"I can only get you so many notepads and writing utensils. Open it."

I lifted the lid on a pair of tan sandals with several thin straps that laced back and forth across the foot and up the ankle. They were accented with an occasional sparkly white rhinestone.

"Try them on," she breathed, her hands over her heart as though I were stepping into my wedding gown.

"Well, they fit and do go nicely with the outfit," I admitted.

She let out a little squeal of delight. "Now, I must paint your nails to match your shirt."

Then she insisted on doing my hair, which, at that point, was fine with me. I expected something elaborate, but she merely put the front up with two clips and let the rest hang down my back.

"Simple but elegant," she said as she fluffed it out.

I nodded as I looked in the mirror. "That works."

I didn't want or need her help in the makeup department, but she seemed to both want and need to help me. I relented.

"You're blessed with a natural beauty, Ana," she said. "Just like your mother," she added with a modest batting of her eyelashes.

With black eyeliner, mascara, a hint of blush, and peach eye shadow, she was finished. Then she handed me a tube of pink lip gloss. "Just to give you a little shine."

When she stepped away and I saw myself in the mirror, I was a little surprised she'd been so subtle. I looked better, but without obviously trying, and I could see my resemblance to her. Wondering what parts of me looked like my dad, and knowing I would never find out, felt like a sucker punch to the stomach.

Deciding to put that behind me for now, I said, "Thanks, Mom. It looks really nice." And I meant it.

She clasped her hands together and grinned. I was certain she felt she'd just won a small victory.

"And for the finishing touch..." She reached into her pocket and pulled out a small jewelry box. Inside were two medium-sized diamond earrings.

"Oh, Mom. I can't."

"You're just borrowing them. These were a gift from your dad. Someday, some man, *maybe Ben*, will get you a pair." She elongated his name and looked at me pointedly as she put the earrings in for me.

I was about to say, "It's just lunch," but then—

"I mean, if not Isaac," she added.

My breathing faltered.

When she finished with the earrings, she poked through my half-empty jewelry box. "I haven't seen you wear these in a while," she said, more to herself than to me.

I ignored her. My shoulders slumped.

If not Isaac.

How could I be happy about Ben seeing me, especially after that letter Isaac had written? Did Isaac even mean it, or was it just his way of making me keep the cypher? How was I to know? Was I *sure* he was looking right at me in the basement before I ran?

However Isaac felt about me, I knew how I felt about him: he was my best friend. I was determined to find him, with Ben's help. Besides, what had I accomplished on my own?

Mom pulled out colorful star or heart-topped plastic rings from my childhood and threw them in the trash. "Surely those don't fit you anymore."

Though I rationalized that Isaac was being treated well, I didn't know for certain. They wouldn't have to torture him, though. Yes, he'd resist anyone who wanted to use his research for evil, but he'd do so as only he could—not with physical strength, which he lacked in comparison, but with his mind. No matter who had captured him, Isaac was smarter. He'd figure something out.

Done with the jewelry purge, Mom stepped back with a finger to her lips. "Maybe your hair looks better swept to the side."

At 12:05, there was a knock on the door. Mom flew down the stairs. My stomach flipped despite myself as she met Ben at the door and, this time, allowed him to step inside.

Here we go. I took a deep breath and started down the stairs. Ben looked up at me and smiled. Mom looked about ready to faint.

It's lunch, Mom, not the prom. Though the thundering in my chest mocked me.

Fact-finding mission, nothing more, I reminded myself.

I descended the stairs as quickly as I dared for fear of stumbling over their silent appreciation, only breathing again when I made it to the bottom without incident.

"See you later, Mom," I said, forcing the most normal smile I could muster, which probably resembled a psych ward patient's. I tucked my hair behind my ears and tried to act casual like this was no big deal.

"Have fun," Mom called, watching as we walked to Ben's car. He opened the door and waved to her as I slid across to the passenger seat—a great cover to buy me time. When he sat down and smiled at me, my breath caught in my throat.

Okay, here we go. Off to lunch with Ben Cody. I can do this.

"You look really nice, Ana," he said as he backed out of the driveway.

"Thank you." I searched for something to say. "I like your uniform."

That's what you come up with?

He smiled. "Thanks. They're standard issue."

"Right. Of course."

Change the subject.

"Uh, where are we going?"

"I thought we could have a picnic at the park."

"Oh." I couldn't hide the sadness in my voice.

"Is there something wrong? Oh, shoot. Do you have a pollen allergy? I should've asked first."

"No, I don't have any allergies." I hesitated. "It's just this was something Isaac and I were going to do this week."

"I see." He appeared to mull this over. "We could go someplace else. . . My apartment, I guess?" His forehead wrinkled.

"No, don't worry about it. The park is fine."

His face relaxed. I held back a chuckle and wondered what state his bachelor pad was in when he wasn't expecting company.

"You said you were going to let me know how things were progressing on Isaac's case," I offered.

"Yes. That cabin is owned by a Robert Smythe. We looked him up only to discover he's been out of the country for the past two and a half months."

"You're kidding me." My head drooped.

"But forensics is sweeping the place, looking for prints, fibers, DNA. They'll find something." His tone was encouraging.

"I hope so," I mumbled.

"Maybe now you can tell me exactly what happened last week."

I drew in a breath, held it for a second, then relayed what took place in Isaac's basement the day he was kidnapped, including why the fire extinguisher had my fingerprints on it. Ben whistled at that part. I told him about losing the brown van with no license plate. He shook his head. And I explained how I sneaked into the precinct to leave him the note about Apple Pi in my diary.

"Clever," he said with a broad smile. "To think you were right there and I missed you." His tone seemed mournful. "Now these men who kidnapped Isaac—you said their faces were covered, but did you notice anything else about them? Tattoos? Accents?"

"No," I said. "What about Isaac's neighbors? Did anyone report seeing anything?"

"Nothing. We checked."

If only the Masons had a Mrs. Granville across the street. The case would be closed by now.

"There's been no ransom demand?" I asked.

"No. All the more reason why the working theory is you took him."

I pressed my eyes closed as I shook my head. "So, you didn't tell anyone about me? About how I was, am, invisible?"

"And lose my job? No. Who would believe me? Plus, I have no desire to cause you more trouble. We'll clear your name by finding the real kidnappers."

"Let's hope so."

When we arrived at the park, a notice posted by the entrance read: "Park closed April 7 from Noon to 1:30 p.m."

"Shoot. The sign says the park is closed," I said.

"Don't worry. I'm the one who posted that. I figured it would be easier to eat without other people around to see us, or rather, see me."

"Nice work," I said, impressed by his foresight. I hadn't considered how a bodiless voice and floating food would appear to the casual onlooker.

When we pulled into the empty parking lot, I was grateful to be able to exit through my own door for a change. Ben grabbed an old quilt and a picnic basket from the trunk.

What did Isaac plan to bring for our picnic? Will I ever know? Will he ever get the chance to show me?

"Shall we?" Ben asked.

I mustered a smile and walked with him to a spot under the expansive, flowing boughs of a large willow tree. A gentle breeze rustled the leaves rhythmically, sending dappled light across the well-trimmed grass. Nearby a bird was chirping a pleasant song. I wondered idly if I had strayed into a fairy tale. I helped Ben spread the blanket and we sat across from each other, cross-legged—another point for the no skirt camp.

Ben opened the picnic basket. "I have something special for you," he said, looking at me with a smirk.

"What is it?" Curiosity mingled with cautiousness.

He pulled out a golden delicious apple. "You wrote in your diary that you like this kind."

I couldn't help but laugh. "I do indeed. And I believe you like them also."

"Guilty," he said.

Joking about it smoothed the rough edge off my embarrassment.

"So, did you read my entire diary?" I asked.

"Guilty again," he admitted and looked down.

"I don't think much of that was relevant to your case," I told him.

"I know, but it was so fascinating." His voice rose.

I lifted an eyebrow.

"*You're* fascinating. I've never met anyone whose mind works the way yours does. The way you think about and reflect on things—it's amazing."

I tilted my head back and looked at him sidelong.

"In fact, I have something else to show you." He reached into the basket again, this time pulling out a bundle of newspaper scraps held together with a binder clip. He handed me the clippings. The masthead on one was familiar.

I scrunched my forehead. "These are from our high school newspaper."

"Yes. Look closer."

I scanned the papers. At the top of each was printed: "by Ana Roberts." Beneath my name were titles: "Summer," "A Reflection on Snow Flakes," "Ode to a Fallen Leaf."

"These are all my poems from freshman year."

He looked at me with mischievous eyes. "I wasn't the only one with a secret admirer."

I put a hand over my mouth and shook my head. "But these were terrible."

"I didn't think so." He took them back from me, mildly defensive. "I still don't think so."

"Well, thank you, but I hope I can do better than that now. 'Ode to a Fallen Leaf?' Please."

"Have you written more since then?"

"A bit," I said.

"I'd like to read them sometime."

"Maybe," I said in a playful tone.

Not a date.

Then I turned serious. "You really kept all my poems?"

"I made a point not to miss one. I really liked them."

"Why didn't you ever say anything to me?"

"One could argue that you never said anything to me, either," he countered.

"That was different. I noticed you for other reasons." I felt my cheeks redden and looked away. "Besides, you were a senior. I was only a freshman."

"True. You are a few years younger, not that it makes much difference now."

I tilted my head down, trying to hide my smile.

Still not a date.

"And, well, my friends told me some unflattering things about you."

"You mean how I'm crazy?"

"Everyone said you were a bit out there."

"And so I am." I sat up straighter.

"No one told me you were brilliant, just quirky."

"Brilliant, huh?" I smirked at him.

"Yes, Ana. I think you're incredible. The way you write. Even your vocabulary." He sighed. "I'm sorry those guys kept me from talking to you back then. I figured it's unusual for a guy to appreciate poetry, since none of my friends did, but I could tell you were something special." His voice lowered. "I did almost talk to you once, though."

"You did?" My gaze shot up at him.

"It was my last day of senior year. I wanted to tell you how much I enjoyed your writing and how I would miss reading your poems. I found you in the hallway before last period, but as I was walking toward you, Isaac appeared, and you walked away together. I looked for you again after school, but I never saw you."

I remembered Ben's last day of school well. I searched for him also, hoping to get one more glimpse before he was gone, but I never got it.

I looked out through the willow tree branches. "If you had come up to me, I probably would've just spluttered."

"I really doubt that," he said.

I shrugged. We'd never know, but I had a good guess.

"I'm flattered you paid so much attention to me. I'm not sure I deserved it," he said.

I shook my head. "All those things I wrote about you. I didn't even know you. You must think I'm a silly girl."

"You're not silly, Ana. You're astute." His face turned a delightful rosy hue.

I snickered.

"Not because you... like me. I mean..." He floundered.

"It's fine. I know what you meant." I took a bite from my apple to stop myself from laughing.

After a few seconds he said, "So, I've been wondering. Why is it I can see you now?"

I almost choked. I coughed and swallowed hard.

"Uuuhh... I think it's because you've gotten to know me so much better. Like, from reading my diary and what-not. Isaac said that could happen." That was mostly true. I held my breath.

His forehead wrinkled. Then he nodded. "That makes sense. I do feel like I know you really well now."

I exhaled. Who was I to tell the guy his true feelings for me? Especially when this was *not a date*.

He pulled water bottles and two sandwiches from the basket. "Ham or turkey?"

I grabbed the turkey. When I removed it from the plastic bag, I couldn't help but laugh.

"You cut the crust off? Do you always do this?"

"No, but it was the only way I knew how to make it fancy. I'm sure your mom makes much nicer sandwiches."

"I occasionally make sandwiches myself, you know."

"I'm sure you do, but you told me your mom is a great cook. She also seems like someone who would be... particular."

I grinned. "That's accurate. I'd say she needs a hobby, but cooking *is* her hobby." I paused, my voice quieter when I spoke again. "Food is really important to her because she grew up dirt poor with a single mom. She never had enough to eat. She would hunt for crumbs on the kitchen counter and floor or under the table."

"Whoa," Ben breathed. "That's rough. And really sad."

"Now when she grocery shops, she picks out the ugliest produce that no one else would buy. I complained about it once, wondering why she would get the stuff that almost looked like it should be thrown out. She said it was because if she didn't buy it, no one else would. She couldn't stand the idea of food going to waste."

Ben was silent as I swatted tears from my eyes. Mom had it rough. I didn't give her enough credit for that.

"All her clothes came from thrift stores," I continued. "And she had to wear them even when the sleeves and pant legs were too short. She was made fun of a lot, especially in grade school. But in high school she was pretty, friendly, and determined to win everyone over. She succeeded. Things eventually improved for her mom too."

Ben reached across the blanket to give my hand a quick squeeze. "You didn't mention any of that in your diary," he said.

All I could do was shrug.

"What about your dad? You wrote little about him. What is he like?"

My face clouded. He noticed.

"I'm sorry. Should we not talk about him?"

I breathed in and exhaled slowly. "My dad is mostly at work all the time. And..." I hesitated.

"And what?" His voice was gentle.

I bit the side of my lip. Why should I tell him this? Then again, why not tell him? He already knew many of my most intimate thoughts. "He's not even my real dad." I stared at the sandwich in my hands. "I just found out I was donor conceived."

Ben sucked in a breath. "Wow. That must've been a shock."

"You can say that again. But I'm handling it." A brief, unexpected rush of anger rose in me, but I tamped it down. "I'm handling it," I said again, more to myself this time. Why ruin a beautiful picnic with this topic? "Why don't you tell me about your parents?"

He waited a moment. Then he said, "My parents are much older than yours. They had me when they were in their forties."

"That's unusual."

"Yeah, I was definitely a surprise. I have two older brothers and an older sister. They're all married with kids. I've been an uncle for a long time. In fact, I have a nephew who is older than I am."

"Weird."

"I know. It's kind of crazy. But I love my big family."

I chased away a sudden surge of envy. "Is that why you came back here? I mean, you did really well in school. You could've joined a police force anywhere."

"Not anywhere. Or even nowhere."

"What do you mean?"

"Have you heard of the Cody Cop Clan?"

"Yes, actually. The Hinckley news made a big deal about it when you joined the force."

"Like so many generations of Codys before me." He looked away, frowning.

"You don't seem happy about that."

"My big brothers and sister were. It was a huge relief to them when I announced I would become a cop, and our parents would stop giving them a hard time for not joining the force. Finally, the Cody Cop Clan continues." Ben waved his arms in the air in mock enthusiasm.

"You joined the police because your family pressured you into it?"

"Yes, but it's actually not so bad. It's not what I would've chosen, but I do like it despite that."

"What would you have chosen?"

"Vet," he said.

"A veterinarian? That's so cute."

"I like animals," he said with a shrug and a little extra color in his cheeks.

"If you didn't feel like you had to be a cop here, would you want to live someplace else?"

"And miss out on Buzzard Day?"

I snort-laughed. "Of all the things for Hinckley to be known for."

"I know, right?" he said. "But every town has to have something."

"To be an annual stop-over on the turkey vultures' migration path is *really* something."

"Home sweet home," he mused. "It might be exciting to be a cop in a big city, though."

"And scary."

"Well, maybe just a bigger place than here."

"That's not saying much," I said.

He grinned. "What about you? Are you a lifer?"

"Hardly," I said.

"Where would you go?"

"Anywhere. You?"

He smiled at me. "The same."

"Well, that really narrows it down." I smiled back at him, and when our eyes met, my heart started beating like a marching band in double time.

Keep it together.

I finished my sandwich. It was easier to eat than I thought it would be.

"Tell me what it's like being a cop."

"Well, aside from the paperwork it can be really boring."

I smirked at him. "How many kittens have you rescued from trees?"

"Oh, now that's my specialty. They call me the 'Cat Whisperer' down at the station. I think I have a record. There was talk about getting me a plaque."

"Now that's something to be proud of."

"I haven't done anything very exciting or out of the ordinary except for this one case."

"Oh?"

"Yeah, it involves a mysterious, beautiful, and extremely bright young woman who is invisible to the rest of the world."

"I'm riveted. Who is it?" The corners of my lips pushed up my reddening cheeks.

He laughed and my heart swelled.

Not. A. Date.

He leaned forward and held my face in his hand like he had in the car the day before. A sudden heat shot into my cheek and raced like wildfire down my neck to my chest. My breath stuttered in my throat.

Not a... what now?

"I can't believe I'm lucky enough to be sitting here with you. I doubt there's a man in the world who wouldn't want to be in my shoes."

"Now you're just exaggerating." My cheek was still burning, so I pulled it away, afraid he'd notice. I turned that side of my face away from him.

"You know, it wasn't just your poetry that made me notice you. You really stood out."

"Because I'm tall?"

He chuckled. "No, not because you're tall. Because of how stunning you are. I couldn't help but notice. And I saw you a lot in school. Outside of the classroom, it's like you were everywhere I was."

"Hmm..."

I wonder how that happened.

"And you carried yourself with such strength and determination, like you didn't care what anyone else thought of you. I saw kids pick on you, and you just ignored them. I think you rolled your eyes once, but that was it. I noticed they weren't even worthy of a mention in your journal."

I shrugged. He was spot on, though. But only because I'd gotten used to the taunts. Or they simply didn't bother me as much once I had Isaac.

"For a freshman, that was pretty impressive. I'm sure most girls would've been crying in the bathroom for an hour. You were so much more mature than your classmates. Heck, you were more mature than *my* classmates."

I was at a loss for words. "Thank you," was all I managed to say.

He actually noticed these things about me? I wonder if he *keeps a diary.* I smiled wryly.

"Come on, I want to show you something." He stood and held out his hand to me. I looked at it for a moment, amazed and in disbelief that I'd get to hold it. When I did, he pulled me up.

"Have you been to the lake before?"

"I didn't know there was a lake here," I said, struggling to focus on his words rather than the strong, warm comfort of his hand in mine, the sensation of our skin touching.

"You're in for a treat then." His smile of pure innocent delight made my heart flutter.

He didn't let go of my hand as he led me through a line of trees, their branches bursting with new leaves, and down a narrow grassy path. At the end was a short, wooden dock, gray and weathered like a wise old matriarch. It jutted into a large oblong lake glistening with sunlight.

"How did I not know this was here?" I gazed in wonder at the sparkling water.

"It's one of our best kept secrets. My dad and I would come fishing here on summer mornings when I was a kid. While most kids were at home watching cartoons, we were sitting on this dock, talking, catching fish."

"Did you catch very many?"

"Some, mostly small, but it was still a good time. It's a treasured memory of mine."

"I'm sure it is. This place is great. It's so peaceful and quiet. There's no one else around. It's like Walden Pond."

Ben shot me a crooked smile. "I was almost certain you'd say that."

"Really? Have you gotten to know me that well?"

"I'd like to think so." His smile reached his eyes, giving them an added glow.

"You're not going to start reciting Henry David Thoreau, are you?"

His smile faltered as he cast his eyes down at his feet.

I pressed my free hand to my chest. "Did you memorize poetry for me?"

He rubbed the back of his neck. "I thought girls liked that sort of thing."

"Well, let's hear it." I crossed my arms and bit my lower lip to keep from smiling.

"I think I've forgotten it now."

"You're adorable," I said with a laugh.

His cheeks flared. "Um, hey, do you see that family of ducks over there?" He pointed to the bank several feet to our right.

I turned to see six baby ducklings follow their mother into the water and paddle along after her.

"Should we get them closer?" he asked.

"How?"

He grinned as he pulled a small bag of cereal from his pocket. When he threw a Cheerio toward the ducks, the mother moved closer to investigate. Another piece landed to her left, then several more dropped in the water closer and closer to us. The mother and her ducklings swarmed around the food, splashing water on each other and quacking loudly. Ben led them to within three feet of us, but they wouldn't come any nearer.

"Would you like to feed them?" he asked, holding the bag out to me.

"Definitely." I grabbed a small handful of cereal then sat on the dock to get comfortable. He sat next to me. We laughed as the ducklings clamored over one another for the food.

When the bag was empty, I frowned, until Ben, with a smile, handed me a second bag. Soon ducks from all over the lake joined in on what became a feeding frenzy.

Ben leaned back on his hands and watched. One piece of cereal bounced off a duck's head. "Nice shot, Lebron," he said.

I bounced a piece off his face.

"Try again," he said.

I threw another and he caught it in his mouth.

"You're better at this than they are," I said.

"Years of practice." He scooted closer until his shoulder was against mine. I accepted the invitation and rested my head against him.

Fact-finding mission. Of what his shoulder feels like.

I closed my eyes. *Or am I dreaming for real this time? If so, anyone who wakes me, dies.*

"This is an incredible day," I whispered.

His lips brushed my forehead. My heart caught fire and radiated heat through my entire body. His arm enveloped me, drawing me closer. My forehead nuzzled against his neck. The ducks went along quacking and splashing. Sunlight played across my face. The breeze tickled my hair against my cheek. Ben's fingers brushed it away, tucking it behind my ear and leaving a trail of warmth where his skin had touched mine.

I sat up to look at him. "Ben, how did this happen?"

His eyes were soft as he said, "You turned yourself invisible, and I finally found you."

CHAPTER 12

Kissing, at that point, was inevitable.

So much for this not being a date.

Normally I might think it too soon, but in truth, this was years in the making. Despite all my fantasizing about this moment, I felt completely unprepared. My heart pounded. My breathing was shallow. I looked at his delectable lips and licked mine like a hungry cat.

Ohmygosh did I really just do that?

But he didn't seem to notice. He leaned in a bit. I leaned in. He leaned in again and my eyes fluttered shut. Somewhere a part of my brain was giving a girlie squeal. I sensed his lips a millimeter from mine.

"Son, I don't know what kind of things you've seen in your line of work, but I think it's time you had a vacation."

We jumped. An old man in a fishing hat carrying a pole in one hand and a tackle box in the other stood before us. We hopped to our feet.

Ben let out an awkward, nervous laugh. "You may be right."

I pressed a hand across my mouth. My other hand covered the first as back-up.

Ben cleared his throat. "I assume you have a fishing license?"

"I got it right here," the man said, patting his vest pocket.

"Very good. I'll just get out of your way then."

We edged past him. He watched Ben walk by and shook his head.

I clung to Ben's arm and burst out laughing once we cleared the trees and were back in the park.

"I hope that guy never gets his cat stuck in a tree," Ben said. "Come on. Let's get our stuff and get out of here."

On the way home, I could've told Ben about only having one day to get an antidote, but I couldn't bring myself to do it. I didn't want to ruin this amazing day. Plus, at the moment, none of that seemed to matter. It was hard to imagine death or insanity could be looming, not with Ben around. *He* was my antidote.

When we arrived, I scooted out his side of the car. He knocked on the front door, and it swung wide within seconds.

"Hello, Mrs. Roberts," Ben said in a polite tone. "Is your daughter at home, by chance?"

"I'm sorry, Office Cody," Mom recited, "but I haven't seen Ana in days."

I gave his hand a squeeze before stepping inside.

"I see. Thank you, ma'am. Good day." He tipped an invisible hat to her and winked at me before turning toward his car.

Mom shut the door and turned to me, her eyes alight with eagerness and curiosity. "So, it went well?"

"Nothing super solid on Isaac yet," I said.

"Oh." She looked down, clasping one hand in the other.

"But they're working on it."

"Okay," she nodded. "Working on it as in, they're getting close?"

"Maybe."

She stopped fidgeting and stood stock still, looking at me.

"Yes, Mom. They're close. It shouldn't be long now."

"Good." She breathed again. "So, what else did you two talk about?"

I struggled with how exactly to answer her. Before I could come up with something, there was a knock at the door. Puzzled, Mom opened it. Ben reached in and handed me a golden delicious apple. "To remember me by," he said.

I smirked. Like I needed help remembering him. I held it to my chest and smiled.

"Goodbye," he said and nodded to my mom, pulling the door shut behind him.

"I'd say it *did* go well," she said, turning back to me with a sly expression. "Tell me all about it."

I gave her a withering look.

"Or as much as you want to." She held up her hands. "I don't mean to pry."

"It was really nice, Mom. We had lunch at the park, and then we fed some ducks."

"You fed ducks," she said in a flat tone.

"Yes, and it was amazing." I turned on my heel and started up the stairs.

"That's it?" she said, her voice plaintive.

I reached my bedroom door and called back, "Oh, and he showed me all my poetry he'd saved from my freshman year."

"Oooooh."

"I should change now." I shut my door behind me. It was cruel, but I didn't want to talk about it. I just wanted to revel in it. I lay on my bed and closed my eyes, not wanting to look at Isaac's stars right now. If my diary hadn't been taken, I'd be burning a hole in the pages with feverish writing. I could start a new one, but I couldn't risk Ben getting his hands on that one, too. I did *not* want him to know what I was thinking now. Instead, I reviewed every second of our time together, locking each in my memory, and relishing the particularly nice parts—at length.

And what would Isaac think of this new development?

The thought intruded its way into my mind. I pushed myself upright, not sure how to answer. But the response was obvious: He wouldn't like it.

A knock sounded on my door.

"Come in," I said automatically.

"I see you're taking your time changing clothes," Mom said.

I blinked, mystified by her sudden appearance. "Oh, yeah." I looked down at myself then at the clock on my desk.

How has it already been an hour since I got home?

"I guess I forgot."

"Mmmhmm," she cocked an eyebrow at me. "I'm making chow mein for dinner. It requires a lot of prep work. Why don't you come give me a hand? That is, unless you need more time getting dressed?" She crossed her arms and smirked.

"I'll be right there."

"Okay." Her tone was skeptical as she shut the door behind her.

I stood and stretched my stiff limbs. I changed into comfortable jeans and a T-shirt and headed to the kitchen.

"Nice to see you with a spring in your step," Mom said.

I grabbed a red and white checkered apron from her outstretched hand and tied it on. "What do you need me to do?"

"You can start by slicing that baby bok choy."

I grabbed a knife and could feel her eyes on me as I began cutting. Her mouth opened and closed several times.

"Forget it, Mom. I'd rather just keep it to myself for now," I said without looking up.

She exhaled through her nose audibly. "Fine." After a minute, realizing I wasn't about to change my mind, she started prattling on about something. Perhaps she thought she could catch me off guard with a suddenly inserted question.

Maybe her strategy would work if my mind weren't a million miles away, or at least as many miles away as Ben was. I paid enough attention to hear and follow her instructions when given. Otherwise, I wondered when I'd see Ben next and daydreamed about what would've happened had that fisherman not interrupted us. I smiled to myself thinking how ridiculous Ben must've looked puckered up to kiss empty air.

Mom plunked her wooden spoon on the stove top, evidently done with her monologue. "Come on, Ana. Give me something," she pleaded.

I put her somewhat out of her misery by sticking with the basics about the meal and the lake. When Dad arrived home, Mom was bursting to tell him what little she knew.

"He can see you?" Dad said.

"He's in *love* with her," Mom said, beaming.

Why I had divulged that to her I'd never know.

"Well, well," Dad said. "And do you like him?"

"I guess so," I said, keeping my tone mild.

"Oh, you should've seen her," Mom said. "She was just beside herself getting ready. We spent *hours* perfecting her, and she was beautiful. Weren't you, Ana? And what did Ben say?"

"He said I looked very nice," I responded truthfully. Later on he said other things, but I didn't need to tell them that.

"Very nice. Pah." She waved her hand through the air. "You were stunning, and you know it. He knows it too. He was just too polite to overwhelm you."

Dad smiled into his chow mein bowl. I suspected he, too, thought Mom was being silly. If he could see me, I was certain we'd be sharing a covert smile.

Mom continued on like this throughout dinner. Once she stopped to ask Dad how his day was, but before he could answer, she began describing how Ben knocked on the door a second time to hand me an apple. "An apple." She repeated.

"Did you eat the apple?" Dad asked me.

"No, not yet. Why?"

"Just be careful when you do. There could be an engagement ring inside."

I almost spit my food out. Mom, on the other hand, was not amused. She glared at us.

After dinner, I helped clean up and hurried to my room. Mom's one-sided conversation for the past few hours had done little to help me think of anything other than Ben, his curls, his *lips*. This massive distraction, coupled with Ben's confidence that the police would discover clues at the cabin, helped me relax. They had to be close to finding Isaac. But as much as I'd convinced myself that Isaac was safe and in his high-tech-lab-at-his-disposal glory, I was eager to know for sure.

I grabbed a Ralph Waldo Emerson book from my shelf and tried to concentrate on that. Before long I was swept up in his flowing poetry and transported to another place and time. I was surprised, when Mom came to my room to say goodnight, that it was already 9:45.

"Hey, kiddo," she said and pulled a hand away from my book to hold it in hers. "I'm," she hesitated, "a little scared." Her voice cracked.

"I know, Mom." I squeezed her hand. "It's going to be okay. Somehow Isaac will make it all okay."

"Are you sure?"

"If anyone can do it, Isaac can."

That seemed to appease her. "All right." She gave my hand a little shake before releasing it. "Goodnight."

"Night, Mom."

When she left, Dad stepped in after her. "Mind if I come in?" he asked.

When was the last time he'd set foot in my room? I sat up straighter in bed.

"Sure. Sit down." I gestured toward the end of my bed, but he pulled out my desk chair.

Oh, right. He can't see me.

"I just wanted to be sure you and I are okay," he started haltingly. "That you weren't mad at me for not being your real father."

"Oh, Dad." I set the book down next to me. His eyes bulged when I let go of it.

"I wish you were. It really stinks not knowing who my real dad is."

He shuffled in his seat.

"You've been a great dad to me, though. The truth came as a shock, is all." I paused. "But I still love you." I couldn't honestly say I wasn't mad at him. Part of me still was.

"What about the reason we had you."

I pursed my lips. "Right. That."

"What your mom said was true. We didn't want to be social outcasts in such a family-friendly company. But, as she told you, we had been trying on our own."

"I know," I said in a quiet voice.

"And it makes no difference to me who your biological father is. You'll still always be *my* little girl."

"I know," I said again. I wanted this conversation to be over. He might as well have been giving me The Talk for all the discomfort I felt.

He chuckled. "We've had some good times together, haven't we?"

"Yes," I admitted.

"Sometimes torturing your mom," he said with a smile.

I smirked. "Those were the best."

"Plus, you have no idea how badly your mom wanted a daughter. She probably would've died if you'd turned out to be a boy."

I whipped my head up. This was news.

"Mom really did want me—a daughter anyway? I wonder how she feels now that I haven't lived up to her royal expectations."

"Nonsense. She loves you just as you are."

That seemed questionable. "But what about you, Dad? Would you have preferred a son?"

He shook his head. "Didn't matter. I was just happy to be a father."

I considered that for a moment. "Thank you. That makes me feel better."

A little, anyway.

His shoulders relaxed. "Well, good." He got up and headed to the door. "By the way, I found your window screen outside. It must have fallen out. I put it back in and tightened the fasteners."

"Oh. Great. Thank you."

"No problem. Sleep well, Ana."

"Dad."

He stopped. "Yes."

"I thought you really liked Isaac." He often insinuated that he wanted an invite to Isaac's lab, but Isaac never went for it. "When Mom and I were talking about him at dinner the other night, you hardly said anything. I'm surprised you're not more concerned about him."

"I wouldn't worry about it, Ana. I'll bet Isaac's fine."

Despite the reassurance I had offered Mom, I still said, "I hope you're right."

"Of course I am. Don't you know dads know everything?"

I half-smiled. "Thanks, Dad. Goodnight."

"Goodnight."

When he shut the door behind him, I thought I heard him exhale heavily. I did the same. I was glad we'd finally talked, but it wasn't like the pain from the lie and not knowing my true parentage had just disappeared. That would take time. But it was a start.

To try to put the whole thing out of my mind, I read for another half hour before getting ready for bed.

As I came out of the bathroom, I heard something strike my window. It sounded like... *It can't be.*

My heart leaped in my chest. I pulled back the blinds as another pebble hit the glass. I slid the window open.

"What are you doing?" I whisper-called to Ben. "I think you're stalking me."

"I learned from the best," he called back with a snarky grin.

I shook my head and smiled, then gestured for him to come to the front of the house. I opened my bedroom door quietly and checked for light under my parents' door. There wasn't any. I tiptoed down the stairs and carefully undid the lock. When I opened the door, Ben slinked around the front hedges and slipped inside.

"What are you thinking, you crazy man?" I whispered.

"I had to see you," he said. "I couldn't stop thinking about you. Are your parents asleep?"

"Yes, I think so. How'd you know I wouldn't be?"

"Because *I* wasn't." He shrugged. "Plus, your bedroom light was on."

"You *are* a stalker." I grinned. "Where's your car?"

"I parked down the street. I didn't want to wake anybody or make the neighbors suspicious." He put his arms around my waist and pulled me closer. "Besides," he said, "unless there's an old fisherman lurking around here somewhere..." He peered into the darkness as if making sure. It was so adorable I almost couldn't stand it. "We have some unfinished business to attend to."

I laughed and quickly tucked in my lips to stop myself. "Nope. No fishermen here."

"Good." He leaned down and kissed me.

It happened so fast I wasn't able to psych myself out. I was grateful for that. I went rigid with surprise at first. Then I relaxed into his arms and wrapped mine around his neck. He pulled me against him, our bodies melting together. I could no longer tell where I ended and he began, nor did I want to separate from him ever again.

It was really happening. I couldn't remember how I'd pictured this in my head, so many times, for so many years. But it didn't matter. Whatever I'd imagined, it couldn't possibly be as good as this. His lips were tender, smooth, and warm. They felt perfectly molded to mine. Everything about his body felt perfectly molded to mine. I could've stayed that way forever.

Until my knees began to buckle.

Ben broke away and held me up. "Whoa, you okay there?"

My cheeks burned like magma. "Sorry. I just forgot how to use my legs."

"Would you like to sit down?"

"Yes. Umm." The most obvious choice would be the chairs in the foyer next to us, but being behind a closed door would mean not having to whisper. And the farthest door from my parents' room was mine.

How do I invite him up without sounding skeevy?

"Let me show you the stars in my room."

"Okay." He seemed genuinely interested—in the stars, I mean.

He followed me to the stairs. "Quietly," I warned.

He nodded.

Note to self: Do not *tell Isaac you used his romantic gift to lure another man to your room.*

Once inside, I shut the door noiselessly behind us. Ben sat on the edge of the bed. "Look up," I instructed. I turned off the light. It was pitch black and silent for a few seconds as our eyes adjusted. Then the glow from the ceiling took over, and Ben became visible. I liked having him suddenly appear in my room—now.

"Impressive," he said. "Come sit next to me."

I eagerly obeyed. He scooted backward to the wall. "It's easier to look up from here." He lifted me around the waist, pulling me next to him with ease. I rested my head on his shoulder.

"Someday we'll have to do this with real stars," he said.

"Agreed," I murmured.

"It's the summer constellations, right?"

"Yeah. How did you know? Did you and your dad do a lot of stargazing when you were a kid?"

"No. I took an astronomy class in college. I needed a science lab, and I figured that one had to be the easiest."

"You don't know your way around a Bunsen burner, either, eh?" I said.

"It's a good thing you and I were never lab partners. We'd have failed for sure."

"We would've had fun, though," I said.

"I'm sure we would have." He gave my shoulder a squeeze and kissed the side of my head.

I let out a contented sigh.

"The stars are sort of off, though," he said.

"What do you mean?"

"You see Libra, there?" He pointed to the one shaped like a table.

"Yeah."

"It's at the wrong angle. The underside shouldn't be facing Scorpius so directly. It should have more of a downward tilt than that."

"Huh. Isaac put those up. I wouldn't think he'd have made a mistake."

"Did he do it all at once?"

"Yes. It took forever, though he looked at the picture on the star package for a full ten seconds before setting it aside and putting the stickers up from memory. I suppose it's possible he could've messed up." Though it seemed unlikely.

"Maybe he was getting tired," Ben said.

"Maybe."

We gazed at the stars for a minute in silence, though I wasn't really seeing them. Ben's fingers were absently, slowly stroking mine, which sent strange sensations up my arm. It was quite distracting.

"Ana, there's something I need to tell you." His tone was serious as he removed his hand from mine, to my disappointment.

A lump formed in my throat. "What is it?"

He got up and turned the light on, then looked at me. "The forensics team didn't find anything at the cabin. It was wiped clean."

I got up too, gripped the back of my chair and leaned forward, struggling to breathe for a moment. "So, we're back to square one." In my mind, the tiny candle of hope I held blew out. If Isaac still hadn't been found after all this time... And without Isaac and his antidote...

"Ana." Ben put his hands on my arms. "We'll come up with something."

"What about traffic cameras? Maybe you can find the van on those."

"Footage from traffic cams isn't saved. It would be far too much data to store. We can watch traffic as it's happening, but if we don't know where the van is to start with..." He left it hanging.

"I should've never let them take him. I should've tried to stop them."

"It sounds like you did." His tone was adamant. "And what more could you have done against three grown men? If you hadn't run, they would've grabbed you too."

I turned to him, lifted my hands, and dropped them helplessly. Tears welled up.

He gripped my shoulders and looked me in the eye. "It's not over yet. We'll find the van some other way. See if a vehicle matching its description has been reported stolen."

"What good will that do?"

"If it was taken from in front of a store that has outside cameras, we can get a look at their film, maybe catch these guys' faces."

I nodded and wiped my eyes. It wasn't much, but...

Then I remembered something. I swept past him and sat on the bed.

"Ben," I began slowly. "I have something to tell you too." I bit my lower lip and stared at the carpet.

"Okay." He sounded uneasy.

"Isaac and his parents have had a plan in place for years where they would pack up and leave town should something happen to him. Something nearly did once before." I waved the thought away. I didn't want to explain. "Anyway, I think it's clear this situation qualifies."

"So, when Isaac is rescued, they're taking off. Okay." His look said, "What's your point?"

I grabbed the end of my blanket and began rolling the tasseled edge between my fingers. "I feel really bad now, after today, after..." My cheeks grew warmer. "I had no idea this was going to happen. I wanted it to, but now I feel guilty."

"Why would you feel guilty about today? We both had a good time, I thought," He sat next to me.

"I know. I really did." I gripped the tassels. "The thing is, I'm a part of the Mason's plan to leave too."

"Why? Why would you have to go?"

"He's my best friend. I'm all he's got, really."

"He has his parents. They'll go with him," he said.

"But he's eighteen. They don't need to anymore. Besides, it's safer for them if they stay away."

Ben stopped my fidgety fingers by putting his hands on mine. "And safer for you, too, Ana. It's not your job to protect him."

"Then whose is it? The police?" I regretted it as soon as I'd said it.

He stiffened. "You know we're doing everything we can."

I put a hand to my brow. "I know. I'm sorry. That wasn't fair of me. The whole situation is frustrating."

Ben said nothing for a while. "You don't *have* to go with him." His voice was quiet. "Like you said, he's an adult."

"I don't want him to be on his own."

His voice rose. "Why are you babying him?"

"I'm not babying him," I almost yelled, but caught myself, turning it into a loud whisper instead. "He's my best friend. For years he's been my only friend." My eyes pleaded with him to understand.

"And what am I?"

"You're important to me too." I grabbed his hand in both of mine. "Isaac has spent enough of his life feeling alone, and I understand that all too well. When this is over, I can't just abandon him."

Ben pulled his hand from mine and walked to the window. He stared out into the darkness. "It's not fair."

I stood next to him, putting a tentative hand on his back. "Let's compromise then. If Isaac's parents decide to move away with him, I'll stay. But if they don't, I'll go with him."

He turned, his eyes flinty. "I hope they decide to leave with him then." He looked past me as he wrapped his arms around me. "It's my turn now."

I breathed him in as I hugged him back. "I'm sorry, Ben. Really, I am."

He rested his chin on the top of my head. "I still don't like it. Just promise me if you go, you won't stay away for too long. Help him get established somewhere and come back."

"I promise if I leave, I'll come back as soon as I can." I held my voice steady, but my heart was cracking like the San Andreas Fault.

He moved his hands to my face and tilted my chin up. His kiss was soft and tender but laced with sadness. Then he hugged me briefly. "I should go," he said.

I nodded and led the way downstairs.

"Aren't you worried what your coworkers might think, seeing you coming into my house this late at night?" I asked.

"What are you talking about?"

I lifted the edge of the foyer curtain and peered through. "It's gone now. I guess they took the night off."

"What's gone?"

"The car that's been parked across the street, just there." I pulled back the curtain and pointed to the empty spot, visible in the streetlight. "Two policemen have been watching my house the last couple of days."

"I don't know anything about this."

"Maybe they don't tell you everything?"

"I guess not," he said as he opened the door. "Anyway, goodnight." He gripped my hand.

"Goodnight," I said in a quiet voice. Our hands stayed together until he was out the door and his fingers pulled away. Mine fell limp at my side. He trudged down the sidewalk then turned and lifted his hand in final farewell. I waved back. I doubted he could see my face in the darkness and was glad of it. I didn't want him to see my tears.

CHAPTER 13

0 Days

Sleep didn't come easily that night. My mind kept repeating: *Isaac. We still have to find Isaac.*

Ben had been the best possible distraction, but who was I kidding? Without my best friend, I hardly knew myself. Plus, an invisible life was no life at all, especially if cut short or spent in a loony bin.

My clock read 10:37. I had merely a few hours to find Isaac and get the antidote. I pulled off my blankets and sighed. I might as well get used to being invisible, for as long as I still knew who I was.

I yawned as I wandered downstairs in my pajamas, wondering if I should bother wearing regular clothes again. At least the bathrobes asylum patients wore on TV looked comfy.

The sound of screeching tires shook me further awake. I raced to the foyer window and threw back the curtain. Across the street, a police car came to a jerking halt in front of the blue sedan, blocking it in against the car parked behind it. The two men in the sedan took off running. A half-eaten powdered donut and a coffee cup spilled onto the street.

Ben and another officer flew out of the police car. The other cop grabbed the sedan's driver. Ben sprinted after the second man. Fifty feet down the sidewalk, Ben leaped and tackled him. His skills as a high school linebacker hadn't worn off.

Both men were handcuffed and dumped into the back of the squad car. Ben looked up at me with a somber expression as he got in the car. They sped away.

"What was that all about?" my mom asked, her voice just above a whisper. I didn't realize she was standing next to me.

"I don't know, but one thing's for certain, those men watching our house were *not* cops."

"But why were they here? Who do you think they are?"

I shook my head, but I knew. They were Apple Pi's men. I was sure Mom knew it, too, but neither one of us wanted to say so. They were still after me and the key. A chill ran down my spine.

"At least they're gone now," I said.

Mom nodded, then walked back to the kitchen on unsteady legs. After a moment I followed. She flung a cookbook onto the counter and pawed through it. I kept an eye on her as I grabbed a blueberry bagel on my way out of the kitchen. She let me leave without comment. Clearly, she was rattled. I bit off a chunk and headed to my room. Sitting on my bed, I glanced toward the ceiling. I froze mid-chew, tossed the bagel onto my pillow, and dropped to the floor.

Running the length and width of my bed was a drawer. I flipped my blankets out of the way and yanked on the handles. Everything inside was a mess—more so than usual. The guy tossing my room had been in here too.

I sifted through the old yearbooks, notebooks, report cards, and grade school art projects until I found what I was looking for: the star sticker package. I held it up to compare Isaac's handiwork to the picture.

Ben was right. Libra was off.

On the package, Scorpius's head formed an arrow pointing toward the side of table-shaped Libra. But on the ceiling, the arrow pointed *under* Libra.

I dropped the package and checked under my desk. Nothing. I scraped my forearm reaching under the bottom drawer, feeling around for a taped-on piece of paper. Still nothing. Frustrated, I plunked onto the chair and pulled open the top drawer, running my hand along its back wall. I came up empty again.

There had to be something here. I was sure of it.

I pulled the drawer out farther, and it fell onto my lap. I groaned. It was always a pain to get back in. Whenever I got one side on, the other wouldn't fit. I slid from the chair to the floor and blew my hair from my face. I lifted the drawer and ducked my head for a better view. Then I saw it—an envelope taped to the underside of the desk, normally hidden by the drawer.

"Oh, Isaac," I said with a smile. "How did you sneak this up here without me noticing?" I tore the envelope open, hoping for a clue to finding him.

But it wasn't. Quite the opposite.

Ana, I don't know when or if you'll find this note. Maybe it will be discovered years from now in some dystopian future where your desk will be broken apart for life-saving firewood. But if you find this before then, please listen to me.

So much of what I do is a secret, even from you. I'm sorry for keeping you in the dark, but it's for your own protection. I'm working on something now that if successful, will be massive. At that point, I don't know how long I can remain anonymous. There may come a day when I disappear. If that happens, <u>don't</u> come looking for me. It will only lead you to trouble. Just let me go. Stay safe, and stay away. I'll be fine. And when I can, I'll find you.

Love, Isaac

Well, that was cheery. But it was also prophetic. I dropped the letter to my lap and stared out the window.

Too late, Isaac. And too bad. We're not in the science lab anymore. Out here, I don't take orders from you.

I stood and began wearing out a path in my carpet. What was happening with those men Ben and his partner grabbed? When would I find out? Would Ben tell me? Should I call? Maybe I should wait. But how long *could* I wait?

Not long. I used the phone in the den and tried Ben's cell but got his voice mail. I was tempted to call the station, but that could be dangerous. I was still a wanted woman. Mom, on the other hand, was not.

I found her in the kitchen kneading dough like it had wronged her.

"Hey, Mom," I started cautiously, "how about asking the police what was up with those guys outside?"

She stopped and stared at me. "Excellent idea." She grabbed the phone without washing her hands and punched in three numbers.

"I want to know what's happening with the men who were arrested in front of my house this morning. I live at— Yes, it's an emergency. They were right outside my home—" She sighed. "Well, can you connect me then?" Another sigh. She hung up and shot me a look before hitting three more digits.

She was the only human who still used 411.

"Hinckley, Ohio," she said in a wannabe pleasant voice that would fool no one. "Police department."

A moment later she was in. "Hello." More cheerful now. "I live at 183 Eucalyptus Avenue, and I'd like to know why two men were arrested outside my house this morning... Thank you." She looked at me and whispered, "I'm being transferred."

We waited. She tapped her foot. I dug my nails into my arms and looked at the clock every five seconds until she started speaking again, repeating her initial question.

"Uh, huh. I see. Can't you tell me any— I did mention they were outside my *house,* didn't I? ... Someone will let me know?" She ground her teeth. "Thank you!" She slammed the phone down, leaving it covered with patches of flour and small globs of dough. One plopped to the floor.

"They won't tell me anything. Can you try calling Ben?"

"I already did. No answer."

She went back to kneading with greater gusto. I watched, feeling more and more like that dough, while the clock ticked away the hours until it was too late for me.

I could only hope it wasn't too late for Isaac.

After three more calls to Ben went unanswered my panic level reached Code Red. It had been hours.

Why wasn't he telling me anything?

I tried to clear the mental image forming, but it forced its way in: the men reaching forward from the backseat, using their handcuffs to strangle Ben and his partner, Ben veering off the road into a tree, his lifeless body fallen across the wheel, the car horn blaring. Gleeful criminals pawing through Ben and the other cop's pockets for the handcuff keys, freeing themselves and running away unscathed, back to my house, feeling less patient this time.

A metallic grinding noise wrenched me from the horrible image. I ran to the window. The blue sedan was being hitched to a tow truck. I searched the street, half expecting to see the two men coming to reclaim their car, but no one was there. The tow truck operator picked up the donut and empty coffee cup still lying in the road and tossed them on the front seat of the car. Mid-hitch, he paused and stared down the sidewalk. I followed his gaze to a small item on the ground. He retrieved it—a cell phone, from the spot where Ben had tackled the second man. Before the tow truck operator dropped the phone in his pocket, I saw the police logo on the case. Ben's phone.

"No wonder," I said in relief. Mom, standing next to me, followed my logic and nodded.

We watched the rest of the process in silence until the tow truck hauled the car away.

"Where are they taking it?" she asked.

"Police impound, I imagine." I tried to sound unconcerned.

She turned to me. "Why are people after us?"

"I don't think it's us. I think it's just me."

"I don't like it. Enough is enough." Her voice rose. "We should get out of here. Pack your things. I'm calling your dad." She turned to go.

I grabbed her arm. "No, Mom. We can't leave. When Isaac is rescued," I said in a slow steady voice, "he needs to know where to find me. We need to wait."

She stared at me. "Fine." She tramped back to the kitchen.

I looked out the window until my own breathing steadied. Mrs. Granville's curtain fell back into place.

Tick tock. Tick tock.

I paced in my bedroom. I paced in the kitchen. Mom tried the police station once more but again got nowhere. She whipped up a meringue by hand instead of using the mixer. I was tempted to ask if I could have a turn.

Why wasn't Ben calling me from the station? Was he too afraid to tell me Isaac's... gone?

At 3:30 I gave up. I slumped on the counter just like I had seven days ago after failing to follow Isaac's kidnappers. It was all but over. I'd lost myself, and probably Isaac too. Who was I kidding thinking he'd be all right? That I could ever be normal again? What was the point of anything anymore?

Several sharp knocks sounded on the front door. Mom and I jerked upright and rushed to the door. When she opened it, Ben, looking frantic, grabbed my hand.

"We gotta go. We know where Isaac is."

"Really?" My heart leaped. Hope surged in. I snatched my gloves hanging over the coat rack and glanced back at Mom as I ran. Worry creased her forehead. I tried to give her a reassuring smile, but I doubted it was convincing. What would we face there? Would it be another letdown? If we still didn't find Isaac after so long... Would we make it in time? For him or for me?

Ben and I didn't bother with the car door routine. I jumped in the passenger side of the still-running car. He threw it in reverse and backed onto the street before slamming it into gear and switching on the siren. We didn't brake for stop signs. He raced through town and onto the highway. I clung to the door handle and armrest like we'd just made the jump to hyperspace.

"We're already behind," he said. "I want us to be there when they go in." He glanced at me. "I want you to be there."

"Where is he?"

"Cleveland. Those men we picked up eventually turned on each other. We separated them and offered each a deal." He shook his head. "Such idiots. They don't know much about what's going on unfortunately. Their orders were to watch your house for anything suspicious, like doors opening and closing by themselves. They had a number to call if they saw anything. Someone was trying to find you."

"Why would I matter?"

"You're proof."

I shuddered. "But how do they know about me?"

"They didn't. They were following orders they didn't understand, but they sure were curious."

"Oh no," I said.

"Don't worry. They don't know what's going on."

"But the police? Are they asking questions now too?"

"They think these guys are nutjobs, who had just enough information to be useful. I wouldn't worry about it. The good news is we traced the number they were given to an old industrial part of the city. One of them admitted hearing about a genius kid there being made to do something. I'm sure we can guess what. And he was certain they're still there now."

"We're on our way then." My eyes came alight.

"Yes, Ana," Ben said. "It's almost over."

His tone was confident, but his expression was torn. I didn't question why. I didn't need to.

"Did they say who was behind all this?" I asked.

"All they knew was one name: Apple Pi."

"Of course," I said. "But why didn't you call me?"

"I'm sorry. I can't find my cell, and I couldn't risk being overheard calling you from my desk. But I didn't have much to say until now anyway."

"The tow truck driver found your phone on the sidewalk."

"Ah, that explains it."

It did. And now to get Isaac.

Flying down the highway was awesome. The cars cleared a path like Moses parting the waters. My adrenaline was pumping. I felt like I could get out and run faster than the car. I wished I could try. Isaac was there. They were sure this time. There could be no mistake. He *had* to be there.

"It's going to be crazy. Not like last time. There'll be cops everywhere. The Cleveland force sent a drone past the building and spotted seven men with automatic weapons. It's impossible to tell how many more there are without getting closer, but we can't risk tipping them off. Police are setting up a perimeter as we speak. We're not taking any chances or letting anyone slip through our net." He set his jaw. "We'll end this."

He looked at me. I nodded my response then folded and unfolded my hands and nibbled my bottom lip.

He reached over and grasped my hands in one of his. "On the plus side, you've been exonerated. Everyone knows you're not behind this now."

But who is?

"It's not much farther."

We exited the highway. After several blocks, he turned off the siren. We entered an old section of the city. The buildings looked more run-down and empty the longer we drove. Soon the only signs of life were a few homeless people. The occasional blackened skeleton of a burnt vehicle lined the street. My excitement dwindled.

Isaac was somewhere around *here*?

We drove to a barricade. Ben showed an officer his badge. The policeman waved to two other men, who lifted and moved the wooden blockade out of the way. After we passed through, they carried it back into place.

Soon we arrived at a staging area. A couple dozen police vehicles were parked off to the side, as well as a giant SWAT truck and four ambulances lying in wait.

"Holy cow," I said. "All this for Isaac?"

He'll be so proud.

"It's clear these guys aren't going to give him up without a fight. Bringing this much fire power shows how valuable he is. They must be taking decent care of him," he said, speaking to my deepest fear. He pulled over and killed the engine. "Come with me."

I checked to be sure no one was looking before I slipped out. I jogged to catch up with Ben. We approached Lieutenant Wallace who was speaking to an officer with thinning gray hair and a presence matching his roughly six-foot-four stature. The uniform stretched across his solid frame held even more colored pins than Wallace's.

"Which building is it?" the man asked.

"It's one block in, the old paint factory," Wallace said, pointing.

"Are your men in position?"

"We have every entrance covered."

"Good. Are they keeping out of sight? In this part of town, an undercover bum on the street would tip them off to our presence."

"Yes, Commander," Wallace said. "We won't go in until you give the word."

"Problem is, we have no eyes inside. We won't risk a full assault until we know exactly where they're holding the hostage. We can't have him caught in the crossfire."

"Forward-looking infrared?" Wallace asked.

The commander shook his head. "Even with helicopter-mounted FLI, these concrete buildings are too thick for thermal imaging. What we need is to get someone close enough to attach the sound detector so we can hear what's happening in there. That will narrow down what part of the building he's in and help us choose a point of entry."

I tugged on Ben's sleeve and tilted my head in the direction Wallace had indicated. Ben's eyes widened and he shook his head several times. I nodded rapidly. Ben leaned his forehead toward me. His nostrils flared. I glared back at him. He crossed his arms and widened his stance. I crossed my arms right back.

"Officer Cody, is there a problem?" Wallace said.

I raised my eyebrows at Ben. He narrowed his eyes. I tilted my head toward Wallace. Ben stared at me, then sighed in defeat. I smiled in triumph.

"Lieutenant Wallace, a moment please?" Ben said.

Wallace looked wary but came over to us.

"This better be good, Cody."

"I may have a solution to Commander Bryant's problem," Ben said. He lifted a hand toward me and took a deep breath. "Ana Roberts is here."

Wallace looked around and stepped closer. "What are you talking about, Cody?" he said in a low voice. "Have you lost your mind?"

"Lieutenant," I said and lifted his arm to shake his hand. His body went rigid and his eyes bulged. He dropped my hand and looked around, sucking in a breath.

After taking a moment to steady himself, he said, "I see your mom was telling the truth after all."

"Yes, sir. She isn't crazy. I can get to the building unseen. I volunteer to attach your sound detector device. No one will know I'm there." I had no idea what a sound detector was, but if it would help rescue Isaac, I was all in.

Wallace leaned back on his heels and stared at the ground. "What do you think, Cody?"

"I don't like it, sir."

I gave him the stink eye.

Ben sighed. "But she can get the job done."

"Thank you, Ben."

Wallace rubbed his chin for a moment. "Let me have a talk with Bryant."

When he walked away, I clutched Ben's forearm. "Oh no. Maybe this wasn't the best idea. Now someone else is going to know about me."

He squeezed my hand. "Is there a better option? Because if so, I'd sure like to know."

"Me too, but there isn't time."

He gave me a questioning look, but I didn't elaborate. I had roughly fifteen minutes to get Isaac's antidote, if he even had one.

Commander Bryant was speaking with another policeman. Wallace pulled him aside and pointed toward us as he spoke. Bryant shot a look in our direction and then back at Wallace. He seemed angry. Wallace talked fast, and with his hands. When he finished, Bryant stared at us, or rather, at Ben. He didn't look convinced. I picked up the walkie-talkie strapped to Ben's shoulder and pulled it and its cord about a foot away from Ben's arm. Bryant's eyes bugged out. Wallace swatted the air, gesturing for me to put the walkie-talkie back. I tried, but it was easier to take off than put back on. I thought I had attached it, but it fell. I caught it and tried again. I fumbled with the clip. Ben tried to help.

"I got it."

"No, let me." Our fingers bungled together. I giggled. Finally, the walkie-talkie was back in place. Ben put his arm around my shoulders and pulled me to him.

"You goof," he said with a smile and kissed my forehead.

Then we remembered where we were. Ben stiffened. We looked back at his commanding officers. Wallace was shaking his head. Bryant's mouth hung open. Ben dropped his arm, and I stood up straight. Bryant called over another man, gave him an order, and the man ran off. Wallace gave us a stern nod. Soon the runner returned and handed a small black box to Bryant. Bryant held the box and spoke to Wallace, jabbing a finger at him. We couldn't make out the words, but the tone was clear. Wallace nodded again and again.

"That looks unpleasant," I said.

Bryant pointed in the direction of the building and then at a black van parked near them. Reluctantly it seemed, he handed Wallace the box. Bryant watched, his hands balled against his hips, as Wallace walked back to us.

"Here it is," Wallace said. He held it out in my direction. When I took the box, Wallace's head darted back and forth. He moved to position himself between me and any possible onlookers who would notice a floating box. "Can't you put it in your pocket?" he said through clenched teeth.

"Unfortunately, that won't work." I handed the box to Ben and removed one of my gloves. "Open it, will you?"

Inside the box was a large diamond-shaped white crystal. A paper-thin sheet of plastic, forming a circle, was attached to the wide end of the crystal. The plastic was clear but with lines in it like a spider web. On closer inspection, they were tiny electrical wires.

"The point of the crystal goes against a window. The plastic suctions it in place. Find a place to stick it where it won't be noticed," Wallace said, barely moving his lips.

"Could you hang on to this for me?" I handed Ben my glove.

Wallace sucked in his breath when it left my grasp. I grabbed the crystal with my bare hand. Wallace blinked and shook his head. "Unnatural," he muttered. He took the box back from Ben and spoke to him, though his words were directed at me. "We can pick up sound waves with a parabola inside that van." He pointed a thumb toward the vehicle. "Inside is a machine that will translate the sound waves into voices. They'll tell us what's going on inside the building and likely inform us where your friend is. Then we hope to extract him safely, with as few casualties as possible."

As few casualties as possible.

"Thank you, Lieutenant," I said.

"This can't fail. Do you understand me? That's an expensive piece of highly sophisticated equipment we're dealing with."

"Yes, sir," Ben and I both said at once.

As Ben and I walked to the edge of the barricade, he said, "Are you sure you want to do this?"

"I've got to. What other choice do we have?"

"I still don't like it. Stick the thing to a window and get right back here, okay?"

I nodded.

"I'll be waiting. Be careful."

I turned to leave, but he gripped my arm for a second, glancing at the officers milling around. No one seemed to be paying attention to us, or rather, to him.

"What is it?" I asked.

"Remember when I told you about wanting to become a vet?"

My forehead scrunched. "Yeah?"

"It's because when I was six my dog was hit by a car. I couldn't do anything to save him."

"Okay?" Sad, but the clock was ticking. Why was he telling me this now?

"Later I thought about becoming a doctor, figuring saving humans was even more important."

I nodded fast, wanting him to get to the point.

"But I'm not a doctor, Ana. I'm just a cop. If you get hurt." His voice broke off. "I won't be able to save you."

"Oh," I breathed and clutched his hand. "It's going to be all right." I mustered a smile. "I'm invisible, remember?"

He didn't seem reassured, but after a quick squeeze, I slipped my hand from his and ducked under the barricade.

Jogging down the middle of the street was eerie, like an Old West ghost town, only modern and industrial. I went around the corner in the direction Wallace had indicated and spotted the paint factory. The sign above the main entrance was hanging at an odd angle, one of the chains holding it having rusted off who knows how long ago. The paint was chipped and crumbling. I smirked at the irony.

I slowed as I approached and surveyed the area. It was a two-story building sandwiched between two others. There were three windows in the front on both levels. Men were standing guard at the upper windows. A man on the street stood near the door, smoking a cigarette with one foot propped against the building and a machine gun slung over his shoulder.

I stepped with care to avoid kicking a rock or crunching an empty beer can. The nearest window was only two feet from the guard. I crept to it, keeping an eye on him. I peered inside. It was difficult to see anything in the dim light. I squinted and made out what appeared to be a shop front. There was a counter and an old cash register. They did more than just manufacture paint here. It was once a store, too, it seemed. Beyond the counter was a hallway. Another man with a gun stood guard at its entrance. A light was on somewhere down that hallway.

Isaac is in there.

I turned back to the smoker. He took another drag. As I watched him, I opened my fingers one by one. The smoker looked down at the sidewalk and flicked ash from the end of his cigarette. I placed the crystal, tip first, against the corner of the window and smoothed the plastic suction down around it. Sweat beaded on my forehead and fingertips. I couldn't let my hand touch the glass. It was covered in dirt and grime. If it disappeared, the guard would notice.

I let go of the crystal and it stuck fast. The man took one last pull, dropped the cigarette, and ground the butt into the sidewalk. He turned and swung the door open. I looked through the window. The guard inside nodded to the man as he came in. I dashed to the front door and slid inside before it slammed shut behind me.

Sorry, Ben. I can't wait.

"Still no progress, huh?" the smoker asked the guard.

"Nah. This kid's a real pain. I don't know why we don't just waste him and get out of here."

"The boss says he's valuable. I'm not going to cross her."

The guard shook his head. "If this kid's such a genius, why hasn't he produced any results yet?"

"Who knows, but we have our orders. He gets more time—for now."

The smoker walked down the hallway. I scanned the floor. There were several sets of footprints cut through a thick layer of dust. I took one step at a time, making sure I kept within the existing footprints. I held my breath and tried not to make a sound as I tiptoed past the guard. I crept down the hallway toward the light and a growing noxious odor: something like sulfur mixed with B.O.

Moving slowly was agonizing. On the inside, I was running, any lingering doubt of Isaac being here gone.

The hallway ended at last in an immense open room with walls stretching to a two-story ceiling. An armed guard stood at the top of each of five sets of metal stairs leading to large stainless-steel vats. These connected to conveyor belts that joined smaller vats. A dozen paint mixers lined one wall. More men with guns patrolled the floor. In the center of the room, at a vast wooden table lined with beakers, test tubes, graduated cylinders, and bubbling chemicals, stood Isaac.

CHAPTER 14

I stifled a gasp. The way his clothes hung from his body, I wondered if they'd fed him at all. He wore the same worn-out jeans and T-shirt he'd had on when he was kidnapped. Now they were dirty, torn, splattered with color—blue, green, and a sickly orange—and scorched in several places, leaving brown-tinged holes.

I needed to get closer. Footprints covered the floor, cutting so many ruts in the dust and dirt that I could step with less concern of being noticed. I maneuvered around the roaming guards and stopped when I reached the table. When I faced Isaac, an imaginary broken test tube jabbed my heart. Dark half circles hung below his eyes. Black streaks lined his face, probably from wiping away sweat with dirty hands. His hair was greasy, matted down in places and sticking up in others.

He focused on pouring a foaming yellow liquid from one beaker to another. He saw me and his eyes widened. The beakers smacked each other with a loud clank.

"Careful," someone shouted. "What are you trying to do?"

"Sorry," Isaac said in a hoarse voice.

I winced at the pitiful sound. *How could I have thought he was fine?*

He set the beakers down and picked up two test tubes. I reached out, about to give his wrist a shake that said "I found you" when I remembered my bare hand and jerked it back, bumping one of the tubes. Its contents splashed me.

"Oww!" I yelled, unable to stop myself.

"What's going on over there?" A guard stepped closer.

"Sorry. Nothing," Isaac said.

I flailed my wrist, trying to relieve it of the burning liquid penetrating my skin, seeping into my bone.

What was that? Acid?

I locked my watering eyes on Isaac, pleading with him to make the searing pain stop. He hesitated then dumped the contents of the other test tube over my burn. I exhaled in sweet relief and smiled at him in thanks.

He returned the smile with a cringe as though about to witness a car crash.

"What is it?" I said with my eyes.

Then I straightened. I saw it too.

A brilliant light blazed like a halo around the top of my head. As I watched, helpless, it worked its way down my body, passing my eyes like a solar flare. I gazed in awe as it traveled across my torso. A million tiny crystals filled with the entire spectrum of sparkling light shot rays of color that illuminated the room. I was transfixed by its dazzling glow as it traced a path down my legs until all that remained radiated from below my feet.

The blaze extinguished in a single flash and the room seemed black in comparison. Quiet ensued as my eyes adjusted to the sudden dimness.

The silence broke as a gruff, dead voice commanded, "Grab her."

My eyes widened. Everyone was staring at me.

Awesome.

I ran for the exit, but a guard snatched my arm. I stomped on his foot. He loosened his grip just enough for me to twist away. I dashed three feet before another guard grabbed me, pinning me against him with one arm around my neck and another around my stomach. I wriggled in his grasp. He snickered.

The man with the gruff voice lifted my chin with a cold finger. "Give it up, girlie. You're not escaping us this time."

I recognized the voice. He was the leader of the group who kidnapped Isaac.

I glared at him. "How's your head?"

A flicker of irritation crossed his face. "Throw them both in his cell," he said. "She didn't come alone, so get ready."

Isaac and I were hustled away as the men mobilized. Half a dozen ran up stairs leading to the windows, taking up positions with guns at the ready.

"Aren't fifteen armed guards a bit much for one person?" I yelled, hoping my voice would carry over the commotion.

Our escort didn't answer. He led us to a dark side room and shoved us in, slamming the door. A lock turned behind it.

To my dismay, Isaac's prison was much like I'd imagined. The walls were a cold, gray concrete with one small, barred window near the ceiling. A thin mattress with a fraying pillow and a single threadbare blanket lay on the floor. All that was missing were the scratch marks in the wall, indicating the number of days Isaac had been there. And the rats. I looked around to be sure. There didn't appear to be any.

"What was that stuff that splashed on me? It felt like liquid fire." I touched the places it had landed. The skin was still tender, but there was hardly a mark.

"Half the antidote for invisibility. I was in the process of putting it together for you. All I needed was to combine them. I guess I accomplished that."

"Cutting it awfully close, don't you think? I was minutes from the deadline."

He looked up from examining my wrist. "What do you mean?"

"Seven days. You said I had seven days to permanent invisibility. I swallowed that pill around 4:00 a week ago."

His mouth twitched. "I never said it was exactly 168 hours."

I squinted at him.

"That's seven days times twenty-four hours."

"Ah."

"You might've had till midnight, maybe the early morning hours."

I smacked my forehead, though I wanted to smack his. Why did I assume it would be so exact?

"Or maybe it would've been pretty much 168 hours," he said.

"Thanks for humoring me. But I could've gone insane or *died*."

He gave me a blank stare.

"You said," I nearly shouted, "that Einstein could go insane or die if he stayed invisible forever."

"Oh, that. I was just talking worst case scenario. I can't be entirely sure how the formula would affect Oryctolagus cuniculus."

My turn to stare blankly.

"Domestic rabbits. It wouldn't have that effect on humans."

My fingers curled, itching to make contact with his face, but by the looks of him, a hardy sneeze could knock him over.

"Ana." He sounded disappointed, almost reproving. "Do you really think I would've taken that chance with you?"

Of course Isaac would never do anything to hurt me. Why hadn't I trusted him? "But I already thought I was going insane, seeing things."

He cocked an eyebrow at me. "Well, to be fair, you kind of do that a lot already."

I closed my eyes and counted down from ten. Being friends with Isaac might be all that was needed to drive me over the edge.

I plunked down on the mattress, easily feeling the hard floor below it. "I was driving myself crazy thinking I was going crazy." I put my face in my hands.

Isaac's weight landed next to me, and he briefly rubbed my shoulder.

"Weren't you at least concerned about Einstein eating the antidote?" I said.

"One thing I can always count on that rabbit for, is being hungry. But, just to be on the safe side, I laced the antidote with a bit of sugar too."

This news was a relief. He didn't really think he would harm Einstein.

"Sorry I stressed you out. But wasn't being invisible kind of fun?"

"No," I snapped. "Not really. And even if I wasn't in danger of completely losing my mind or dying, how was I supposed to get the antidote from you? You've been locked up."

"Not for long. I had a plan. Speaking of..." He leaned over me, threw off the pillow, and picked up a syringe hiding underneath. In one swift motion, he grabbed my arm, pushed up the sleeve, and plunged the syringe in above my elbow.

"Ow! What was that for?"

"It's an antidote." He gave his head a quick tilt. "Another antidote. It was to be mine in the off chance my calculations were incorrect. I've infected the air with a toxin, slowly poisoning these guys. In another hour they would've fallen over, and I'd have just walked out on my own, found you, and undone the invisibility."

I gaped at him. "You... You didn't need me to come. You weren't waiting for someone to rescue you. You were ready to leave on your own. All this time. I've been so worried." I shook my head at the far wall. "I should've paid attention to your note. You told me not to come. You said I should stay away for my own protection and that you'd be fine."

"So, you found one of my notes. Where was it?"

"Under the desk in my room. There were others?"

"Sure." He shrugged. "I like to take precautions. You figured out the constellations, then. Good girl. And, hey, great to see you. I assume you brought the cavalry?"

I nodded.

He stood and pressed his ear to the door. "They're really scrambling out there."

Was the crystal doing its job? Did the police know what was happening? Would Ben forgive me for coming inside? If I'd stuck the thing to the glass and gone back to the barricade, none of this would've happened. The guards would have no warning that cops were ready to storm the place. More people would get hurt because of me. Police might die. *Ben* might die.

"What have I done? I thought I was here to rescue you."

"It's okay. We'll still get out. I'm sorry I didn't escape sooner. I had to wait for them to bring me enough chemicals to make the compound. Also, if I released it all at once, they'd detect a smell. I guess it wouldn't have mattered. Soon after, they'd all be knocked out anyway, but there's a certain finesse to these things."

"You created a sleeping potion?"

"Yes, you could call it that. It would put them out for days. I'd just given out a heavier dose before you came in. I calculated the weight of each man with one small dose for myself, plus a little more for good measure. That would've been enough to make you fall over. Good thing I had some extra antidote handy."

"What were they making you do?"

"Recreate my invisibility pill, of course. But I stalled, saying I needed my notebooks because I couldn't remember the formula."

"What about your periodic table?"

His brow creased. "What periodic table?"

"The police went to school and searched your locker. I saw them looking at your highlighted elements. Wasn't that the key to your formula?"

To my surprise, and irritation, he laughed.

"I almost forgot about that," he said.

"Aren't you concerned it was just lying there for someone to find? I thought you'd be more cautious."

"That table is garbage."

"What?"

"It's a decoy, a red herring. I left it there on purpose just to throw anyone who came looking off the scent."

"Well, it threw me."

He knelt in front of me. "It's okay, Ana. Did the police take it?"

"No. *They* knew it was worthless. I can't believe *I* fell for it."

"I don't think my captors knew about that, but they did bring me my suitcase of notebooks."

"Really? They must've broken back into your house and taken it from the basement."

"Precisely. So, I had no choice but to create a pill."

"What? You did?"

"I had to give them something. I left out the secret ingredient of the recipient's blood. They made one man swallow it. When he disappeared, he started dancing like a fool, while the rest of us watched. It took him five minutes to realize he was only invisible to himself. It wore off in two and a quarter hours. In a way, this forced captivity has been in line with my own desire to perfect my formula. Now I've made it so I can control, to the minute, when it wears off."

"*Now* you can."

"I haven't been able to test it fully yet, but I feel confident my calculations are correct." He smiled in satisfaction.

"You've been *happy* about this? But it looks like they haven't been feeding you." It also smelled like he wasn't given shower breaks, but I kept that observation to myself and tried not to breathe through my nose.

"That's true. I haven't been eating regularly, but when I'm in the middle of a project, I often forget to eat anyway."

I couldn't believe it. He didn't need me.

My heart leaped with a sudden possibility. Isaac proved he could take care of himself—sort of. Maybe I could stay with Ben.

Isaac sat down next to me. "How'd you get here? How'd you find me?"

"Men were watching my house. Police arrested them, and they gave up your location."

"But how did they know who you were?"

"From the news. You've been in it for days, and me too, because I'm also," I made air quotes, "missing."

He groaned. "I'm so sorry. I shouldn't have asked you to come to my house. I should've never gotten you involved."

"It doesn't matter now. I'm no longer invisible, and you're all but rescued, so it's over."

He looked away from me, then down at his hands. Finally, he said, "Thank you for coming. You probably shouldn't have, but still, I'm glad to see you. I've really missed you."

And he hugged me.

At first, I stiffened from the shock. He always kept a respectful distance. But I relaxed and hugged him back, grateful to find him, safe and sound, even though we weren't technically rescued yet. Then it hit me.

I had my best friend back.

"I'm so glad you're okay," I sniffled. "I was so worried."

He pulled back and dried my cheeks with the torn hem of his sleeve. "I wouldn't let anything *permanent* happen to me," he said, "because without me, you'd probably blow up the chemistry lab and burn down the school."

I gave him another gentle squeeze. "Oh, Isaac."

That's when the shooting began.

We covered our ears and huddled closer together. The noise was deafening. The brief pauses between gunfire were filled with shouts, and worse, exclamations and moans as someone was hit. Something heavy thudded against the door. Our guard must've been taken down.

I crammed my eyes shut and wondered if it would ever end.

And if Ben was okay.

About twenty minutes later we lowered our hands as the shooting came to a non-climactic halt, followed by more yelling.

"That toxin you put in the air to poison these guys, it won't hurt the cops, will it?"

"Nah, there ought to be enough open doors and broken windows in this place to flush it out. It'll be harmless, but I wasn't going to take any chances with you."

"There's something else I wanted to ask you," I began slowly.

"I'd say, 'shoot,' but that hardly seems appropriate." He grinned.

I gave him an exasperated look. "Why did you make *me* invisible? Why didn't you make a pill for yourself? Then you could've escaped when they came for you."

"I was in the process of creating one for me, but I ran out of time." He examined my hand. I'd been unconsciously rubbing the tiny scars on my thumb and forefinger from when I'd picked up the gear that cut me.

"You figured it out, did you?" he said in a low voice.

"Yes, I found your lab, the hidden one."

"I knew you had it in you." He frowned at my wounded fingers. "I'm sorry I did that to you, though."

"It's okay. It didn't hurt that bad."

He wrapped his hand around mine. I stared at our hands together, unsure how to feel.

"Listen, Ana, I have to leave. School, town, everything. It's not safe for me here."

"I know. Operation Descartes."

"That's right. Except it's not the government I have to worry about. Someone might make another attempt on me."

I drew in a breath and braced myself for what was coming.

"I thought I wanted to be on my own, that it would be better that way. . ." His words sped up like they were running the last few steps down a steep hill. "But now I know that's not the case. You were never under any obligation to join in Operation Descartes, but I'd like it if you came with me." He paused, as though having reached the ground. "Will you?"

I considered how resourceful he was, how he was about to escape on his own, how he wasn't really in any danger. Maybe I didn't need to go with him, certainly not to keep him safe.

Then I took in his frail form. Would he remember to eat if left to his own devices?

But it wasn't to be looked after that he wanted me with him. It was because we were best friends. And he loved me. He didn't want to go alone, any more than I would.

I lifted my chin. "If you need me, I'll be with you."

He pulled me into a fierce hug, surprising me with his strength. "That's wonderful. Thank you. I couldn't imagine starting over somewhere without you."

I returned the hug and smiled when he released me, but looked away as I swallowed the lump in my throat. I was about to ask if he thought his parents would come too, but the door to our cell lurched open. Lieutenant Wallace strode in and extended a hand, pulling me to my feet. "It's nice to see you, Ana," he said. "Apparently everything didn't go according to plan."

I half smiled. "I guess not."

Isaac scrambled to his feet.

"Good to meet you, Isaac," Wallace said, shaking his hand. "Please come with me. We'll have medics look you over."

Wallace led us from the cell into the main room. Policemen were everywhere. I searched for Ben but couldn't find him. Others, dead or wounded, were crumpled on the floor. In one place, a long streak of blood ran through the dust. I averted my eyes, only to see blood splattered on the walls. My stomach turned. Some men were being led away in handcuffs. Where was Ben?

I looked for him again when Wallace ushered us outside to an ambulance and handed us over to medical personnel. "We'd like to speak with you when you're done here," he told Isaac.

"Yes, sir," Isaac responded with no enthusiasm.

A medic helped Isaac into the ambulance. "Miss, would you like to come up?" she asked. "I'll take a look at you too."

"No, thanks," I said, distracted. "I'm fine, really." I touched Isaac's knee. "I'll be right back, okay?"

He nodded, though his brow furrowed.

I ran to a large group of policemen and threaded my way through, scanning their faces. No Ben. I spun around, searching, dodging people, jogging between clusters of men and women in uniform. When it seemed I'd checked everyone but there was still no sign of Ben, a jolt of panic shot through me. Where could he be? Where hadn't I looked?

I faced the assembled ambulances and my heart sank.

No. Please, no. Please, please, no.

The sun went out and the world turned silent. What had I done? If he was hurt, or worse, it was all my fault. My eyes brimmed with tears. Haltingly, I took a step forward, and another, afraid to reach my destination.

Ben appeared around the side of an ambulance, his face heavy with concern. A cry escaped my lips. He was okay! He spotted me and we both started running.

When we reached each other, he put his hands on my arms and checked me over. "I was looking for you. Are you all right?"

"I'm fine, Ben." Tears streamed from my eyes.

"You sure?"

"Yes," I nodded and sob-smiled, hastily drying my face with my hands.

"Thank goodness." His arms encased me, and a hand burrowed in my hair, radiating warmth through my whole body. I closed my eyes and sighed, tension leaving me as I leaned against him. I breathed deeply, soaking him in.

Mmmm. His manly musk was on high alert, but not in a nasty sweaty way.

"You're okay, too, right?"

"I am now. But I was never in any real danger. They kept the rookies in reserve."

My fingers touched something wet on his back. I pulled my hand away and stared at it. My mouth turned dry and my throat closed.

Blood covered my fingers. I tried to speak but it came out as a croak.

Ben grabbed my hand and wiped it on the side of his shirt. "Don't worry, it's not mine. I helped someone to an ambulance."

I started breathing again.

"Sorry for giving you a scare. Is Isaac okay?"

"Yes. He seems to be, relatively anyway." I curled my arms to myself. "He's getting checked out." I nodded toward the ambulances.

"That's good," he said. "So, I guess you're not invisible anymore."

I'd nearly forgotten. "When'd you find out?"

"We could hear it from the sound waves. At first, we thought something was wrong with the machine when it went silent. Then someone said, 'Grab her,' and I realized what had happened. You have no idea how freaked out I was."

"Yeah. It was a shock for me too."

"I thought I was going to lose you. Why'd you go inside?"

"I'm sorry. I know I shouldn't have, but I saw an opportunity, and I took it. I thought maybe I could come back and give you all an idea of the layout, but then..." I gestured to my body. I had also hoped Isaac would hand me an antidote I could take once safely outside, but that hardly mattered now.

"We heard them take you and Isaac to another room and you shouting how many guards there were. I wasn't happy you went inside, but you did manage to get Isaac to a safe location and give us a better idea of what we were heading into."

"Then you're not mad at me?"

He shook his head. "I'm not sure I like that everyone can see you again, though." He wrapped his arms around me. "I enjoyed having you all to myself."

I knew what he meant—no competition with Isaac. "I'm still here." *For now.* I let go of him and stepped back. "Did you catch the leader?"

"We have the guy who seemed to be in charge. He's over there." Ben pointed to a hand-cuffed man. It was my old friend with the gruff voice. "He's insisting he's not the boss, though."

"Wait a minute. One of the guards mentioned a 'she.' Did you find any women inside?"

"Not that I heard, other than our cops and you."

"I didn't see one, either." A chill came over me. Whoever was behind this was still out there.

"You sure you're okay?" He put his hands on my shoulders and peered at me.

"Yea." I gave him a weak smile and reached up to twist one of his curls around my finger. "I've always loved your hair, you know."

He grinned. "Yes, I do know."

I let my hand fall. "I should probably check on Isaac."

"All right. See you soon." He gave me a quick kiss that left me yearning for more.

I returned to the ambulance to find Isaac alone. His face and hands were clean, and he was hooked to an IV.

"Can you believe this?" he said, holding up the tube. "I know I've depleted my glucose stores, but I'm still functional."

"Don't complain, Isaac," I said as I climbed in. "Everyone wants you back in perfect health."

"Of course," he looked out through the open doors of the ambulance, "so they can pick my brain apart. This isn't going to be pleasant—for either of us. How many people knew you were invisible?"

"Just my parents—at first."

His look was disapproving.

"They kind of found out." That was true. Even if I hadn't told my mom, there was no hiding it from my dad.

"And who else?"

I paused a moment. "Just three policemen."

Isaac sucked in his breath. "I specifically told you—"

"I needed their help," I insisted. "I never would've found you on my own."

He shook his head. "I didn't need you to find me at all."

I bit the side of my lip. "I know." The ambulance filled with silence. It felt like a deep pit, and I was sliding in.

"We've got to get out of here," he said. "I don't want to tell these people too much. We should go while we have the chance." He yanked the IV line out of his arm. "I think I'm full anyway." He hopped out of the ambulance and turned to help me down.

"We're not leaving yet, are we?" I asked.

His forehead creased. "Why not?"

I couldn't help but search for Ben. Instead of finding him, my eyes landed on a familiar car pulling up. "For starters your parents are here. You should probably go talk to them."

"Great," he said with a heavy sigh. "I guess I'll have to. I'll try to make it fast."

"I'll be over here." I had no interest in seeing Isaac's parents. Just the thought of his dad made me shudder.

I found Ben again and caught his eye. He came toward me. "What are Isaac's parents doing here?" he said.

"Wouldn't one of you guys have called them?"

He shook his head. "That's not protocol." Another officer called him, and he turned away. All the cops seemed to be focused on what was left of the bad guys as they were lined up in zip ties outside the building.

I looked back at the Masons. Instead of tears of joy, they looked irate. Was it over the pitiable state the kidnappers had left their son? That would be understandable. But they weren't looking at Isaac's weakened form. They appeared to be angry with *him*.

Isaac stopped short and turned, his face aghast. He started to run, but Mr. Mason lunged and caught his arm. With his other hand he covered

Isaac's mouth and forced him into the backseat of the car, yanking the door shut behind him. Mrs. Mason sped away.

Several things clicked together in my brain: the basement tidied up after the break-in, the ease of getting Isaac's notebooks to him. The kidnappers broke in without a trace because they had a key. What's more, when Mr. Mason was getting into the car, I caught a glimpse of something familiar in his jacket pocket. Something deadly.

"Ben," I shouted. He ran back to me. "I know who Apple Pi is."

CHAPTER 15

"It's them. Isaac's parents. They're the ones after his formula. Mr. Mason has a gun," I choked out. "They've taken him again."

Ben's forehead crinkled. "I'll alert Wallace." He dashed off.

I squeezed my arms again, suddenly nauseated, as Ben searched among a nearby group of cops. He gripped one man's shoulders and jumped for a better view. He asked one officer after another. They all shook their heads. Finally, one pointed back toward the building. Ben stared in that direction. He shook his head and put his hand on the officer's shoulder as he spoke.

My world was spinning. Just when we'd rescued Isaac after a week of worry and uncertainty, he'd been kidnapped all over again. And by those whom everyone thought were so kind for taking him in after his real parents' death.

It became clear now. Giving Isaac a lab to foster his gifts was pure selfishness. Mrs. Mason complained that her husband had promised her riches from his inventions, but he'd come up empty. Mr. Mason seemed sure Isaac would make up for his lack. And he was right. Now they had Isaac again, and with each passing moment were getting farther and farther away. Losing him the first time was awful. This was outright torture.

Ben ran back to me. "I can't find Wallace, but Mitchell said he'd get word to him. Come on." He grabbed my hand and we rushed to his car.

It was blocked in by a Cleveland police vehicle.

"Son of a..." Ben took off again. After several agonizing minutes, he found the right cop who ran to his car. I stood back and watched, using all my willpower not to scream, as the officer navigated the tight turns at a crawling pace. Back and to the left. Forward a little. Back and to the right. Forward. And back again.

"Come on, man." Ben banged on the trunk of the car.

My fingernails dug into my palms.

The other vehicle clear at last, we leaped into Ben's car. He drove backward half a block before making a sharp turn around. Gravel spewed behind us.

"More of our guys will follow soon," he told me. "They'll need clearance since there's still a lot to do here, plus," he paused, "we don't know *for sure* the Masons are behind this."

I glared at him through blurry eyes.

"I believe you," he said at once. "Of course I believe you. But I didn't see what you saw, and you're a civilian who's been under a lot of stress."

My entire body became hot all at once. "After everything I've been through, do you really think I'd—"

He lifted his hand. "I'm only telling you the way Wallace is going to look at it."

I opened my mouth to protest but changed my mind. We'd reached the outer barricade only to find it pushed off to the side, and not because the officers had been warned we were coming. There was no one standing guard, only bodies, three of them, lying on the ground.

Ben jumped out. I lifted in my seat. He checked for a pulse on each one, but I saw the pools of blood. He muttered an expletive. My stomach turned, and I dropped back down.

Ben pushed the button on his walkie talkie as he ran back to the car, his face ashen. "This is Officer Cody reporting a 1290. Three officers down at the outer barricade."

"Confirmed dead?" a somber voice asked.

He took a breath. "Affirmative. All units respond. In pursuit of suspects now."

I stared at Ben, sure my face was green.

"You okay?" His voice sounded too loud.

I swallowed hard. "I will be."

"You'd think as a cop I'd be better prepared for this sort of thing," he said as he weaved through the barricade. His face had also taken on a sickly cast. He gunned the engine once we were clear. "They'll believe you now. Wallace will be told immediately."

I felt somewhat better. Back-up would be coming. Still, those officers.

"Did you know them?" I asked in a quiet voice.

"No, but I didn't need to." His eyes were flinty.

I understood. They were fellow boys in blue.

We ignored stop signs. The siren blared as we raced through downtown Cleveland. Traffic moved aside as we slid past. At last, we were making serious progress.

Then we reached the highway. It was a near standstill.

Rush hour.

I sank in my seat. Ben banged his fist on the steering wheel. Even with the lights flashing, we made little headway. We got up to seven miles per hour, when we were moving at all.

"The Masons must be stuck in this, too, right? They can't have gotten far ahead of us," I said, hopeful.

Ben didn't answer right away. "We're assuming they came this way. What if they didn't?"

My heart stopped for a moment.

Ben got on the radio and called Dispatch. "We're on 71 heading south, in pursuit of a silver Toyota Camry." He turned to me. "Did you catch the license plate?" I shook my head. "Plates unknown." Back to me. "What's Isaac's address?"

"3745 Knoll Road."

"Dispatch, please send uniforms to 3745 Knoll Road to intercept two suspects, armed and dangerous, with a hostage. They may be headed there."

"Copy that," came the response.

"Our force is spread thin, but someone will get to Isaac's house." He smacked the steering wheel again. "I shouldn't have looked for Wallace. We should've just taken off right away." His knuckles were white on the wheel. "Let me try to get to the shoulder." But with the siren shrieking, several cars had moved off to the side, blocking our way.

"They must think I'm after them." He turned off his siren and reached for the bull horn. "Clear the shoulder. Clear the shoulder," he shouted through his open window. The cars meandered back into the slow lane. With our path clear, we moved faster but had to hit the brakes now and then to avoid blown truck tires and other debris.

The plodding pace drove me mad. At best we hit thirty miles per hour, but never for long. After what felt like an eternity we were off the highway and flying down the streets of Hinckley. I clutched the sides of my seat as the houses whizzed by. We even caught air going over a hill. But when we turned on Isaac's road, Ben slowed to a crawl.

As we got closer, a wave of relief hit me. The silver Camry was in the driveway. We parked three houses down and jogged the rest of the way. On the back seat of the Masons' car lay the marked-up periodic table from Isaac's chemistry book. The trunk was open, with several suitcases stacked inside. Any hope they had for a quick getaway was dashed by a police vehicle blocking their way. No one was in sight.

"We need to be careful. We don't know what we're walking into."

I nodded. I missed being invisible. We half-crawled to a window at the side of the house. Ben ducked his head around for a quick peek inside. He looked at me, his expression bleak. I peered in too. The Masons were near the front of the house. Mrs. Mason was pointing a gun at Officer Riley. He lowered his gun to the floor and kicked it toward her. She picked it up and tucked it in the back of her pants. Mr. Mason stood next to her with his arm around Isaac's neck and a gun to Isaac's head.

I clamped a hand over my mouth and slid to the ground.

"I can't *believe* there's only one officer here," Ben said through gritted teeth.

"But now there's two." I tried to muster an encouraging smile, but I was torn. Isaac was in trouble, but Ben would be too once he stepped in to help.

"I'll check the back door," Ben whispered. He disappeared around the corner of the house and returned several seconds later, holding a key—my key.

"It was locked, but I found this under an ugly frog statue. Amazing that people think leaving a key under something two feet from the door counts as hiding it."

"Huh, yeah."

"Stay out of sight." He crept to the back of the house again.

What was his plan? Sneak up to Mrs. Mason and put a gun on her, tossing Riley's back to him? Then what? Hostage exchange? I guess that could work. I nibbled my thumbnail.

Ben must've received training for situations like this, but part of me wished he'd stay out of it and be safe, while the other wished he'd hurry and rescue Isaac. I wanted to pull my hair out. Two of the men I loved most in the world were in danger. I couldn't just sit there.

I crawled to the front of the house. The door was ajar. I peered through the opening. Riley stood to the side with his hands on his head. Isaac and the Masons were facing him. I recoiled at the sight of an ugly purple bruise under Isaac's eye.

"This would've been much easier if you'd just shared your formula with us," Mrs. Mason said.

"I knew there was something off about you two. I didn't want to believe it, but somehow, I knew."

Mr. Mason snickered. "You really are a genius."

Mrs. Mason scowled at her husband then took a step closer to Riley, her gun still trained on him. "Now look what you're making us do," she said to Isaac.

"I didn't make you do anything. Is all this worth killing cops for?" Isaac clawed at Mr. Mason's arm.

I watched, not breathing, as the back door swung open a little at a time.

"I'll just add them to the list," Mrs. Mason said.

Isaac paled. "Who else have you killed?" He sounded afraid to ask.

As she turned from Riley to Isaac, her eerie smile made my blood run cold. "You really don't know?"

"Know what?" His tone was wary.

"You poor, foolish boy. How could you not see?"

"Helen." Mr. Mason's voice was a sharp warning.

The back door was fully open. Ben set a tentative foot inside.

She shrugged. "What does it matter now?" She sneered at Isaac. "You think your parents' death was an accident? We ran them off the road. It was so simple."

My mouth fell open. I stopped watching Ben's cautious entrance and stared at Isaac. His eyes filled with tears.

"You what?" His voice caught in his throat and his knees buckled. Mr. Mason yanked him upright. "But why?"

"To get at that brain of yours, of course." Mr. Mason said. "Your talents were wasted on your parents. They didn't deserve you. We had better plans for you."

"And you were following them nicely at first," Mrs. Mason said.

Isaac squinted at her.

"You don't remember? The first project we had you working on at our lab in Florida."

"You mean the leukemia thing? When you tried to force me to find a cure for cancer?"

"That's right, and you gave up. We kept poking and prodding you to keep going, to finish your work, but you refused."

"Because it can't be done. If it could be, it would by now. People have tried. Many people."

"But you're not like most people," she shouted. "You're different. You're special. Just like our boy was until he was taken from us. You were supposed to fix things."

Isaac looked at her with a pitying expression. "Even if I could do what you were asking, it wouldn't bring your son back."

"You think I don't know that?" she shrieked at him. "But if you did, no one else would have to suffer the way we have."

"It wouldn't change what happened," Isaac told her.

"No, well maybe this will change things," she said with deadly calm as she raised her gun to his forehead.

"Helen," Mr. Mason said. "You know this isn't the plan. Things didn't work out, but we can still use him."

Not taking her eyes off Isaac's, she moved the gun away. "Fine."

"But why did you have to kidnap me?"

"Because you weren't telling us anything. We'd have to take your invention from you and then let you come back home to us, none the wiser."

"You're insane," Isaac said. Mr. Mason punched him in the side. Isaac groaned and fell forward, but Mr. Mason yanked him up.

Ben was three feet from the end of hallway, his gun at the ready. My breath caught in my throat as he took another step and froze. His face twisted into a grimace. A floorboard had creaked.

Mrs. Mason turned toward the sound.

I didn't stop to think.

"Hey," I yelled as I pushed the front door open.

Isaac's face fell. I didn't dare look at Ben, though I could imagine his expression. More importantly, the Masons didn't look at him, either.

"You." Mrs. Mason's voice was serrated. "Figures you'd show up, you little brat. Our plan was flawless, but then you were here too, and those idiots let you escape."

I opened and closed my mouth, saying nothing. I put my arms up as she pointed her gun, waving me toward Riley, who pulled me behind him.

"You came back to spy on us. What did you hear us say?"

"I didn't hear anything. I wasn't normally here when you were. Just that one time." I glanced at Mr. Mason and quickly looked away. "I didn't hear you talking. I only wanted to take care of Einstein."

She barked a laugh. "Isaac's precious bunny? It hopped upstairs, probably looking for food." She smiled wickedly. "Don't worry. He won't ever be hungry again."

Isaac and I exchanged a horrified look.

"You knew about my men watching your house, trying to keep tabs on your movements," she continued. "You told the police."

"I didn't," I said. "I thought those men *were* police."

"Just shoot them both," Mr. Mason said. "I'm sorry I didn't take care of her when I had the chance."

So, it wasn't remorse on his face after he'd taken a shot at me. It was regret at having missed me.

"Turn around. On your knees, both of you," Mrs. Mason told Riley and me.

"No," Isaac shouted as he squirmed and clawed at the arm holding him. Mr. Mason leaned back, lifting Isaac until his toes scraped the floor. Isaac gasped for air.

My horrified eyes met Riley's as we turned and knelt on the floor. The barrel of the gun pressed against the back of my head.

Mrs. Mason leaned down and whispered in my ear, "I'm going to enjoy this."

Not wanting to give her the satisfaction, I resisted the urge to flinch as I closed my eyes.

This was the end. I'd failed. I hadn't saved Isaac. It had all been for nothing. A single tear ran down my cheek. I wouldn't be with either of them. And it didn't matter anymore.

Because I'd be dead.

Through a fog I heard Isaac yelling.

A shot rang out. I toppled forward. A heavy body had fallen across me. I twisted out from under the weight. Mrs. Mason rolled onto the floor. Her lifeless eyes stared at me under a circle of red on her forehead that grew larger every second.

Her shirt had fallen upward, revealing a red birthmark on her side. It was in the shape of an apple.

Another shot. Riley spun and sprang to his feet. I turned and crumpled to the floor, my ears ringing.

Ben tore the gun from Mr. Mason's hand while Riley freed Isaac from his grip. Mr. Mason shouted curses as Riley slammed him against a wall.

Isaac slumped on the floor next to me. He shouted something, but I couldn't make sense of his words. I stared at him as he shook my shoulders.

Ben held out his hand to me. I grasped it, and he pulled me up. His face looked tortured.

Isaac stood and grabbed my arms. Ben's hand fell from mine. I blinked until Isaac's words became clear.

"Are you okay?" he yelled. "Ana, are you okay?"

"Yes, yes. I'm fine." I squinted. "Are you?"

"Yes," he cried. "I'm perfectly fine." He shook his head. "What were you thinking?"

I looked over his shoulder at Ben. My eyes widened at the blood running down his arm. I searched his face, but his mournful expression showed no signs of pain—not physical pain, anyway.

Isaac let go of my arms and followed my gaze. "What's he doing here?"

"He brought me here."

Isaac looked at me sharply. "So now he knows you exist." He studied my face.

I bit my lower lip and hoped he read that as offense, not guilt. In truth, I felt both.

"Right," he said. "It's time for Operation Descartes to take full effect. Are you ready?"

Am I ready? I stared at him as the question echoed in my head.

Policemen poured into the house. Wallace strode in through the back door and barked orders.

Isaac grasped my elbow and leaned closer. "Don't you see? Too many people know you were invisible. They can't be trusted. They'll dissect you for the formula, or they'll use you as bait to get to me."

I stared at him. "Bait?"

But an officer pulled him away. Another drew me to one side and out of the way of the growing crowd. When I spotted Ben on the opposite wall, our eyes locked on each other.

Mr. Mason was being hauled out in handcuffs. He stopped in front of me and spat on the floor. The officer pushed him along. More chaos erupted around us. Police swarmed. Some entered the basement with white gloved hands and made several trips out, carrying Isaac's equipment from his secret lab.

I viewed the activity in abstraction. The noise and chatter of voices, orders being given, heavy footfalls throughout the house, were like a constant wave of sound. I could no longer distinguish where it all came from. I focused on one thing: Ben's blue eyes staring into mine. A medic patched up his wounded arm, but he seemed not to notice. When others walked by, blocking our vision, we still stared. The space between us filled with an unanswered question.

And I needed to decide.

Ben had agreed to let me go should Isaac's parents not be leaving with him. The answer to that question was obvious. But did I still have to leave? I had told Isaac I'd go with him if he needed me. I knew he wanted me, but did he need me? Could I get out of my promise on a technicality? *Could* Isaac go without me?

Did I want him to? Being without him for a week had been painful enough. He was my best friend who'd always be there for me. How could I betray him and not be there for him?

But now Ben was in my life in a spectacular way. Being with him was more than I could've hoped for. Would this be the end when it had only just begun?

I longed to speak with him, to be held by him. My body ached to feel his strong, protective arms around me, his warm breath across my forehead, his smooth lips on mine, his assurance that everything would be okay—eventually.

I stepped forward, my heart in my throat.

Just make it across the room to him.

I managed several steps when someone grabbed my arm. I blinked, swallowed hard, and turned to see Isaac at my side.

"Let's go. Now. Before someone else questions me."

I stared at him. Finally digesting his words, I choked out, "I don't know if I can."

He stepped back and his hand fell from my arm. His expression was uncertain, like he didn't recognize me. Confusion and fear chased each other across his face. The sight was more than I could handle. It reminded me of the look he gave me in the basement, begging me to run and save myself. He sacrificed his own safety by first making an invisibility pill for me, to be sure *I* would be okay. That was true friendship. And love.

In that look, in that moment, my decision was made.

I straightened. "Can I have just one minute?"

His brow furrowed and he looked away. "I'll be in my car," he said in a low voice.

As Isaac walked away, Ben came to my side.

"He doesn't look happy," he said. "Should I be?"

"Ben." I wanted to say more, but no words would form in my mind, just empty, raw, clawing emotion.

"I see."

"He said it wouldn't be safe for me to stay here, not when people know he and I are close, and I was invisible."

"I could tell he was less than thrilled to see me. How do you know he's not just manipulating you to keep you away from me?"

I shook my head. "Even if that were true, it wouldn't change what I have to do."

He drew in a breath and let it out slowly. "You had an agreement. I get it."

It was more than an agreement. It was a bond. But all I said was, "Thank you for understanding."

He looked at me for a moment. "I may regret this, but," and I was in his arms, his lips on mine, not soft and sweet but hungry. I was intoxicated by his ferocity. Everything else faded to nothing. I let my body synch with his, clinging to him, never wanting to let go.

But I knew if I stayed much longer, my resolve would crumble. With effort, I pulled myself away and rested my forehead on his shoulder. "Please don't make this more difficult for me than it already is."

He laced his fingers through my hair. "Come back," he murmured in my ear. "Get Isaac safe and come back."

I lingered, my heart thumping in my chest. "Goodbye, Ben." I stepped back, not trusting myself to look at him, and turned, threading my way through officers. I kept my eyes down, trying to be invisible. Once outside, I ran to the car. Isaac started it as soon as I opened the door. The force of him pulling away from the curb shut my door for me.

I turned back in time to see Ben running to the road, staring after us. We drove around a corner, and he was gone.

I couldn't fight the tears streaming down my face. Isaac's one good eye focused on the road ahead. The other had swollen to a narrow slit.

"We need to put distance between us and them, fast. What they're finding in my lab will raise a lot of questions. The bigger our head start, the better. It's a long drive to where we're going."

"And where is that, Isaac?" I asked in a whisper.

"Boston. And Ana." He waited for me to look at him. "We can never return."

My body sank into the seat like I'd gone boneless. I turned away from him and bit my lower lip, watching my world zoom by and disappear behind us. We turned a sharp corner. Then another. We were on the highway now, heading north, away from home.

And away from Ben.

The End

ACKNOWLEDGEMENTS

I want to first thank my mom, and not just because if I don't, I'll never hear the end of it. She was the one to whom I first timidly shared my idea for this story, asking, "Do you think that's anything?" She thought it was a terrible idea, and so, to defy her, I wrote it anyway. I kid. She has been a staunch supporter from the get-go.

I also greatly appreciate the tireless support of my husband who cheered me on and secretly watched over my shoulder for a new chapter heading to appear. "Oooh, you finished another chapter? Can I read it now???"

Undersheriff Mike Barnett sat with me for an hour, answering all my cop questions, including by follow-up text and email. That was above and beyond the call of duty. Thank you sincerely, Mike.

My early readers sustained me with their enthusiasm and feedback, especially Heather Graves, Shelby Raymond, and Darren Raymond. Darren even volunteered to read multiple drafts. Other supportive friends include Elise Simpson, Jonathan Baca, Jonathan Scallon, and Christine Wood.

I'm so grateful for the keen editing eyes of Mark Petruska, Stacy James, and Mary Booth. The latter gave me the greatest compliment by telling me that she, a teenage girl, was so engrossed in my story that she missed several texts from friends, even though her phone was next to her and not on silent.

Author Florence Heckel Russell, also absorbed, didn't notice day turn to evening or that her stomach was rumbling until her husband came home and asked, "What's for dinner, and why are you reading in the dark?"

Where would I be without my author friends? Bishop O'Connell taught me a lot by returning my first chapter doused in metaphorical red ink. Harry Heckel IV, Bill Powell, Laura Perkins, and Megan Eccles were also a great help honing my early pages.

I appreciated the encouraging beta read from author Julie Holmes and the thought that Isaac should have a record collection. Pediatrician-turned-author Carrie Rubin gave me the tip about Isaac's glucose stores. Agent Elizabeth Kracht's developmental edit was invaluable, as was the feedback from agents Shannon Snow and Anjanette Barr.

If not for my lovely and talented blog buddy, author Cheryl Oreglia, I may not have learned of Black Rose Writing. Thanks to publisher Reagan Rothe, tireless designer David King, editor Mary Ellen Bramwell, and the entire Black Rose team for believing in this project!

And my thanks to God, without whom, none of this would have been possible.

ABOUT THE AUTHOR

At age twenty-one, Ilsa Rey packed everything she owned into her little red Ford Focus and drove from Cleveland to California for good. She is now a recovering chicken owner and a martial artist with a black belt in Taekwondo and a blue belt in Jiu-Jitsu. Her favorite things are writing, training, and teaching self-defense to young women. She lives in southern California with her husband, four children, and the ghosts of chickens past.

Find her online:
X: @IlsaReyAuthor; Instagram: @Ilsa_Rey; Blog: IlsaRey.com

NOTE FROM ILSA REY

Word-of-mouth is crucial for any author to succeed. If you enjoyed *Wish I Was Here*, please leave a review online—anywhere you are able. Even if it's just a sentence or two. It would make all the difference and would be very much appreciated.

Thanks!
Ilsa Rey